GREAT SON

BOOKS BY EDNA FERBER

Autobiography
A PECULIAR TREASURE

Short Stories
NOBODY'S IN TOWN
BUTTERED SIDE DOWN
CHEERFUL—BY REQUEST
HALF PORTIONS   GIGOLO
MOTHER KNOWS BEST
THEY BROUGHT THEIR WOMEN

The Emma McChesney Stories
ROAST BEEF MEDIUM   PERSONALITY PLUS
EMMA McCHESNEY & COMPANY

Novels
GREAT SON
SARATOGA TRUNK
DAWN O'HARA
FANNY HERSELF   THE GIRLS
SO BIG   SHOW BOAT   CIMARRON
AMERICAN BEAUTY   COME AND GET IT

Plays
THE ROYAL FAMILY
(with George S. Kaufman)
MINICK
(with George S. Kaufman)
DINNER AT EIGHT
(with George S. Kaufman)
$1200 A YEAR
(with Newman Levy)
STAGE DOOR
(with George S. Kaufman)
THE LAND IS BRIGHT
(with George S. Kaufman)

Great Son

BY EDNA FERBER

GARDEN CITY, N. Y. 1945

DOUBLEDAY, DORAN & COMPANY, INC.

To
DOUGLAS BEMENT
who loved Seattle.

Introduction

THIS BOOK should have been a trilogy. Certainly it was intended as a tome, at least. But sometimes the vast dimensions of a people or a region prove so unsurmountable that a writer, in bafflement or defiance or defeat, decides to attack with a slingshot instead of a more proportionate and formidable weapon.

No book, to my knowledge at least, has been written that encompasses the majestic background or the amazing people that form the story of America's Northwest. That which has been written has, for the most part, taken the form of history. But people are history. In writing a story whose background is the city of Seattle the difficulty is that the human chronicle is so romantic, so improbable, so fantastic, and, at the same time, so touching that the would-be writer reels. One of those 1,800-page romances might have accomplished it—the awesome and bulky type of volume that is so tough on the stomach muscles when read in bed—with a map in the front and an index in the back, and footnotes explaining the meaning of Chinook Indian words.

There are certain American historical events too fabulous for fiction. Anyone who dips into the colorful record that is Seattle's past must thumb old newspapers, records, maps, memoirs, and quasi-histories. No one who reads of this region can fail to find especial enrichment in the American Guide series volume entitled *Washington,* compiled by the Writers' Project of the Work Projects Administration; and in *Northwest Gateway,* a fascinating book by Archie Binns, himself descended from Puget Sound settlers.

Everything in and about Seattle—its people, its scenery, its spirit, its politics, its energy, its past, its future—is larger than life. Curiously enough there is, too, about the region a dreamlike quality baffling to the outsider. This quality, misty as Rainier herself, imparts an unreality to the whole. Romantic, robust, the people and the city have an incredible past and a future beyond the imagination. The present completely escapes the chronicler. It is so vast that one cannot see it in perspective and must be content with a worm's-eye view.

This may be an inadequate excuse for a slim book on a gargantuan subject. Here, in capsule form, is that which should have been a lavish and prodigious feast.

Back and forth, in and out, weave the people in this book, appearing, disappearing, vanishing into the mists of Mt. Rainier or never really taking on human dimensions. This, then, is not so much a novel as a character outline of what will, someday, at other hands, be a stupendous and dazzling piece of Americana.

The people in this book are no more unlikely than Seattle itself. But Seattle actually exists. They never have existed outside these pages.

Treasure Hill
Easton
Connecticut
1944.

GREAT SON

1

THERE WAS TOO MUCH of everything. But not for Vaughan
Melendy. Himself of heroic stature, he fitted well into the gor-
geous and spectacular setting that was the city of Seattle. Towering and snow-capped like the mountains that ringed the city, he
seemed a part of it—as indeed he was. Born into this gargantuan
northwest region of towering forests, limitless waters, vast mountains, fertile valleys, he himself blended into the lavish picture and
was one with it. He loved it, he understood it. Breathing deep of
its pine and salt air, a heady draught, he digested it like the
benevolent giant he was.

Eastern visitors, accustomed to nature in cozier mood, were
vaguely frightened by this colossal pageant. Certainly a recital of
the region's natural charms, no matter how restrained, always
gave the effect of a Chamber of Commerce pamphlet gone mad.

To begin with the least of its astounding features, the city of
Seattle boasted two canals, man-made both (if Seattle had ever
deigned to boast of so paltry a possession). Next, two ample lakes
lay glittering and dimpling in its midst where even one would
have been redundant for this town whose water front led to the
Pacific. Water-ringed though it was, with Elliott Bay, Puget
Sound, the Strait of Juan de Fuca forming an aquatic background breath-taking in its beauty, Seattle still sulked over the

fact that the actual Pacific Ocean lay more than a hundred miles distant.

As though its founders had tried to rival the fantastic splendor with which Nature had encircled it, the city itself was built on seven hills higher than the classic seven hills of the Eternal City. Houses and gardens and trees and vines clung to the steep slopes or perched on the pinnacles. Garages were built on roofs. Automobiles, parked in front of houses or shops, clutched the asphalt in defiance of the law of gravity. Dwellings, looking like toy cottages stuck on a Hans Christian Andersen hillside, peered impishly down upon the roof tops of towering apartment houses below. Unwary pedestrians panting up a perpendicular street found themselves confronted with a dizzy flight of steps that seemed to scale a sheer wall but that merely led to the street's higher level. Always, on the downslope, the streets fell away to the waterside and always the gaze was met with that dramatic water front lined with docks and ships of every description, and beyond this the mountains.

In this panorama there were rivers—the Duwamish, twin-mouthed, was in itself a sizable body of water—but for such puny spawn of Nature Seattle had little respect. It took for granted, too, the immense black patches shadowing the distant hills and valleys that, like deep velvet thrown down as a background for jewels, were the forests of giant firs and cedars and spruce and hemlock. With a final godlike gesture Nature had flung up not one but actually two separate and complete mountain ranges that flanked the city, one east, one west. To the west lay the Olympics with their snow-covered ridges. The Cascade Mountains, blue-green in the distance, lay east. In this last stupendous feat there was a kind of Jovian insolence. It was too much.

Above the whole, with the dramatic finality of a complete masterpiece—above canals, rivers, lakes, bay, straits, hills, forests, and mountain peaks—loomed the queen peak, Mount Rainier, eternally snow-crowned. Being a queen she knew she must not show herself too commonly; she rarely permitted her subjects to see her glorious face. But they knew she was there, majestic and beautiful, hidden behind her curtains of cloud and mist. On brilliant days she swept aside her concealing folds of gray chiffon and emerged a dazzling creature, her face and form glittering with a million jewels of ice and snow. Then all Seattle turned its eyes up to her; they paused in the busy canyons of the downtown streets; they faced her, blinking, from the hills; they peered from their windows and they called to each other, "Look! Look! Rainier's out! You can see Rainier!" Unconsciously the town took on a holiday mood. The Rotary Club, chewing its soothing cigar after a session of corned-beef hash, said, "See Rainier? She sure looks good." Tearoom ladies over their creamed chicken patties used adjectives that usually they reserved for their favorite movie stars. School kids, frisking, yelped, "Looka! Rainier!"

The tourist from the East had considerable difficulty in digesting this overlavish scenic feast spread for his delectation. "Uh—— Olympics!" he stammered. "But I thought you just said they were called the Cascade Mountains."

"Not those. Not this bunch. Over there, those are the Olympics, see, and the ones you saw a while ago, those are the Cascades. There are two."

"Two! Two what?"

"Two different mountain ranges."

"I never heard of such a—— Say, wait a minute! Are you trying to kid me for a tenderfoot? A while ago you showed me Lake Washington and then you said Lake Union. Now don't tell me you've got two——"

"Yes, we have. Two lakes, too. That's Washington and this one's Union." Almost feebly the tourist said, "I see."

Salmon in the near-by rushing streams; shrimps and crabs and oysters in the bay; game in the forests; fruit in the valleys. In the mountains lay gold and silver and lead and mercury and platinum. Granite and limestone and marble.

Overwhelmed by all this, and feeling vaguely resentful, the visiting tourist would return to his hotel filled with the desire to pull down his bedroom shades and lie quietly for a while with his eyes shut; or hoping, perhaps, to find a cozy dim little basement bar with a view of nothing where he could call for a drink and sit thinking only of tiny things such as buttercups, thimbles, snail shells, and postage stamps. He was then told that there was no such thing as a single drink purchasable in Seattle. One had to buy a bottle. It was the law. Maddened by this insistence on profusion, the visitor was likely to break into a tantrum.

"Good God, does everything come wholesale here! This town is suffering from giantism!"

It was indeed a colossal feat of Nature. It was a godlike production. It was too much for the average man. But not for Vaughan Melendy.

Like the trees and mountains all about him, he stood more than ordinarily tall. Even now, past seventy, he was well over six feet, and straight of back and flat of stomach. The men and women of his family all had been tall. Perhaps the hewing of wood and the drawing of water had developed their muscles and lengthened their limbs. Perhaps the mood of exaggeration which touched all nature in this region applied to man as well.

It was a new town, Seattle, even for the United States and even for the West. Yet it had somehow the look of an old city. The ageless sea and the timeless mountains gave it a mellow glow, misted it and shaded it and colored it so that its modern skyscrapers and its imitation Queen Anne and gimcrack Victorian mansions took on the patina of time. Of all American cities it was, perhaps, the most American. All nationalities had come there, from the Orient, from the Far North, from the South, from the West. Even as you stepped off your train to enter the city you saw that your redcap and all the other scampering little porters were of a cast of feature unfamiliar to you. Filipinos, you learned, and Hawaiians. Japanese were the market gardeners and the household servants. Down at Fisherman's Wharf the halibut and salmon fleets were manned by Norwegians and Swedes and Finns. Irish, Italian, German, French, English, Chinese, Negro, all were ingredients of this savory dish.

A city not yet a century old, its skyscrapers taunted Mount Rainier while Indian tepees could still be found in the forests and the Alaska Thlinget totem pole down on the Skidroad was not an anachronism. It was the kind of city pictured by untraveled Europeans as an American city. It was fantastic, it was thrilling, it was absurd, it was majestic, it could have been the most beautiful city in the world—it might yet be, one day.

Her citizens were fond of saying, "We're the last frontier. Step off the water front and you'll find yourself swimming it for British Columbia or Alaska or Siberia. We're the city of Seattle in the state of Washington and, like the fella says, we're all there is. There isn't any more."

2

THE STOCK that bred Vaughan Melendy had landed at Alki Point in 1851 when there existed no state of Washington, no city of Seattle, no anything other than wilderness, water, and Indians. At the other extreme of the continent New York City went in silk and broadcloth, rode in carriage and pair, politely applauded the opera, aped the manners and customs of Europe. Yet here in the nameless Northwest there was no sound of civilization, there was nothing to break the silence but the footfall of the Indian in the forest, the pad of the wild beast, the splash of salmon in the streams.

Alki. Those first bearded boys who settled this wild new land had picked up the word in the Chinook jargon. *Alki* meant by-and-by. A prophetic instinct must have told them even then that a handful of years would see amazing changes. And now, in 1941, there still lived a woman who had seen the wonder wrought. Vaughan Melendy's mother, old Madam Melendy they called her, respectfully. Mrs. Exact Melendy had outlived the miracle itself, through ninety years and more. Out of nowhere, out of nothing she had beheld the gigantic engineering and architectural feats; she had witnessed the building of massive dams, bridges, parks, museums; the ornate old houses on Queen Anne Hill and

Capitol Hill; the golf clubs, the colorful markets, the luxurious private estates just outside the city. Herself a sort of civic monument, Madam Exact Melendy was living proof of the Aladdinlike myth of the founding of what the city fathers mellifluously (and somewhat undemocratically) called the Northwest Empire.

Not only did this ancient dame live to tell the amazing tale of the town's beginning, but she told it (her grandson Dike Melendy said) at the drop of a conversation. She had become a terrific snob about it all, she considered herself pioneer royalty, queened it all her life over members of the Mercer Girls' expedition who had arrived in 1865. No important civic gathering or public project was complete without a glimpse at least of the monolithic Madam Exact Melendy enthroned on the platform, her ample silken skirts spread in statuesque folds, her lace jabot clasped by very large, very good, very blue-white though somewhat dusty diamonds (set in gold that her son Vaughan Melendy had himself brought out of Alaska).

In the past ten years it was noticed that she claimed to remember events which she could not possibly have witnessed even in her infancy. Doubtless she had heard her parents speak of them and now they had become part of the colorful tapestry that was her own life. Newcomers to Seattle, bored with local lore, sometimes dismissed the whole pattern with the flat statement that Seattle had no history—that nothing was history so long as there remained alive a participant in the entire pageant of events. Hints of this skepticism having come to the ancient's keen ears, she had boomed in her astonishingly powerful voice, "Oh, so they want me to die to please the history books, eh! Well, they can save their breath and their wreaths as well. I'm chockful of good pioneer blood and these newfangled vitamins. I'll live to be a hundred and more. What's a hundred these days!"

She will, too, the town agreed with grim admiration.

This monumental old lady had been an infant in the arms of her young mother when she was brought ashore at Alki Point

from the schooner *Exact*. It was early in the morning, chill
autumn, the rain had come down unrelentingly all night so that
it made a gray and gloomy curtain between the wistful faces at
the ship's rail and the waiting men on shore. Above the squirming
flanneled bundle in her arms the face of the young mother was
weary and not a little frightened. She and the other women passengers had expected to see the outlines at least of a civilized settlement: houses, smoke curling from chimneys. But there was only
a wilderness of forest with no sign of a decent dwelling unless you
dignified by that name a roofless cabin of rough pine that was like
a raw gash against the impenetrable black wall of giant tree
trunks.

The rain had not ceased with daylight, and the little company
that had just stepped ashore in open boats from the anchored
schooner was sodden and dispirited. The neat calico sunbonnet
that the young wife had starched and ironed before coming on
board was a limp rag now. The water from its fluted peak trickled
dismally down her nose. The infant, too, shield it though she tried,
was soaked within and without.

Months had gone by since she and her young husband and
their neighbors had made the agonizing overland journey from
their native Illinois to Portland, Oregon. The young bride had
stayed in Portland amid the safety of its two thousand inhabitants
while the husband had gone on to stake his claim to land and land
and land in the new wilderness beyond. Now, in November, she
had embarked at Portland with the others of that young company, mere boys and girls, though married. The Pilgrim Fathers
themselves, more than two hundred years before, had not landed
in a wilder or more savage spot.

On the voyage from Portland to this Alki Point the young
wife had endured such discomfort and squalor on the little two-
masted schooner that she had prayed only for the stability of the
ground beneath her feet once more and the shelter of her husband's arms. She and the others had been terribly seasick from

the rough voyage and from the rich fat smoked salmon which the passengers had thriftily purchased from the Indians before sailing from Portland. They had cooked it on board on the one little stove in the midst of the smoke and smells of the crowded cabin. Even now the thought of what had followed caused her to feel faint and sick.

The bearded boy who rushed forward to meet her on the beach had never seen his child, for he had left Portland before her birth. There were tears in his eyes, his face was twisted with emotion as he took the squirming bundle in his left arm while his right encircled the girl, so that the three stood embraced as one. Then, "Phew!" he said. "Salmon! You smell of smoked salmon like an Indian!"

At that she began to cry, what with weakness and disappointment and wounded vanity and fear of this wild country. He kissed her wet face, he patted her convulsive shoulder, he joggled the baby, who needed nothing less than joggling at the moment. "Don't! Don't cry, Hetty. Look, you haven't even told me what you called it. I don't even know my own baby's name."

"It!" she wailed, every fiber of motherhood offended.

"Her," he corrected hastily. "I don't even know what she's called."

The girl lifted her face drenched with tears and rain. "I didn't name her. I wanted to wait till we could name her together, properly. I just call her Baby." A belated sob rushed up to join its predecessors. "Course, if she'd been a boy like you—like you wanted—why, he'd have been called after you. That's why I didn't name him—her, I mean. I don't know. I thought maybe Mary. Laura's nice. Abigail like your ma? Louisa? Sophia?"

He was holding the infant and now, as though in protest, it lurched in his arms, emitted a vigorous shriek, struck out with a fist suddenly free of the flannel cocoon, and clipped its astonished male parent neatly on the jaw.

"Heh! Well, gosh! She ain't a boy but she sure hits like one."

The waving fist now landed a glancing blow on his left eye. Shouting with laughter, the young father jerked back his head, and his gaze fell on the schooner *Exact* riding at anchor in the bay, a tough little craft barely seventy feet long, grimy and battered from her rough trip around Cape Flattery and up the Sound. "Say! Exact! That's it! That's the name for her, after the ship that's brought her to me safe and sound. It's a name'll bring her luck. A name like that, a girl can't help but be a stanch little craft. Exact. Look, she's smiling!"

The drenched and weary young wife still had the spirit to remonstrate. Outraged, she murmured something about Lydia. Too late. With the others he had turned shoreward, and she followed the dispirited little company that began to trudge up the beach in the cold rain.

"Where's the house?" she asked. "Our house."

He waved his free arm in the direction of the single roofless pine cabin through which the water was pouring, a deluge. "There."

"House! That!" Hysteria broke her voice.

"Shipshape by night. We'll finish it now in a jiffy. We didn't have a frow for splitting shakes, so we couldn't get the roof on. Now the schooner's brought us tools it's soon done."

The girl turned her eyes back toward the ship that now suddenly seemed so safe, so snug, so desirable. "Those men—those other passengers who didn't land with us—they're miners. They sang and yelled and played poker the whole way, a scandal. They're on their way to Queen Charlotte Islands; they say there's gold there, great lumps of gold, there are Indians called the Haidahs, very fierce, but still—gold . . ."

But his set young face was turned sternly away from the ship that even now was preparing to be on her way. His eyes were on the land, on the forest that covered this Alki Point and the hills beyond. As they walked, their boots squashed with the water in them, the rain ran down their soaked clothing, the infant squalled, the young wife stifled a desire to scream and run. Run where? They trudged toward the roofless cabin.

"Gold! Gold can come later, maybe. Maybe there's gold right here. There's everything for the taking. Land! Land! I've wanted it all my life, and plenty. Now I've got it. Little Exact here, she'll have a thousand miles of new land to grow up in."

3

AND NOW, past ninety, here she was, Exact Melendy, Seattle's oldest pioneer, queening it on Queen Anne Hill, Seattle's highest point. From her broad, thick, plate-glass windows she could survey her domain, misted or sun-drenched by day, sparkling with a thousand lights by night. Her son Vaughan's house was high, but hers was higher. It stood on a knoll that was almost another hill in its own right, the land sloping away from it on all sides so that the house perched like a miniature medieval castle. Madam Melendy, the town called her, rather pretentiously. A society reporter on the *Post-Intelligencer* had started it in order to avoid confusing her with Vaughan Melendy's wife, Emmy. There were three Melendy women, and one or all three seemed always to be popping into the society or club columns. Mrs. Exact Melendy, the widowed matriarch; Mrs. Vaughan Melendy, her daughter-in-law; Mrs. Dike Melendy, wife of Vaughan's son. Committees, chairmen, and reporters were quick to seize upon the title for old Exact.

Madam Exact Melendy, Seattle's oldest resident and well-known pioneer, was guest of honor and addressed a few words to the members of the Northwest Pioneer Association at their banquet . . .

The family, though they had used it at first only in fun, now accepted it and even addressed her by it sometimes. Her great-grandson Mike Melendy found it a real convenience. Emmy Melendy was Grandma to him, but one couldn't very well address anyone as Great-Grandma. Madam, he said. Hi, Madam Melendy!

They formed quite a little colony up there on Queen Anne Hill, the Melendys. They occupied three separate houses, and there was even a fourth which town gossip always connected with the family. That was Pansy Deleath's house. Local townspeople or civic welcoming committees, bent on showing the sights to visitors, always included the dazzling view from Queen Anne Hill, but the view included not only Mount Rainier (if they were lucky) and the docks and the bay and the mountains and the lakes and the clustered city itself, but the homes of the Melendy clan. As the visitors descended from their cars and stared at the view and at the dwellings they were regaled with a spicy routine.

Up there, that's old Madam Melendy's house, she's Seattle's oldest pioneer, she came here a baby in Fifty-one, she's terrific, smokes a pipe, wears satin and diamonds to breakfast, runs the whole shebang, she's over ninety and rich as dirt they're all scared of her. . . . That big house there is Vaughan Melendy's, he owns half of our downtown real estate and salmon canneries up in Alaska, and lumber and so on, he struck it rich in Alaska in the gold rush just like in the movies, he comes of old pioneer stock, but they lost their shirts didn't hang on to their early land claims, but he got it all back and more after Ninety-eight. . . . That newest place, that's Dike Melendy's, his real name is Klondike, that's the name they gave him, can you beat it! His wife's an actress in New York they're kind of separated anyway she's gone most of the time, they have a son Mike it's like the song—you know—Dike and Mike they look alike, only —you see that house down the hill a ways, the kind of storybook-looking one with all the madroña trees and vines? That's

Pansy Deleath's house they say she's been old Vaughan's mistress for thousands of years and Dike Melendy is really her son that old Vaughan and his wife Emmy adopted. . . . She was a dance-hall girl, Pansy I mean, up in Alaska, that's how they met and I must say young Mike the grandson looks the image of Pansy, I guess it skipped a generation, he's eighteen or nineteen, just a kid. He's got a kind of square jaw just like her and eyes deep blue they're almost purple, they say that's how she got her name up in the Klondike, Pansy on account of her eyes. . . . Her mother came to Seattle an opera singer back in the Eighties. . . . A lot of people wouldn't talk to Pansy years back, the women used to snoot her but she never let on she even noticed, she just went her way, gave her money whenever needed. . . . Yes, she's rich, too, made it up in the Klondike and owns a slice of Seattle now and could buy and sell a lot of us. Folks like her now and respect her, you can't help yourself, she's got a kind of gay way with her, warmhearted and a good head on her, too. . . . Queen Anne Hill could tell a lot of stories. Up here this used to be the fashionable place to live, that's how they built all these big houses, but it's not such a fashionable neighborhood now, they're building out farther Highlands way that used to be considered way out of town. But the Melendys have stuck. They say young Dike, that's Vaughan's son, was going to build a big place out there before his wife left him for New York. . . . Well, anything can happen here in Seattle. Anyway, just about everything has. . . .

Every morning, fair or foul, Vaughan Melendy came out of his fine house, crossed the lawn and garden, and stood bareheaded on the huge flat-topped rock that formed the highest point of the ledge. That ledge had long ago been transformed into a rock garden by Emmy with the help of the Japanese gardener. Summer and winter the rocks were brilliant with the colors of tiny clinging blossoms in that mild moist climate, made mild in spite of its northerly latitude by the warm air of the Japan

Current. From this vantage spot Vaughan surveyed every morning the panorama of sky and mountains and water and forest. Every morning it was a source of fresh joy and wonder to him. He lifted his head and breathed deep, and as he drew in the lung-filling breath of salt and pine air the voice of his wife Emmy floated out to him like a querulous ghost in the mist. "Vaughan! Your hat! You'll catch your death!" With quite unconscious analysis he sometimes thought grimly, "I bet she wishes I would."

His gaze, though appreciative of the beauty that lay spread before him, was a practical one. He marked the weather portents. He thought, well, no Rainier today with this fog; or, she'll be out if the sun keeps warm, about noon, maybe. His keen eyes searched the docks; they saw the funnels of great ships; he had seen the ships of all nations down there, but that had passed as the war in Europe spread so that its evil growth threatened even these remote shores. He spoke of these ships in the nautical terms of a seaman. Foreign bottoms, he called them. Here in Seattle the Orient and the Occident met. The great liners had come from Japan, from China, from the Philippines, Alaska, New Mexico, South America, Europe, Africa, Australia. Into this port they had poured the riches of continents—silk, rice, tea, coffee, sugar, spices, hemp, rubber, furs, oils, copper, ore, gold. The great cargo ships of the world were familiar names to Vaughan; their precious freight was part of his successful and widely diversified business life; he spoke of them as you would speak of acquaintances—the *Santa Floura* for Ketchikan; the *Kaiuo* from Yokohama; the *Santa Rosa* for Mazatlan; the *Mauna Ala* for Honolulu; the *Niles* from Buenos Aires; the *Nansonville* from Oslo. He knew the ports for which they were bound, the lands from which they had sailed. He knew not only the ships but the waters on which they traveled, for he had piloted in his youth, and that was tricky work in these waters of every depth and width and current. Useless Bay and Cultus Bay where many a ship had met her fate. He knew the story of the clipper ship *Windward* that had gone aground off Cultus. Towed at last into Seattle Harbor, she actually was buried upright, masts and all, as the land was filled, and he knew as truth that she now lay under the concrete streets of Seattle. What other city had an upright clipper ship buried in her heart!

Standing there, he stamped on the stony ground beneath his feet; he liked the feel of the earth and the nip in the heady air and the taste of the fog in his mouth. There were people who rose from their beds and washed and sat down and ate their breakfast. Not he. Too many years of his youth had been spent in the open, wrestling with the forces of Nature. Years on the water; years logging the woods as a lumberjack; years in the bitter hardship of Alaska. At thirteen, fourteen, fifteen he had known the feel of the early-morning air as he stumbled sleepily out to work before daylight. Now it was part of his daily ablutions.

Dike. Dike, he reflected, got his exercise out at the Highlands Golf Club. Swung a mean mashie, Dike did, and even young Mike had respect for his father's backhand at tennis. Vaughan turned to look at his son's house; he could just see the upper stories, for it stood below his house as his own stood below his mother's house. A more modern house than his, having been built more than a quarter of a century later. But he wouldn't swap, not even today. Dike was coming home from the East today with his wife. It was a pattern repeated often in the past twenty years. Funny, you never thought of Lina as Mrs. Dike Melendy. It was Lina Port. Well, she had a right to the name; she had made it for herself; it meant something back East. People who went to the theater knew her name. She wasn't a great actress; she never had been a star; she never would be. She was good. Pansy had explained it to him on one occasion—one of many—on which Lina had packed up to rush to Hollywood for a bit part and then had gone to New York to play a full year in Snow in June.

"Lina isn't only an actress," Pansy had said when Lina had

again left her husband, her luxurious house, her son, her snug, secure life to play throughout a stifling summer or a freezing winter on what was generically referred to as Broadway. "She's stage-struck. She begins to feel restless, and Dike thinks if he gives her another bracelet or a big sapphire clip or a trip to San Francisco, why, that'll fix everything, she'll forget all about the stage. But it never works. It's like the way you feel in the spring when the salmon begin to run; you know they're good red kings and you know the canneries up there will get along without you fine, but you keep thinking of that three hundred miles up to Kodiak in the rough sea with the swells running high, and you know you're better off here, and Emmy fusses and your ma has a fit, but pretty soon you can't stand it any longer, and you go down and you get aboard the Alaska boat that couldn't be more uncomfortable and stinks of fish, and off you go with a native boy and a good engineer and a bum cook, and you're happy."

"Yeh," he had said, and now for the first time he understood Lina Port and felt akin to her. "Yeh, I see."

This morning as he stood there, hatless, on the ledge overlooking his world he was conscious of a new feeling, and it was not a pleasant one. It was a feeling of insecurity; it was nothing you could name exactly, it was like the feeling you had when you passed a bunch of kids, they were kind of quiet and innocent-looking and doing nothing, but as you passed there was a crawling, shrinking feeling in the back of your neck where you felt that snowball was going to land.

"Vaughan! Breakfast!" Emmy at the bedroom window.

"All right. I'm coming." But he did not move. As he stood there silhouetted against sky and bay and mountain he was like a statue labeled The Northwest. He looked great, but he wasn't thinking great thoughts. He was a worried man of seventy, healthy, rich, respected. Must be my liver, he thought. Hell, no, I never had a liver, not going to start now, like an old woman. I didn't sleep much last night, funny thing for me. Guess that's why

I feel logy this morning. A cup of coffee'll fix me up. Seventy was no spring chicken, but it wasn't that. The world. It was getting to be such a crazy-acting place you couldn't keep track of it. Things used to be plain and simple; you did a thing and you knew how it would turn out. But not now. The world was changing. Seattle was changing before his eyes. Not changing the way it had in the last fifty, sixty years. Look at Ma, she could remember when it was a howling wilderness full of Indians. Ma certainly had made a monkey of those fellas in the Bible with their three-score and ten. At seventy she had just got her second wind. Now another twenty years piled on top of that and twenty more to go, likely as not.

It was curiously quiet up there this morning. Still. It was as though the whole city, the entire region as far as his eye could see, opalescent in the morning light, were suspended in space, waiting for something. He missed the hoarse hoots of the ships in the bay, the deep bass growl of the ocean liners, the throb of a thousand pulsing engines. There was a different sound nowadays; you heard the throb-throb of new engines, but the ships they drove forward were up in the air, thousands of feet up in the air, and young kids were piloting them—kids like Mike, who were air-crazy. When young Mike said ship he meant an airship. Mustn't let new things scare you, Vaughan told himself. Sure sign of old age, that was. Take 'em in your stride, accept them, try to understand them.

Who could tell what anything was going to be, the way the world was headed? Who could tell the way the world was headed, for that matter? Look at old London, smashed up. Look at Rotterdam, pleasant a little town as you'd want to see; he and Emmy had admired the sturdy, ornate buildings—quaint, Emmy said —and the narrow streets and the docks and wharves. He had been especially interested in the shipping. Well, look at it now. Mashed. Who could tell what might come through the air to us right here—to Seattle even? Japs might take a notion to get go-

ing. Folks laughed at him when he said things like that. Well, if
ever they did get together with the Nazis, why, good night.
Everything here right out in the open; no defense that you could
call defense. Good-by, Seattle and San Francisco and Vancouver
and pretty little Victoria and Alaska, too, likely as not, and the
whole damned West coast. No use warning them. Nobody would
listen. But he had a feeling. A funny feeling at the pit of his stomach.

"Vaughan! It's all getting stone cold!"

"All right! All right!"

He turned toward his house. He looked at it as though he
never before had seen it. He knew now it wasn't as fine a house
as he had thought it when he had built it with such pride many
years ago, after he had stepped off the greasy Alaska boat with
a poke of gold in either hand. Like a figure (he now realized)
in a Klondike gold-rush movie, kind of ridiculous, but true and
wonderful, too, like a lot of things in America. Sometimes he
thought maybe his whole life had been sort of ridiculous and wonderful but true. The richest man in the biggest damned house on
the highest hill in the greatest city in the state of Washington.
That was Vaughan Melendy. A bigger house even than Jim Hill's
house, and finer. A library full of expensive books, the bindings
good as money could buy. Emmy's linen closets and china cupboards and silver chests stuffed full of the best there was, too.
Crystal chandeliers flashed their emerald and scarlet and gold
and sapphire. Big, soft oriental rugs on the shiny hardwood floors.
Big, soft chairs. Radio in every room including the kitchen.
Kitchen so full of gadgets the Japs hardly had to lift a finger.
A cake practically whirled itself together and jumped into the
oven under its own power, all those electric mixers and so forth.
Electricity. By God, time the war in Europe was finished proba-
bly would have all that electricity at Bonneville Dam and Grand
Coulee roped and tied so a fellow wouldn't have to work at all.
Electricity would do everything for you by then, open and shut

the door, put your coat on for you, breed your children for you, likely as not. That would have suited Emmy fine, he thought with grim humor. Emmy, who had never given him a child.

There on the side porch was Yoshitaka in his white house coat so neat and stiff, bowing and sucking in his breath and saying, "Breakfast ready, please Mister Melendy," and not being able to pronounce the letter *r*. As Vaughan came nearer the man shook his head. With the napkin in his hand he made dabs at the lapels of Vaughan's coat.

"What's the matter, Taka?"

"Wet. Missy mad."

Both Taka and his wife, Masako (May, they called her in the household), spoke English like Japanese stage servants, but their son William and their pretty daughter Grace, both American born, spoke without a trace of Japanese accent. The two were students at the University of Washington. William was going to be an engineer. Now, in his off hours, he earned his tuition by working as gardener for the Melendys, acting as informal chauffeur when his father was busy with household jobs. He and young Mike Melendy just next door were great friends; their talk was all of planes, engines, motors—it was unintelligible talk to the men of Vaughan's generation.

Most of Seattle's Orientals—Japanese and Chinese—lived in the shacks south of the town's business district. The Nakaisuki family lived in one such tiny house, and every square inch of the infinitesimal plot of ground around it was planted with fruits, vegetables, flowers. It produced a fantastic variety and abundance of crops. The vegetables they sold in the Farmers' Market. Early in the morning Taka and May appeared quietly at Vaughan Melendy's home; they performed their duties with utter perfection; they departed in their little secondhand car when their work was done at night. Even Emmy, the finicking, the faultfinding, could discover little to criticize in their conduct of the house.

Now Taka showed his square yellow teeth in disapproval of

Vaughan's iron-gray hair misted with fog and the shoulders of his coat damp with it. It was difficult to tell whether Taka was approving or displeased. His grin was the same for both emotions. He pointed toward Melendy's head and made little sounds.

"Afraid I'll catch hell from the missus, heh?" Vaughan said. He ran his palm over his hair and it came away wet. He bent over and shook himself like a great mastiff and the tiny drops flew. The thick vigorous crown of hair with the wave in its forelock had begun to grow iron-gray after he returned from the Klondike back in Ninety-eight, though he was then a virile giant not yet thirty. Sometimes even now he found himself staring as at a stranger at his own reflection in the mirror as he shaved. "Funny thing," he would mutter. "Used to be jet black. Now look! White as a whale's belly."

In the early days women had liked it and remarked it. It made his pink cheeks seem pinker, his blue eyes bluer.

"What you got for breakfast, Taka? Something good and hot?" He wiped his shoes carefully on the mat before the door, this side and that. Taka stooped and picked a bit of leafmold from the cuff of his trousers. Emmy was not one to tolerate a muddy footprint on her carpets. Emmy's floors, windows, furniture, curtains, glistened, crackled, shone. Quite a feat in that moist climate and with those windows. Plate glass ten feet wide and thick enough to stand the winds on Queen Anne Hill. No one need go out of doors for the view; it came into the house; it filled every room with sky and mountains and water and sun— when the sun chose to shine through the mists.

Through the big front entrance hall floated delicious breakfast smells. It was more than an entrance hall, it was a rotunda of dimensions which you ordinarily would find in a public building. The four-story staircase with balconies running all the way around formed an impressive well. The enormous, absurd house was stuffed with expensive furniture bought in New York, in San Francisco, or here in Seattle. There were great Chinese vases and lumps of ivory and jade from Gumps's. Tusks, moose heads, stuffed salmon, Indian relics—proof of Vaughan's prowess— leered or glared at one from walls and corners. Years ago Vaughan had got hold of the steering wheel and lamps of the old *Portland,* the ship that had brought the first ton of gold into Seattle Harbor from Alaska. The nautical lamps in the lower hall, the wheel on the ornate balcony off the second floor seemed stark and incongruous in the midst of the carved banisters, the tortured newel posts, the beams, mantels, marbles, metals, spears, oriental hangings, potted ferns.

Taka held open the door, then managed to whisk around Vaughan and now stood behind his chair, waiting to shove it neatly under Vaughan's knees as he seated himself at the breakfast table.

"Good morning!" said Emmy, just as though she had not seen Vaughan less than half an hour ago wrestling with his underwear in their bedroom. Emmy said good morning in the morning to everybody. She said good morning to her husband and to her son Dike and to her grandson Mike and to Taka and May and to William and to the butcher when she telephoned him, and to her friends. Young Mike, her grandson, found this mildly amusing and irritating at the same time and essayed to break her of it, forgetting for the moment that Emmy was a humorless woman.

"Good morning! Good morning!" he would say with a horrible heartiness. "And a very good morning to you, Mrs. Melendy, if I may presume to call you that. And how are you this morning?"

But then Emmy would tell him how she was, in some detail. Dike, if he happened to be present, would say to his son, sotto voce, "Serves you right, Smarty Pants."

Emmy was a good woman and a wonderful housekeeper and a crashing bore. She sat now at her breakfast table, and everything she wore was fresh and in perfect order, and everything

on the breakfast table was shining and exquisite, and Vaughan
knew that the orange juice would be cold and the eggs would be
hot. The mahogany woodwork shone. The mahogany table shone.
The silver glistened; the plants in the window shone with health
and castor oil. Itsybitsy, Emmy's toy Pekinese, sat on the floor
at the side of her chair, brushed and silken, rolling his moist and
protuberant eyes greedily and making snuffling sounds. Vaughan,
who had known the malemutes and huskies of the Alaska days,
despised this tiny beast.

Vaughan picked up the *Post-Intelligencer* folded so neatly at
the side of his plate. He was more eager to read it than to eat
his good breakfast, but he first essayed polite conversation because he knew it was expected of him and he felt constrained to
do so and hated it and would have admitted none of these things
if confronted with them.

"Uh, didn't see William around this morning. Too wet, d'you
think?"

"Oh, Vaughan, for heaven's sake! You know perfectly well
he's gone down to meet the train."

"That's right. Dike and Lina. Forgot for a minute."

"Well, I didn't. Honestly, I don't know where Dike's pride is.
To let that woman make a fool of him over and over again. I
don't know where he gets it. I'm not like that and neither——"
She stopped. She actually had forgotten that Dike was not her
own flesh and blood. Vaughan glanced up from his paper and
saw that she was not embarrassed or shocked at what she had
started to say. She had stopped abruptly merely because Taka
had re-entered the room with the hot breakfast dishes. Emmy's
code included the rule that one must not discuss family affairs in
the presence of servants. She now coughed genteelly and assumed
a tone of casual conversation. "I thought I'd have them to dinner
tomorrow noon, Sunday. The whole family to welcome her, Mike
home from college and everything."

"Well, say, maybe she'd rather stay home and rest and get

unpacked and so forth. That's a long trip by train from New York. Why didn't they fly, I wonder."

Taka had left the room again for the kitchen. "Because she won't reach here so soon by train, that's why," Emmy said viciously.

"Now, Emmy, you don't understand. Lina's an actress; the theater's in her blood; she loves it. A household isn't enough to——"

"Mhm. And a husband isn't enough and a son isn't enough and Seattle isn't enough—or good enough, I should say."

"Now, Emmy." He plunged into his paper with a clear conscience. He needn't listen to this. He had heard it for twenty years.

On and on in her very feminine, querulous voice—her Baby Snooks voice, Mike called it. Emmy had been a very pretty girl; she was pretty even now in her late sixties; it was remarkable how she had kept her trim figure and her clear, fresh skin. Her prim little pursed mouth was somewhat withered, the pale blue eyes were less appealing in their nearsighted wistfulness now that she wore her eyeglasses constantly. But her soft, pale brown hair was hardly touched with gray. Her pink face was small; her nose was tiny so that the pince-nez had difficulty in maintaining a hold. It literally pinched the skin of her nose, wrinkling it in a way that had annoyed Vaughan for years and years and years, though he did not realize it. Emmy was as completely dressed now at eight in the morning as though she were going to an office or a social engagement. Fresh and neat at the shining breakfast table in her blue dress with its crisp white collar and cuffs.

Emmy was always dressed. Once, years ago, Vaughan had realized with a shock that in all their decades of married life he never had seen Emmy uncovered. He had seen her undress in bedrooms, in train compartments, in steamship cabins, but she was the kind of woman who, disrobing, uses her nightgown as a tent. In corset, petticoat, pants, and stockings she pulled her

nightgown over her head and primly withdrew inside it. Busy
elbows and knees produced strange outjutting angles but never
a glimpse of bosom or thigh. Finally her head emerged flushed,
triumphant above the nightgown that covered her from shoulders
to floor, above the little heap of discarded garments that lay,
harmless and innocent, at her feet, now that they were merely
things of cloth and silk and (discreet) lace.

Now as she talked on and on in her high childlike voice she
was pouring his coffee, a rite. She had pretty little hands, plump
and white and dimpled in spite of her years. She was enormously
vain of them, she loved to watch them. They fluttered over the
coffee cups, over the sugar, the cream, flutter, flutter, flutter.
Taka served the hot bread, the eggs; there was a sizzling bit of
smoked salmon for Vaughan's scrambled eggs, part of the last
catch sent down from the Melendy canneries in Alaska.

". . . and I'll ask Dave Dreen if you want him—that's six"—
she was enumerating her Sunday noonday dinner guests—"and
—phew! That salmon! I hate the smell of salmon in the morning!
—your ma and Reggie, that's eight—Pansy is nine——" She
looked at him sharply as she had looked at him for almost half
a century at the mention of Pansy's name.

Emmy, Pansy, Madam Melendy—the three women were held
together in a terrible bond of love for this man, a bond inter-
woven with strands of jealousy, affection, hate, admiration, resentment toward each other. Emmy held him with the bonds of
helplessness. This childless wife had, through the years, tried to
slip into the place of the children she never had borne.

What do you think they'd like for dinner? . . . Do you like
this hat, Vaughan? I'm sort of tired of blue so much. . . . I
wish you'd speak to that man who brought the porch chairs. . . .
Where are you going? . . . I don't know what you're talking
about. You twist around everything I say. . . .

A neat and fussy housekeeper, completely feminine, and abys-
mally dull, as are all completely feminine women. She was

crumbling a bit of bread in her fingers. Emmy ate almost no breakfast, drank her coffee black, had a way of making a hearty breakfaster feel guilty. Now she gathered up the little scattering of crumbs into a neat heap, every tiny one, swept them with the side of one hand into the palm of the other, deposited them on her plate, spatted her pretty hands together.

Abruptly Vaughan pushed back his chair, rose. He hadn't meant to. He had not even finished his first cup of coffee. Napkin in hand, he was rather astonished to find himself standing there.

"What's the matter?"

"Why?"

"Aren't you going to finish your breakfast?"

"I've finished."

"You've only had one cup of coffee. You haven't even drunk that."

"Uh—I guess I'm not hungry this morning. I didn't sleep so good last night. I don't know."

She, too, stood up now. "I don't see what I've said, if that's it. Now you'll go and tell your mother——"

"Oh, Emmy, Emmy."

"I don't care, I think Dike's wife is a scandal to the family. Leaving her husband and child months at a time; why, even when Mike was a baby she——"

"That was the understanding, wasn't it, when she married Dike years and years ago? She told him she was crazy about the stage and would go right on being an actress. My God, what're we talking about this now for, eight o'clock in the morning, when Dike and Lina have been married twenty years? Dike's—why, Dike's over forty-five; Lina must be crowding forty. What the hell are we talking about!"

"Forty or not, I'll bet she won't stay. She'll go off again, mark my words, first chance she gets in a show. Paint herself up and flounce on the stage in some cheap play——"

"I thought you liked the theater. Always go to everything comes along, and on our trips to New York, why——"

"You always twist around everything I say."

He looked down at the napkin still clutched in his hand, he tossed it to the table, came over to her, stooped and kissed his wife's cheek, the soft pink cheek so strangely unlined in a woman of her years. "Maybe you're jealous, Emmy. Maybe you wish you could have skylarked off like Lina, not worrying about your menfolks and—what's that they call it?—expressing yourself."

The tears—those ready weapons with which she always slew her opponents—now sprang to the pale blue eyes. She took off her glasses; she dabbed at her eyes with her napkin; she fumbled for her handkerchief and opened it, so fresh, so delicate, so neatly laundered. "Vaughan Melendy, please remember who you're talking to! Please remember my family. I'm no fly-bynight. Please remember Mama was a Mercer Girl."

4

"Mama was a Mercer Girl," Emmy always said, and her voice was rich with pride. Everyone in Seattle knew what she meant. It wasn't that Mama's name had been Mercer before her marriage. Not at all. She had been Miss Abbie Griggs of Massachusetts, one of that intrepid and fantastic shipload of bombazine belles who, shepherded by Asa Mercer and chaperoned by him, had sailed from New York Harbor to Seattle in 1866. Perhaps no aquatic journey in the history of the world had ever had such qualities of comedy, melodrama, romance, and downright ludicrousness as this one. One hundred virgin New England spinsters, prim, corseted, hoop-skirted, virtuous, had set sail on the sixteen-hundred-ton steamship known as the *Continental,* and the object of their journey—though clothed like themselves in the conventional garments of polite verbiage—was simply and starkly the acquiring of husbands. For of men in this new wild Northwest Territory there were enough and to spare, but of marriageable women there were almost none. It was Asa Mercer, one of those bearded boys who, in their twenties, were pioneers in the Northwest Territory, with whom the idea of this bizarre pilgrimage had originated. It was he who, after a year of disappointment and insult and heartbreak, had sailed in triumph with a hundred frightened but determined females.

They had been terribly seasick off Hatteras; they had stopped at the magnificent harbor of Rio de Janeiro; the wallowing ship had fittingly enough rounded Cape Virgins; had battled her way through the powerful tides and the storms of sleet and bitter rain that bedevil the Strait of Magellan; past mountains, past jungle shores, into the Pacific. The lurching tub touched the Galapagos and went on for another five thousand miles north. Though she had sailed from New York Harbor January 6, 1866, it was spring and April before the *Continental* entered California's Golden Gate, and even later before the last of the intrepid girls was safely landed in Seattle. They stepped off the ship intact, inviolate. In the town bells were rung, whistles tooted; the whole population was down at the dock including certainly every un-wed male. These were arrayed for conquest in their best store clothes and their satin store ties, and those who had no such fine feathers with which to attract the eye of a possible mate had bought new overalls. They had greased their boots; they had greased and slicked their hair; their faces were shining with eagerness and yellow soap.

It had been Asa Mercer's idea. Perhaps nowhere but in America could a plan so much like the possible plot for a comic opera and at the same time so fundamentally sound and practical have been formulated and brought to a triumphant conclusion.

Here in Seattle, Washington Territory, was this Asa Mercer at twenty-three the president of the Territorial University. He had grubbed out stumps for the university on Denny Hill; he had carried lumber for the university buildings. And here, in Washington Territory, there were ten men to every woman. And on the other side of the great country hundreds of thousands of young men were dying or had died on the battlefields of the Civil War. The entire South, the entire Eastern seaboard was being decimated of its young and virile males.

"I'm going to Washington," Asa Mercer announced. "I'm going to Washington city and talk with a man I know. He'll see my meaning plain."

"What man's that?" asked Asa's older brother Tom.

"Abraham Lincoln, President of the United States."

"You've gone clean out of your mind."

"Not me. You very well know when I was a boy back in Illinois I sat on his knee and he told stories that made everybody holler laughing. It might be he won't remember me, but I'll never forget the sound of his voice, kind and gentle and slow, and the feel of his hand, strong but gentle, too, like his voice."

"What's that got to do with hauling girls from back East clear around to Washington Territory? He'll have you thrown out."

"Likely. But maybe not. Abe Lincoln knows, if anybody does, that thousands and thousands of New England boys are dead and rotting at Gettysburg and in the Wilderness and at Spotsylvania. And there's the young girls, thousands of them, too, knowing they'll die old maids back East. And here are our young men in Seattle with good cabins to live in and plenty of food, and strong and healthy and wanting good wives. He'll understand. He'll help me."

And so the young Lochinvar set out. It was a jubilant letter his brother Tom got of Asa's safe arrival in New York April 17, 1865.

DEAR TOM [he wrote]. *Here I am in New York at last. A long wait for the steamer at Aspinwall, and a long trip on her, but here and well and hopeful. As soon as I got my hotel room and washed up I bought a ticket for the morning train to Washington. It may well be I'll have to wait days in Washington before I can see President Lincoln. They say he is overwhelmed with people pleading to speak with him on all manner of matters, all as important as mine, and I daresay many more so. But I'll wait patiently, and when I do see him I've no doubt about the outcome. A good man, a kind man, and blessed with deep understanding. This time next year I am certain that five hundred New England girls who otherwise would have gone unwed through life will be good and happy wives to our Seattle boys— and maybe happy mothers as well.*

Having written his letter, young Mercer, exhausted with travel and intent only on his great plan, shunned the thought of New York's gaieties at night, went to bed and slept the sleep of the young, the healthy, the utterly weary. Refreshed, he awoke with the morning light, and at six he was downstairs in the hotel lobby, ready for breakfast and eager to be off for Washington.

The hotel office was festooned with loops and bands of blackest crepe. On the wall there was a bulletin around which readers crowded, their faces stricken. President Lincoln had been assassinated at Ford's Theater the night before as Asa Mercer slept.

The eight months that followed were a saga of hope, disappointment, courage, despair. The boy—for he was little more than that—moved mountains, worked miracles by sheer determination and a deep belief in his own purpose. I'll see General Grant, he said; and saw him. Grant, a pudgy bearded man forever puffing and chewing at a cigar, knew magically what this young Mercer planned, and sympathized with his cause, for Grant had known, years before, what it had meant to be a lonely heartsick young man at the garrison of Fort Vancouver in Washington Territory three thousand miles away. He had listened, and he had said, "You have a fine plan. I'll help you."

But months went by. The Mercer Girls were as far as ever from Seattle and the new Washington Territory and husbands. Asa Mercer talked with Governor Andrew of Massachusetts, for it was from his state that he expected to bring most of his young spinsters. It was fitting, he said, that Massachusetts, the mother colony of the East, should now be the mother colony of the West.

He saw Edward Everett Hale. He saw Quartermaster-General Meigs. By now young Mercer had publicly made known his plan; he had even selected some hundreds of New England young women who measured up to his strict requirements. No flighty ones; no girls of doubtful background. These future wives of the men and mothers of the children of Washington Territory must be young women of character, background, purpose. He had received an avalanche of applications; he weeded and selected sternly. The months went by, and the important men he saw approved his plan and he had the promise of the ship, the *Continental*.

For Abbie Griggs, in the little town of Marston, Massachusetts, the Civil War was ended, and life as well. With red-rimmed eyes she looked into the future and there she saw a gray mist of nothingness. She wore the dead Isaiah's picture in her brooch with a lock of his hair—the picture he had taken in his uniform with the pancake-topped hat, the goatee beard that made his face seem so stern. New England was now full of spinsters such as Abbie, whose neat, high-necked gowns were fastened at the throat with brooches, and inside the brooch a dim likeness of a boy who never would laugh or love again. The throats would soon be withered above the flat brooches and the flat breasts.

Abbie Griggs was sixteen when her Isaiah had gone off to war. He had been one of the first to be killed—he had died at Manassas in the first Battle of Bull Run in July 1861; he had scarcely gone when they had the news of his death.

So Abbie had sat at home for four years, for five years; the Civil War was over. Her father was bitter about Lincoln; he had called him That Baboon in the White House; he said that Lincoln was to blame for all the ills that had come upon Massachusetts, upon New England, upon the United States, upon the world.

Abbie had seen New England spinsters alive and dead and dead-alive. She had seen spinster tombstones such as dotted the cemeteries all over New England.

POTTS

Jerusha Potts

Beloved Daughter

of

Jotham *and* Sarah Potts

b. 1802—d. 1849

Blessed Are The Pure In Heart

Well, she did not want to be blessed. She did not want to be pure in heart. She had been b. and now she did not want to d. without having known love and marriage and children. These things Abbie Griggs did not say aloud. She did not even say them to herself. She only thought them deep in her innermost frantic mind where the fears and the agonies and the despair ran back and forth and up and down like hideous little mice with ice-cold feet. She felt the warm blood coursing in her young veins; she looked about her and all about her as she looked were girls like herself, women like herself, old maids of sixteen, eighteen, twenty. They'd be thirty—forty—fifty—d. 18——?

"Ma, there's a man named Mercer—Asa Mercer—he has a plan for taking five hundred young women . . . knew President Lincoln. . . . Even General Grant says . . . and Governor Andrew . . ."

"Don't let your pa hear you talk like this. You're a Griggs. You're the daughter of a Potts. If he was to hear of such talk I don't know what he'd . . ."

Puget Sound. Washington Territory. Seattle. Well, people had gone to Europe and stayed there and been happy. Puget Sound was no farther than that, and besides, it was America, it was the United States, it was like the West toward which the women of Forty-nine had gone with their menfolks in the covered wagons. Earnestly, feverishly, she pleaded with her mother.

"Only this is by ship and pleasant as can be. No long, dusty trip across the land, with Indians waiting to scalp and steal. Lucy Withers' sister—the one who's married and lives in Connecticut —knows a girl whose cousin went to the Puget Sound country, she's from Boston and a lovely family. Eleven girls went a year ago with this same Asa Mercer; they're all married now; they're——"

The girl's strained and stricken face, so white now and thin, stabbed the mother's heart. She knew the hopelessness of her daughter's future, yet this wild plan was something her conven-

tional mind could not grasp. Besides, she knew her husband
would sooner see his daughter dead than part of this strange
hegira. To hide her own anguish the mother made her words the
harsher.

"Married to scum and rapscallions and criminals who likely
had to leave a respectable town here in the East."

"That's not true! They're fine young men, young and respectable and strong! Strong and alive! Alive!" Her face worked with
anguish; she clasped her hands to her breast and beat on her
breast as though to release some agony hidden there.

Suddenly the mother was the frightened one. She said, "I know,
I know. But your father——"

"He can't stop me. I'll go. If this Mr. Mercer will take me, I'll
go."

"How?"

"You must help me. A letter. This Mr. Mercer will take only
the most respectable young women. Like me. Respectable and
strong. You'll write a letter consenting——"

"Yes, but——"

"The Reverend Cable will write a letter if you ask him. Father
needn't know. There's no time to lose. Ma! Ma! I'll die here. Like
those others—Beloved Daughter Of. I don't want to be Beloved
Daughter Of. I want to be beloved—beloved wife of."

"Money?"

"Oh, I forgot. Money."

"I've a little put by. Your pa doesn't know. I've a little put by,
the way women do, from the butter money and the wool from
the sheep I raised from lambs. A bit, but it may do."

"Oh, Ma!" The two women, New England women, undemon-
strative, mingled their tears now.

Abbie reached New York only on the day the *Continental* was
sailing, eight months or more later than the time Asa Mercer had
planned and hoped to set sail. Malice and indifference and
vilification and lack of funds and trickery all had done their best

to destroy his plan, but now the *Continental* actually was sailing from New York Harbor. True, instead of five hundred there were only one hundred young women, but they were girls of honorable families; they had refused to be frightened by the false and malicious lies which Gordon Bennett's *Herald* had printed only a week before the expedition was to sail.

The men of Puget Sound are rotten profligates.

A young Satan by the name of Asa Mercer is collecting the flower of New England womanhood for the brothels of Seattle.

Spurn the tempter and stay at home.

Thus the newspaper articles. Four hundred young women put Mercer and his expedition out of their lives. Of the hundred who remained faithful was Abbie Griggs. Up the gangplank she swept, her hoops dipping and swooping with the vigor of her movements. There at the ship's rail were festooned the other ninety-nine girls, their faces alive with a look that was a strange mingling of fright and freedom. They had escaped the living grave of New England spinsterhood. Not one of them had ever been outside her native New England and most of them had never set foot beyond their native town.

As the ship cast off and warped her way out of the dock a cheer went up from a hundred girlish throats; it was more than a cheer, it was a sort of hysterical shriek of happiness. The dock receded, the land receded, their parents, their dead lovers, their ghostly husbands, the prim front parlors, the wax flowers under glass, the sewing bees, the church sociables, the tea drinking that revived but did not stimulate—all faded into the background of the Eastern shore line and vanished forever from their lives.

The *Continental* crept around Cape Hatteras, and the rugged virgins were terribly seasick and doubtless wished themselves on land—any sort of land—but they did not look back with regret upon the icy embrace of the chilly front parlor; they were no longer wax flowers under glass, they were seasick women inured now to human sounds and ugly sights. The wind howled; the ship

creaked; the salt spray doused them; the food was mostly par-
boiled beans. The hundred spinsters were sick, they were cold,
they were hungry, they were happy.

By the time the ship reached Rio de Janeiro they were again
fresh and bright; the air and the sun had brought color into their
faces; the young Spanish clearance officers came on board. They
saw a hundred American girls in their best flounces and bonnets,
their eyes bright, their skins fair, their cheeks flushing under the
ardent Latin looks. A good many of them could have stepped off
the ship then and there, for the young Spanish officers spoke of
marriage and the beauties of the southern climate.

"My, they're handsome!" the giggling girls whispered to one
another.

"I like American boys' looks," said Abbie Griggs.

"But these are so romantic."

"I warrant they wouldn't like walking a baby, nights," said the
hardheaded Abbie.

"Why, Abbie Griggs!"

They cleared Rio, into the Strait of Magellan; the ship bore
west and then southwest; she cleared Cape Pillar and Evangelistas
and headed northwest into the Pacific and came finally into
warmer latitudes and kinder seas. From the Galapagos at the end
of the world she went on another five thousand miles north. A
good thing these had been girls of health and spirit at the start.
Those who had not been so healthy became amazons in these
hundred days. Air and sun and hope and freedom did it, and
though the fare was rough—beans and some pork—they seemed
to thrive on it, perhaps because they were able to buy fruit and
fish in ports here and there.

Spring and April saw the *Continental,* battered by a thousand
winds and icy sprays, entering San Francisco's Golden Gate. Asa
Mercer, the courageous, the invincible, the matchmaker of all
time, had three dollars in his shabby trousers pocket. Somehow,
by lumber vessels and little trading ships that plied between San

Francisco and Seattle, he managed to bring the girls into the haven of the Puget Sound country.

It was from the deck rail of the brig *Tanner* that Abbie Griggs first beheld the splendor of the Seattle shore line—the mountains, the bay, the hills, the forests. As she gazed, her cheeks were peonies, her eyes were pools of electric blue (Emmy Melendy inherited that fine skin of hers from Abbie). The town was down at the wharf. The university bell clanged its welcome; the lumber-mill whistles tooted; the crowd cheered, and Abbie saw that the faces upturned from the wharf below were predominantly bearded faces—young bearded faces above broad shoulders proudly set in new suits of clothes or bright new overalls. These were not mustached dandies with dark, ardent eyes and slim waists and narrow chests such as had come aboard at Rio. These, thought the practical and passionate New England spinster, Abbie Griggs, these were men who could fell a tree or break a colt or build a house or shoot a deer—or breed a boy baby.

In her best bonnet and her tight-bodiced gown she leaned over the rail of the little brig *Tanner* and waved to the upturned faces below—the red-cheeked, clear-eyed faces. She returned the greetings on shore with a wave of her handkerchief; her behavior was maidenly, was circumspect, but she could not hide the exultation that revealed itself in the smile on her lips, the light in her eyes— she did not want to hide it. She had bested that grisly engraving on the New England tombstones; she had gambled with life, and she knew now that she had won.

"Hello, down there!" she called in her clear, girlish voice. "Hello, Seattle!"

5

Vaughan's car was out in front. Taka or perhaps William had managed to bring its surface to a high degree of glitter in spite of Seattle's morning mists. Its four tires clung to the steep hillside like a cat's claws to a tree trunk. Vaughan liked a small car, neat and compact, that could be tucked away in tight corners and manipulated easily in the busy traffic of Pike Street, and Fourth Avenue, and Second, and Pine. You had to be sure of your brakes on Seattle's perpendicular streets; he liked to have not too much weight behind them.

Every morning of his life, through the decades, if he was in the city he had paid his daily visit to his mother, Exact Melendy. It was a compulsion now; he couldn't have stopped if he had wanted to. Actually, he would have been afraid to stop. Now, as he took his way over the familiar path to her house, he became a diminished man. The towering figure seemed actually to shrink; his hands hung limp at his sides; he even toed in a little, unconsciously, as he walked, and stubbed his toe on a pebble and swore under his breath and looked about him guiltily. He was a little boy again, this powerful man of seventy, a little boy on his way to see his mother who would question him, chide him, hover over him when he no longer needed nor wanted guiding or chiding or even praise.

It was incredible—but in the American tradition, perhaps—that so successful and virile a male could be so dominated by the three females who loved him. There they were, pecking at this great structure of a man as birds peck at a thousand-year pine in the forests of the Puget Sound region. There was his wife, that virtuous and destructive female; his mother, still strong in mind and body at ninety-two; and there was the woman he had loved for half a century, Pansy Deleath. No, he reflected now, Pansy did not peck at him—Pansy never had pecked at him. She poured over his wounds the balm of her gaiety and understanding; it was like the soft, clear gum that oozes over the pine bark, rich and smooth and pungent, proving that there still was life in the old tree.

He turned along the path and glanced back at his house, a fantastic structure. Like Seattle itself, there was too much of everything about the house—too much house, to begin with. Too many cupolas, too many gables, towers; too many windows, porches, porte-cocheres; too much scrollwork, saw-tooth, plate glass; too many nooks, corners, chimneys, pillars, levels. Too much of everything. He loved it.

Emmy said the house was a great deal of trouble; she said it was simply killing her; she said she just loved her things, but there were so many really good "pieces," and even with Taka and May (and William helping sometimes, though he didn't like indoor work), it was too much. She said, "Of course I like everything just so. I guess I'm an old fuss-budget. But that's the way I am. I often wish I could learn to keep house more the way Pansy does—sloppy and any-which-way, and dishes piled up in the sink."

She even said this to Pansy, looking guileless and all blue-eyed wistfulness behind that glittering pince-nez.

Pansy was not deceived. "It's a gift," she said. "I was brought up sloppy, and it was wonderful. Ma and I would let things go for days at a time. Then we'd have a cleaning bee with towels pinned over our hair and everything out on the line."

"I'd love to be like that," Emmy said insincerely. "Of course Mama was old New England stock and she brought me up just so." She had said this a thousand times. "Of course Mama was a Mercer Girl."

There was not a drop of malice in Pansy Deleath. "I guess that accounts for the difference. Ma was a mixture of Irish and French and American and Scotch thrown in, but the Scotch never had a chance."

Kitty Deleath. Abbie Griggs. Vaughan, walking toward his mother's house, found himself naming the mothers of the two women, placing their names side by side in his mind as though written on placards. Now what makes me do that? he thought. Mama was a Mercer Girl. He grinned and even laughed a short grunt of laughter, for there came into his mind the lines of a disrespectful little song that young Mike had audaciously improvised at the time of their golden-wedding anniversary. It had gone through the family grapevine, but somehow it had got to Emmy, and her outraged tears had taken on freshet proportions. The words of the song popped neatly and in order into Vaughan's mind. He even hummed the tune and found satisfaction in doing so. Mike's mischievous eyes and long-jawed, serious young face were in his thoughts as he hummed with relish:

> *Mama was a Mercer Girl,*
> *Virtue claimed her as its pearl,*
> *Mama never misbehaved at night.*
> *Mama was an 'itsie dirl,*
> *Mama never had a whirl,*
> *Mama never got a little tight.*
>
> *Mama was a Mercer Girl,*
> *Sound the tocsin, flags unfurl,*
> *Mama's offspring weren't very bright.*
> *Mama . . .*

From the direction of Dike's house Vaughan heard the clank of metal on metal. That must be young Mike down in his basement workshop. He was home from college on one of those odd vacations that colleges seemed to have nowadays. Used to be regular times, he reflected, Christmas and Easter and the summer months and so on. But now Mike said a lot of fellows were leaving to go into the Canadian Air Force and the RAF, and they were even talking about compressing the whole college course into three years or even two years. War. When we get into it, Mike said, as though there could be no doubt.

Mike had wanted to get into it two years ago. Lucky thing he was way under age and Dike wouldn't give his consent and neither would Lina, who was in New York; and the whole family had, as Mike said, gone into a tailspin. Mike knew the name of every man-made flying thing. He knew the names, numbers, power, speed, equipment of American planes, British planes, even German planes. He knew them more familiarly than his father Dike Melendy before him had known the names, make, horsepower of automobiles a quarter of a century earlier.

Vaughan remembered that Dike had rolled them off glibly. "That's a Stutz . . . Pierce-Arrow . . . Cadillac . . . Fiat . . . Packard . . . Buick . . . Gosh, lookit! Hispano!"

Now young Mike, casting an eye upward and squinting a little into the sun, not only knew names and numbers, he knew nicknames. "B-24 . . . P-47 . . . B-17 . . . Pregnant Peanut . . . Mustang . . . Kittyhawk—uh—she can't get up there . . . PBY-5, good old Cat . . ."

Occasionally Vaughan had heard Mike and Taka's young son William Nakaisuki talking their flying jargon, and it was as unintelligible to him as though they had been speaking a foreign language.

"Yeh, and the fuselage is thick and the cockpit's set back even with the wing edge; it's got a vertical fin and the rudder's set ahead of the elevators that's how I can tell."

"The Meph can climb 39,000 she's got a large spinner and a big cowling round the engine the tail plane's cantilever and a retractable tail wheel, average dihedral in the front . . ."

Vaughan could stand it no longer. "Say, what in God's name kind of lingo is that? What the hell you kids talking, anyway?"

Young Mike grinned at him fondly. He liked and admired his grandfather, but the lad's look now was much like that usually bestowed by a parent upon a child when the child, bewildered, says Why? Why, Daddy? Why? No use explaining things a child's mind could not grasp.

"Just flying talk, Tikum," he said. Bits of Chinook Indian jargon had crept into the everyday talk of Seattle people. It was one of the first words Mike had learned when a baby. Tillicum—friend. It had emerged as Tikum in his baby talk, and Tikum it still was.

Now Vaughan passed his mother's house, looking apprehensively up at the windows. He wanted to see Mike first; he wanted, unconsciously, to look into the face of someone young and unafraid, of someone by whom this strange and disturbing new world was taken for granted because from childhood he had known no other. Let's see, Vaughan reflected, Mike had been, well, eight or nine when this crazy Hitler had started his shenanigans, turning the whole world upside down. Airplanes and Hitler and vitamins and television and streamliners and sex were no mysteries to Mike—he took them for granted. The lad had his own plane. Dike had bought it for him on his eighteenth birthday as he, Vaughan, had given Dike a car of his own when he became eighteen. But Mike had mastered the technique of flying long before he had gone aloft triumphantly in his own little plane. He had hung around the Boeing plant and the flying fields as Dike had hung around garages; he knew every airfield between Washington and Kansas. He had flown all over this hazardous Northwest terrain of mountains and water and forests.

Pretty damned wonderful, kids like Mike, the old man reflected. His drooping shoulders straightened; his step became sprightly and firm; his fine head came up; he ran a hand through his thick white hair and found pleasure in the thought that he, like the young Mike, wore no hat.

Mike had a workbench in a separate little room off the garage; it had been built expressly for him with a cement floor, tool racks, drills. Since he was thirteen this workshop had been his toy, his passion, now it was a man-size affair. Dike said his son was equipped to build a battleship or a bomber down there and that he expected any day to wake up and see a plane wing sticking up through his bedroom floor. Hacksaws, electric drills, chisels, punches were Mike's playthings.

Vaughan stood in the doorway. "Hello, Mike!"

The tall, lean figure bent over the bench straightened itself. "Hi, Gramp."

"How come you don't call me Tikum any more?"

The boy grinned, his teeth very white in the smudged face. "I is a bid boy now. That baby talk is kind of vomit making."

"Not to me it ain't."

"What time is it, anyway? I busted my watch on the plane last night like a dope."

"About eight-thirty, I guess. Yeh."

"Cripes, I guess I'll eat. I didn't have any breakfast."

"What time did you get in?"

"Late. After midnight. Had a head wind all the way from Fargo."

He came over to the old man, wiping his greasy hand on his coverall. Vaughan put a hand on the boy's shoulder. "You look good. Thin, though."

"Well, no fatties in our family, is there?"

"That's right."

He loved this boy more than any living thing in the world; his feeling for him was deeper than ever he had had for his own son or for his wife or his mother—for anyone except the quite dif-

ferent emotion he had known in his young manhood for Pansy.
Perhaps his feeling for the boy stemmed from that earlier love, he
thought. The boy strongly resembled Pansy, no question about it.
The family knew it, Vaughan knew it, Pansy knew it, the town
knew it, no one ever spoke of it. The long jaw; the purple-blue
eyes that went black under emotion; the quiet voice whose timbre
struck a sympathetic note in the listener; the rather bony, loose-
hung frame. The humor, casual, gay, warm. The son of Dike and
Lina Melendy all right, but the descendant of Pansy Deleath.
Dike and Mike they look alike, folks said jokingly. Not true.

"You know your ma's due home this morning? And Dike."

Mike, wiping the grease off his hands with a bit of waste, rolled
his eyes romantically. "Ah, yes! Young Master's coming home
with Missy to open up the old manse. Ah, the rhododendrons are
as high as a man's head. See the dark spot on the stairs? They
say they tried to paint it out but it always comes up again. Hear
the wind how it soughs—soos—how d'you pronounce that, anyway? Sounds indelicate, soughs."

Vaughan grinned. "That's a disrespectful way to talk of your
ma and pa, though."

Mike was pulling off his coveralls. "I saw Lina in New York
last week the night her show closed."

"How was she?"

"Good. The show was kind of dumb, though. I'd seen it when
she opened in it. Kind of combination steal on You Can't Take It
with You and Life with Father. The guy who wrote it certainly
had a good memory. Lina was good, but the part wasn't so hot."

"I didn't mean the show, how she was in the show. How was
she herself?"

"Swell. We went to the Stork after the show and all those
withered buds looked old enough to be her mother. How old is
Mother, anyway? I've kind of lost track."

"Well, let's see, she was about twenty when she and Dike were
married; you're going on twenty—Lina's crowding forty or over,

though she certainly didn't look over twenty-five last time she was out here."

"What's the idea of their galumphing in by train?"

Annual honeymoon, Vaughan was about to say, but thought better of it. "More restful, I guess. And Lina isn't a very good flier." He was leaning against the doorway, silhouetted clearly against the huge panorama of sky and mountains and water. His eyes on this, he spoke to the boy as though he were thinking aloud. "I kind of figure maybe your ma's home for good this time. She's no kid any more. I hear the theater in New York is kind of shot to hell. Maybe she's through being stage-struck for keeps."

Mike had been scrubbing his hands at the little sink. Now he strolled over to the doorway and leaned against the opposite side, his gaze glancing up with an airman's eye at the great sweep of sky. He then regarded his fingernails critically; gave them up. The boy's face was serious, was compassionate beyond its years. "Mother's mixed up. So's Dad."

Vaughan pondered this a moment. There was a little silence such as that between two men of an age. "Uh, how do you mean —mixed up?" But he knew. He knew, too, that the boy would not go very deeply into this. They were not very articulate, these kids —not gabby was Vaughan's way of putting it.

"They've been sort of stumbling around ever since I can remember. Mother wanting to go to New York and act whenever she was here, and going on about the quiet and comfort of this house when she was stuck in New York. When I was a kid, Dad was always saying the child has no background and no home life, and then Mother would start talking about her career. Then there'd be a hell of a row, and then they'd make up and I'd feel like excess baggage or something. I learned all about that later. It's called an insecure childhood. Supposed to be bad for you."

"Insecure! Why, say, you had everything a boy could think of! Plenty of money, big house, everything from Kiddie-Kars up to airplanes."

"That's right," said Mike, wishing he hadn't started this.

"Why, Dike's crazy about you. Always was. Can't do enough for you."

"Dad's swell. But he stopped growing when he came home from the war."

"How do you figure that, Smarty Pants? Nineteen eighteen. You weren't born or anywheres near it. Dike wasn't even married!"

"I didn't mean to sound lofty. I just mean the war did something to him—fellows like Dad. They came home and then they whooshed up and down the world in big, fast cars and sat around in speakeasies drinking rotgut. It was as if something had hit 'em over the head."

"You don't say!" Vaughan's tone was quizzical but he was disturbed. "And who's been giving you such an earful?"

"We covered all that in Social Psychology. Once I saw a bunch of them at an American Legion convention. Decent enough guys, but they made you ashamed to look. Horsing around, blowing little whistles, and wearing funny hats like an Elks' convention, and bumping into people and shoving cops and cars, and throwing feather pillows and pitchers of water out of hotel windows. Forty-and-Eight and Mad'moiselle from Armentières; you'd think they'd been on a bloody picnic in Europe instead of in a war. War! War stinks!"

Vaughan looked at the boy. He seemed composed enough, his tone was quiet, even passionless, but here nevertheless was deep disturbance. "You kids, you're so damn smart, you think you know all the answers. All kids think they're smarter than their elders, but you kids are the worst yet."

The lad grinned at his grandfather; it was a smile of great sweetness, it was not a merry smile. "We ain't going to get much education. But boy, are we going to learn a lot!" In his tone, in his quiet, gentle voice, there was a terrible prophecy.

Fear clutched at old Vaughan's vitals. It found vocal expression in anger. "You make me sick. Time I was your age I was up every morning four or five o'clock falling trees in the camps or piloting or whatever. We weren't running around in any cars or airplanes. And your pa settled down to work after a while when he came back from the war down in the office learning the business and so on. He's about the best Admiralty lawyer in the Northwest, Dike is, and he knows his lumber and shipping and the canneries. Director on all the boards. You kids have had it too easy."

"Yeh," said Mike absently, completely without resentment. "It's all been done for us. Everything by machinery. Even the war's all done with machinery. I suppose when I'm through college I can go and sit up in Dad's office and look at real estate and ships and go around finding out whether tenants' toilets work and why the roof leaks and if the place needs painting this spring. And someday I'll be in his place and he'll be in your place and my kid'll be in my place and the hell with it. I'm demi-siècle. All that stuff doesn't interest me. . . . Well, I guess I'll go and eat. What time does their train get in?"

"William went to meet them with the Cadillac. They're driving up from Portland. I'm going over to see Madam. Come on along a minute, say hello to her."

"I'm starving."

"Oh, just say hello. She'll like it."

"You don't want to face Madam alone. You been misbehaving?"

They grinned at each other, two men. A great surge of tenderness for the boy swept over Vaughan; he gave no sign, he did not touch him. Together they walked toward Exact Melendy's fortress.

Of the clan, only young Mike, her great-grandson, seemed to be outside Madam Melendy's power. Through the barrier of decades that separated them, through almost three quarters of a century that lay between them, she tried in vain to reach him, to press a thumb in the clay as she had molded the others. Lightly, gaily, the lad eluded her. He would no more have been rude or unkind to her than he would have kicked one of the grim and massive old edifices of walnut or mahogany with which her house was furnished. Occasionally he called on her dutifully at the urging of his father or his grandparents. To him, she was almost as much of a wraith, a legend, as old Chief Seattle, the Duwamish Indian after whom the city had been named.

As with the others, her long, bony finger tried to caution him, her voice boomed hollowly out of the past. "Now you heed what I say, Michael. You don't know everything. I'm older than you are . . ."

"Oh, I wouldn't say that if I were you, Madam," the boy would reply solemnly. "Look, did you ever think of running for President? Sugar, you're the girl could swing it. Anyway, you'd get my vote."

"Oh, you think you're so smart!" she would retort, inadequately. She had said this to his father, Dike Melendy, a quarter of a century earlier, and to his grandfather, Vaughan Melendy, a half century ago.

Exact Melendy's house, built for her by her son, was like a watchtower. It sat solidly on its knoll and it seemed all windows, all great thick plate glass, so that she surveyed Seattle; she swept Queen Anne Hill with her gaze; her family in their houses could not go in or out of doors that she did not see them; they could not turn a lamp on or off that she could not note it if she cared to. Her vision was phenomenal. Now, at ninety-two, it was too difficult for her to walk up or down the steep, winding path that led to her door. Years ago Vaughan had had built for her an ingenious tiny railway like a miniature mountain funicular. In this she seated herself grandly and was pulled up to her house and trundled down from it. It had become one of the sights of Seattle. Neighborhood children for years had eyed it wistfully. Mike, in his childhood, had been the envy of his playmates. As a rare treat they sometimes had been allowed on Saturdays to ride up and down a time or two. The seat was upholstered in rich green leather; there was just room for Madam Melendy's ample skirts and bulk with a squeeze in for her long-suffering companion, who then became driver and railway engineer. It was quite a piece of machinery, very costly indeed, and to see the ancient dame jauntily disposed therein, sailing down the steep slope to her son Vaughan's house, was a sight so improbable that the *Post-Intelligencer* still ran it occasionally as a Sunday feature. Of late years she rarely used it, but at any suggestion of its removal her remonstrance was, as usual, based on the ulterior motives of which she suspected her descendants.

"The railway! You'll do nothing of the sort. I'm not dead yet and I'll thank you not to forget the fact."

To the family the railway was known as the Mac, a blending of its name—the Melendy, Alleghany & Chesapeake Railway—which was facetiously painted in large white lettering on the side of the little carriage.

Vaughan trudged up the path now with Mike keeping pace by his side. The old man's shoulders sagged a little; his hands hung listlessly. "Pretty soon I'll probably be so old and broken down I'll have to use that damned contraption to get up here to see Ma —unless I ride up in the car like a sissy invalid."

"Don't let her get you down, Gramp. You're a big boy now."

"Don't know what you're talking about."

"Ye-e-es, you do. You've been scared of her for sixty years."

On one of the upper porches that were stuck, like false mustaches, at the front of the house there appeared a girl who briskly waved a bright yellow cloth or scarf. They thought she was waving at them, they waved in return; then it was clear that she was not looking at them, she was merely shaking out a dustcloth. She wore a blue dirndl, and a band of blue made contrast with her clear gold hair.

Mike looked up at her, glanced at his grandfather. "Say!"

"It's Reggie."

"Who?"

"Reggie. She's hired kind of company for Madam."

"She looks like a kid. What's the matter with old Birch?"

"Didn't Dike write you? Miss Birch fell and broke her leg on one of Madam's damn slippery floors. She's laid up at her brother's in Bremerton. Madam said she wanted somebody young around for a change. Freshen her up."

"That's cannibalism."

"Eh?"

The boy was silent. Now the girl on the balcony turned and saw them coming up the path. She smiled and her hand came up in greeting.

"Yoo-hoo!" Vaughan called.

"Hi!" said Mike.

"Hi!" said the girl. She looked down at Mike. He looked up at her. Then she looked down at the bright bit of cloth in her hand, gave it a last cleansing flap into the morning air, and disappeared into the house, shutting the balcony door.

"What do you mean—Reggie?"

"Oh, Regina, I guess. Yes. We call her Reggie for short. She said her mother had called her Reggie. In Germany."

"Say, what is all this? What d'you mean—Germany?"

But they entered the house now, and from the entrance hall they heard Exact Melendy's voice booming out at them. "What are you doing home, Michael? You're late, Vaughan!"

She followed the sun from window to window in this big house. In the early morning she was always to be found seated in the vast bay window of what she called the music room. The term "living room" was not in her vocabulary. Parlor, sitting room, library, music room. Big, square, boxlike rooms filled with glistening mahogany and walnut, lace curtains and heavy silk damask hangings at the windows. A structure and an interior preserved miraculously out of the past, as was the mistress of the house itself.

Exact Melendy was seated enthroned in her music-room window, a museum piece like the mammoth square piano. Its keyboard was time-yellowed ivory as was her parchment skin. A mandolin sat atop the piano, a jaunty cap of golden yellow striped with black. On Madam Melendy's head perched a yellowed lace cap with a coquettish knot of narrow black velvet ribbon. Monolithic, her ample skirts spread about her, she seemed to tower even in her chair. There she sat, doing nothing. There was an impressive quality in her idleness; she was like a living monument, vibrating power, charged with it as a dynamo. Waiting for her son. She was wearing an incredible morning dress of blue faille with panniers of a blue-and-brown striped material forming a sort of overskirt. The strong, abundant hair under the lace-and-muslin cap was less white than that of her son. She might have walked out of the pages of *Godey's Lady's Book*. In front of her was her breakfast tray—an astounding array of massive silver and fragile china. In her lap was the morning paper. As always, she had been reading without spectacles; she seemed to have outgrown them or grown beyond them—a gift which irked her daughter-in-law Emmy to a poisonous degree. The front page that morning was Europe in agony; a shambles of death and destruction; acts of superhuman bravery, of subhuman brutality and knavery; cities blasted to rubble; kings deposed.

"Nothing in the paper," boomed Exact.

"You'll probably find something or other in the next few months, Ma," Vaughan said, wryly for him. "I betcha." He came over and kissed her forehead like a little boy.

Her glance brushed past her son, rested on the lad. "Well!" Mike, too, came over to her. He put his fresh, vital young cheek against her withered one. "Remember me, Madam? Your wayward great-whosis?"

"It's a wonder I do, for all the notice I get from you."

"How about those star sapphires and orchids I keep sending you? Does nothing satisfy you?"

"You think you're smart." She eyed him sharply. "Don't you go to school? Back East in Massachusetts?"

"Yes, chum."

"What're you doing here, then? I suppose you think you know so much you don't have to go to school any more."

He grinned good-naturedly. "Well, yes. But this is vacation."

"Kind of funny time for it."

"Kind of funny world."

This evidently was one of her keen mornings. Now and then the astonishingly alert mind lapsed; it was as though she retired for a time into a quiet and remote world of her own, taking refuge behind her barricade of years, drawing a veil of aloofness over her face as did Mount Rainier.

"I see by the papers where they want us to get into this war over in Europe. Roosevelt and those. I been asked to stand up say I'm against it at the Pioneers' Association dinner and I'm agoing to, you bet."

"That's telling 'em!" Vaughan agreed heartily.

But Mike said quietly, "Look, Madam, I wish you wouldn't."

"Why not, like to know? What's it our business? Same way with the Civil War. I recollect Pa said keep out of it let the North and South scrap it out, none of the Northwest's business, he said. Slaves. What's slavery got to do with us, he said."

"So," Mike drawled, "we imported a lot of Japs and Chinese, and if you think that isn't going to be something someday."

Sharply Vaughan demanded, "What makes you say that? Crazy thing like that!"

Michael was lifting a dish cover here and there on the lavish breakfast tray. The old lady had finished her morning meal, but the remnants evidenced a prodigious repast. A pink curl of broiled ham remained; one of three eggs; yellow cheese; toast; jam. Mike filched the ham, decorated a crust of toast with it, popped it into his mouth, gulped a mouthful from the side of the cream jug.

"Can you pack away a trencher, Madam!" he said admiringly, surveying the tray.

"Old folks have to have their proteins," she said crisply. "Meat and eggs and so forth. Dr. Crosby says it's the newfangled diet, but land! That's the way my ma and pa ate, and Jotham there to the day he died."

She pointed with one long forefinger at the portrait of her dead husband over the fireplace. A black-bearded man, Jotham Melendy, with a little of the look of Vaughan. And now that he stood there facing the portrait, perhaps Mike, too, bore a trace of family resemblance to this great-grandfather of his: the upper head, a fleeting expression. There was a very bad painting of the late Jotham Melendy in every one of the four sitting rooms and a fifth in Exact's vast bedroom. She had ordered them done wholesale at a thousand dollars each; scarcely a day when she did not refer to one of them, with the effect of including him in the conversation with a wave of her great hand.

The heavy paneled folding doors were open between this room and the sitting room beyond. Michael's glance went to this aperture and to the vast mahogany stairway that curved a river's width up to the second story.

"Uh—Gramp told me Birch broke a leg. Tough."

"Good riddance!" said Exact Melendy.

"Now, Ma!" Vaughan remonstrated, shocked.

"Oh, I'm sorry for the girl," Madam Melendy said. A silken pouch bag fashioned of stuff like the panniers of her skirt hung by its cord from the arm of her chair. In this she rummaged a moment and took out a long-stemmed meerschaum pipe, small of bowl, beautifully colored, and a silken tobacco pouch. Neatly, expertly, she filled the pipe, tamped it, and before Vaughan could strike the match for her she had bent and struck a light from the sole of her great flat shoe, using an old-fashioned red-tipped Swedish match which she nonchalantly carried in loose handfuls at the bottom of her bag. She puffed a moment, relaxed in her chair. "Birch is a good girl." Miss Birch was forty-seven. "But she treats me like a baby." Suddenly, with terrifying mimicry, she assumed an expression of spinsterish sweetness; she pursed her withered lips; she cocked her ancient head with awful coquetry. " 'Are we going to have our little nappie now? H'mmmmm? . . . Don't you think that a little teensy-weensy drop too much rye for us? . . . Oooo! Your very best dress!' It's enough to turn a body's stomach."

It was a good show. The two men roared. It was plain how this woman, almost a century old, still could keep a grip on the family lines, still could hold their interest and even their affection.

Still Mike saw no glimpse of a golden head, no blue dirndl descending the stairway. "I hear you've got a new—uh—companion."

"Seems to me you've heard a lot for somebody's just got home."

"Well, I'm spry, Madam, for my age."

"I guess I'll be getting along, Ma. Got to go down earn a living. Coming, Mike?" Vaughan, the dutiful son, had paid his morning visit, there had been little or no fault-finding; he wanted to be off.

"Living!" she scoffed. "Day like this you'll most likely be down at Fisherman's Wharf gabbing with the Swenskies." Vaughan flushed like a boy caught in mischief.

"Bull's-eye!" said Mike. "Look, don't you want somebody to take that tray away? Want me to call somebody or—uh—do something?"

"That girl!" mumbled Exact. "You have to call her for everything." Michael brightened expectantly. Old Exact took the pipe from her mouth and emitted a bellow that would have done credit to a sea captain on the bridge in a hurricane. "Hulda! Hulda!" The look of expectation faded to disappointment. The dining-room swinging door whished and whooshed as the bony Hulda entered, all starched gingham, nodded her gruff greeting, picked up the tray as though it were a toy, and stamped back to her domain. "Good cook, though," Exact added grudgingly. She tapped the ashes out of her pipe. The royal audience was ended. "Time for my rye," she announced somewhat crossly. "Usual thing Reggie's on the dot."

As she spoke the girl appeared. She carried a small round silver salver. On it were a tall crystal goblet, a jigger, a silver spoon.

"Good morning, Mr. Melendy!" She smiled a strangely grave little smile at Vaughan; she looked at Michael; she inclined her head in a conventional bow such as a poised and much older woman might have bestowed.

"Reggie, my dear," Vaughan said. In his tone there was warmth and even affection.

The cantankerous Exact suddenly seemed mollified, though she only said gruffly, "I suppose I ought to be thankful somebody in this house is prompt. Old you're neglected."

"Yeh, you're neglected," Vaughan said huffily; "like Queen Victoria was neglected."

Deftly the girl measured two tablespoons of liquor into the glass, stirred it, moved the small table conveniently to the side of the chair, handed the glass to the old woman. "Keeps my strength up," boomed Exact. "Doctor says." A tinge of guilt was in her words. In the tradition of her day strong drink was for men.

"Pretty soft," Vaughan said, tactlessly for him. "Slug of good rye twice a day."

"I hate it!" shouted Madam Melendy, and coughed genteelly, and shook her head. There was something touching, something startling in the contrast between the girl's lovely fresh young face bent over the withered old one. Golden hair, neat and shining; unexpected warm brown eyes; clear blonde skin; slim, sturdy body. Yet a curious effect of tragedy experienced, of some brutal life force encountered before her weapons of defense had been forged. She had spoken four words only, she made no bid for attention, yet the eyes of the three followed her gratefully.

Suddenly, " 'As the lily among thorns,' " Vaughan found himself saying, to his own surprise.

"What say?" Exact snapped.

"Nothing." Sheepishly. "Nothing. Line out of the Bible." Virtuously. Still, he hoped she didn't know it was the Song of Solomon. "Heh! I never thought to introduce you two young——"

But he was too late.

"Hello, Reggie!" said Michael, and came over to her and held out his hand. "I'm Mike Melendy."

"Hello, Michael," she said. Her firm hand met his.

"Heh!" said Michael. "A bone crusher, eh?" He assumed a look of agony.

"Sorry. Tennis."

"Good?"

"Rather."

"Where do you play?"

"The university courts."

"Oh. Are you at the university?"

"Yes. Eleven to two." Her accent had no trace of the German. It was an English accent such as an excellent British governess imparts to a Continental child, but beneath it there was a dash of the American as well.

"What are you taking?"

"English and drama."

"That's Bennington, isn't it? Gordon Bennington. He's good."

"He's magic."

"Oh. Teacher's pet." But immediately he saw that she had not understood this; he realized that he was not talking to an American girl. Hurriedly he added, "Do you mean you're a writer?"

"I'm trying to be."

"What kind of thing?"

She actually blushed then, as though he had asked her an intimate, a personal question. He thought, my gosh, I haven't seen a girl blush in ten years. She said, candidly enough, "Plays. You know—everyone's writing a play."

Exact had had enough of this. She stood up now. It was star-

tling to see the unfolding of her six feet of height. The decades
had bowed her shoulders a little, the muscles and sinews had
shrunk, yet she was a commanding, a heroic structure as she stood
there.

"So your ma's coming home this morning." She fixed Mike
with a steely eye.

"Yes. They must be in Portland by now. I guess I'll go home,
get my breakfast."

"She won't stay."

Vaughan turned at the door. "Now, Ma, don't start that."

"Plenty of nice girls right here in Seattle, but no, Dike had to
go off East to get a wife."

Mike laughed. "What a gal! You're wonderful, Madam. You
get an idea in that little curly head and does it stick! Lina and
Dad have only been married twenty years." Just the same, he
wished she'd shut up.

"Married!" snorted Exact. "Traipsing off to New York more
than half that time, Lina."

She was an old, old lady. But, after all, this girl was a stranger.
All this talk about his father and mother. Didn't want to seem
stuffy, Mike thought. But the old girl was like a spoiled kid. The
lines of the square jaw tightened. "Good-by. Coming, Gramp?
Good-by, Reggie."

She looked at him, understanding in her eyes. Her face was
good and kind, but merry, too. It said, wordlessly, don't mind me.
I know about old people. Aloud she said, "Time for your nap,
Madam Melendy."

As they left they caught the old lady's trumpeting. "Nap! Nap!
Nap! Sleep my life away! What's for this afternoon?"

"We'll have a drive at three. And then you promised to appear
for a minute at the D.A.P.P.A. meeting. What is that?"

"Daughters of Alki Point Pioneers' Association," boomed
Exact on her majestic march to the stairway. "Me gray silk."

Michael's long legs were loping down the path so that Vaughan had much to do to keep pace with him. The boy's eyes were flying the warning signal, purple to black. "A hell of a life for a swell little kid like that!" Suddenly he stopped, turned, seemed about to go back to the house.

"What's the matter?"

"Her name. I don't even know her last name."

"Well, my God, you'd think she was leaving on the next train. She's going to be here for months—and years—I hope. Anyway, till old Birch comes back, and maybe if she'll stay we can pension off Birch——"

"What's her last name?"

"Why, it's—— Say, isn't that awful! We just call her Reggie —short for Regina—and I know her name as well as I do my own, but it's just slipped—— Gosh, I must be getting old."

But Mike was off up the path. Over his shoulder he said, "It might be Schlumpf!" Up the stairs at a leap, into the hall. Together they were ascending the broad stairway, Exact and Reggie, the old lady stumping ahead, each foot placed flat as a board on each step, the girl following behind, her slim figure silhouetted against the massive flounced structure looming above her.

"Heh!" said Mike. The blonde head turned quickly; her face was lovely in astonishment, the lips parted, the eyes wide. "Heh, Reggie! What's your name?"

Over the broad mahogany banister she looked down at him; the grave dignity of her face was made brilliant again by her smile. "Regina."

"I know. Regina. That means queen. Good here. Regina what?"

"Dresden. Regina Dresden."

"Just wanted to know." He was off.

Old Madam Melendy had by now achieved an about-face on the stairway. "What say? What's Michael want?"

"Nothing, dear. He just forgot something."

Down the path Vaughan, waiting, said, "Dresden. Regina Dresden. You'd waited a second I'd have told you. It came to me minute you'd gone. Kind of a pretty name; got strength in it, too, like her. Jewish, her folks are—or anyway were, back there in Germany, before Hitler killed them."

6

Vaughan hoisted himself rather lumberingly into his car. Carefully and slowly he drove off, using quite a lot of footwork. He never had sat behind the wheel with the masterly ease that marked Dike's driving. As for Mike, an automobile to him was as commonplace as a Kiddie-Kar.

The hill led down past Pansy Deleath's house. He always slowed a bit there and gave the place a comprehensive look. He wasn't hoping for a glimpse of Pansy (he always told himself), he wanted the assurance only that all was right with her, that the house appeared in order, the shades up; perhaps the sound of her radio on the early morning air.

There were houses of every type of architecture on Queen Anne Hill, for it represented the Alaska Gold Rush wealth of Seattle. These huge bedizened structures with their gables and bays and pillars were the realized dream dwellings of bearded men who had come back from the bitter North with sacks of gold in their fists and crude boxes of it in rough wood and metal crates. Cape Cod houses, swollen almost beyond recognition; Tudor, Georgian, bastard Greek renaissance, Deep South verandaed, Victorian. No one had thought of adapting his house to the climate or to the wild, glorious beauty of the region.

There was Pansy's house, a white confection like a frosted

cake, set in a cozy cluster of madroña trees. The glossy madroña leaves, the rich red-skinned trunks made a lavish background. Any Seattle garden thrived in the mild, moist air warmed by the Japan Current. But Pansy's garden was a brilliant picture summer and winter. The native plants were there: Flett's violet and the heavenly bluebell; deep-woods orchids, rock pinks, and sea rose; the tall barber's pole, white and scarlet; starflower, wakerobin, anemone—white, purple, blue. Early, early in the spring Pansy's trillium each bore its single perfect bloom. Roses clambered everywhere, but far outshining them in the spring were the rhododendrons, massed banks of them in rose and pink and lavender and white. More than thirty-five years ago Vaughan had seen to it that Pansy's land was planted with fine specimens of bigleaf maple and vine maple, Oregon ash and Western dogwood. They towered now and spread a canopy of green.

Slowly, slowly Vaughan's car approached the place. At seventy he was behaving like a boy who saunters past his girl's house, assuming blithe indifference but keeping the tail of his eye alert for a glimpse of the beloved figure behind a window curtain or in the garden.

Suddenly, on an impulse, he jerked back the emergency brake, clicked off the ignition, and got out. The neighborhood probably was marking his every move—Emmy, too, and Madam. Hell with 'em, he thought, as he had a thousand, ten thousand times. I'm all upset. Pansy can put me right, talk things over with Pansy.

He went round the garden to the back. A sizable house, it did not shine with the overzealous care in which Emmy found compensation; it had none of the overpowering quality of Exact Melendy's portentous pile.

Pansy Deleath was on her knees painting the kitchen woodwork a tough and brilliant blue.

He came in and she glanced round, her rather heavy face lighted up with her poignant and winning smile; she sat slumped comfortably down on the floor and pushed her hair out of her eyes with the back of her wrist, the paint brush still in her hand. She was wearing oversize canvas gloves—garden gloves—they were paint-spattered, and there were daubs of blue paint here and there on her cheeks, her brow. She was flushed and interested and filled with a painter's triumph as she surveyed her handiwork. Her breakfast dishes were in the sink, unwashed; the morning paper lay helter-skelter on the table; there were growing plants in a stand at the window; her absurd and rakish Scotch terrier with the barrel body and the long head and the bright, merry eyes frisked over to Vaughan, looked up at him adoringly.

Vaughan stooped and rubbed the little animal's neck and chest; the dog lay at his feet close against his shoe as Vaughan sat down. From the room just beyond a tawny Irish setter appeared, came straight to the man and laid his muzzle on Vaughan's knee. Vaughan unconsciously drew a deep breath like one who has been overhurried, exhaled it, and sat back in the chair relaxed, content, at peace.

Pansy Deleath did not say, oh, goodness, how I look! She did not try to tidy herself or excuse the unwashed dishes or chide the dogs. She looked up at Vaughan. "Don't you love blue in a kitchen! Not all blue, but pieces of it, like this. The baseboards, and these three panels. Gay. The painters said they never heard of such a thing, so I'm doing it myself. Painting's wonderful. Makes you feel so talented."

She never talked loudly; if you wanted to hear what she had to say you had to listen; there was nothing strident or sharp about her. Not like his womenfolk, not like Emmy's querulous whimperings or Exact's trumpetings.

He picked up the small dog and set him on his knees, and the beast lay there, content. The man settled in a brief serenity, too. He looked at her, at the woman he had loved for more than forty years, the mother of his only son, his one child. He was relaxed; life seemed simpler and easier as always when he was with Pansy. In all these years she never had reproached him; he had behaved toward her like a villain in one of those old melodramas, he often told himself. Those pansy-purple eyes never had held a fleck of accusation; they looked into his with candor and with devotion.

As she stuck her brush carefully into a little can of turpentine and took off her painting gloves he found himself looking at her, taking stock of her as, queerly enough, he had looked at Emmy this morning, and at Mike and Madam, and at the world, for that matter. Trying to bring them into focus.

I suppose you'd call her a plain woman, just to give her a quick look, a stranger, he thought. Mouth's big and nose kind of big and jaw kind of rugged; always was, even when she was eighteen. God knows she had needed strength and ruggedness those days in the Klondike. Pansy, the boys had called her up there in Lousetown, because of the incredible blue of her candid eyes. Her mother actually had named her Isolde, after the heroine of the opera whose robust soprano was far beyond Kitty Deleath's sweet, fragile vocal powers. At the thought of the inappropriate name he grinned, unknowing.

"What're you smiling at, all to yourself?"

"Was I? I don't know. I was just thinking of your real name. Isolde. No more fits you than if they had called me—uh—Percy."

She did not press this; she did not pry further into the little path of quiet thought through which he was trying to find a clearing.

She moved lightly about the kitchen for a woman so big-boned. With her bright pink enveloping bungalow apron, splashed with flecks of blue paint now, she wore inappropriate dangling earrings. Her golden hair was frankly dyed. Touched up, she called it. She never had had it cut short as most women had. She sometimes wore it in a coiled knot at the back of her neck, sometimes piled on top of her head. Occasionally she had a rather wooden permanent wave.

"I haven't got a mite of style," Pansy sometimes admitted ruefully. "Put a thousand-dollar dress on me and it looks like a bungalow apron. When I used to go traveling in Europe, back before the war, I'd always buy me a couple of dresses at a swell place—Vionnet or Lanvin—but I looked like a dressed-up horse. The girls there would be so polite and Frenchified, but they were snickering inside. I didn't blame them. Now Lina—she's got what I call style."

If she happened to be talking thus to Emmy she encountered immediate resentment. "Lina! If you call that kind of extreme dressing good style. I don't."

Pansy's house was like her clothes—good and clean but careless. When you came into Pansy's house you didn't have to think of the carpets or the floors or the silver or the furniture or your pipe smoke and ashes. She had known the mud-wallow streets of the Klondike and rough wooden floors into which the mud was so trampled, ground, and pulverized that it became part of the wood itself. Shacks blue with smoke, heavy with smells. One-street shanty towns where a bathtub was a bucket.

She had learned values there, right enough. Perhaps that explained why, if there happened to be a particularly fine sunset, she would sit out in the garden enjoying it and had her supper an hour later, two hours later. Sometimes the dishes were washed at once, sometimes they piled up for three meals, four. Plenty of clean sheets, but often she made her bed at night just before she got into it.

"That's what comes of living alone," she confessed ruefully. "Sloppy. But it's kind of wonderful, too, in a way. Peaceful. Too peaceful, maybe. Like being dead."

A natural cook, there always was good food in Pansy's house —a cold chicken in the icebox, a heel of succulent ham, beef for a midnight sandwich. She ate heartily as a man, liked her food without fripperies, and despised Emmy Melendy's dishes though she never mentioned this, certainly not to Vaughan, whose loathing of what he called Women's Club Food amounted to a phobia. Emmy liked the recipes you saw illustrated in the women's magazines; in her cuisine mayonnaise mingled with pineapple slices and whipped cream and chopped nuts; maraschino cherries mated with lettuce; she approved that miserable miscegenation of chocolate pudding and vanilla sauce.

He sat stroking the dog in his lap; now and then his hand rested on the silken head of the setter nuzzling his knee. He did not talk. The morning mist was lifting. The sun came in at the east window; the new paint smelled fresh and clean.

"Have a cup of coffee, Vaughan?" Pansy said in that quiet voice of hers. Vaughan had always thought it a thrilling voice; it was somewhat husky but it had in it a curious note that hit you, ping, right here. Up North, when she had sung Mighty Lak a Rose, the miners used to weep into their beards.

Now he said, as though thinking aloud, "Your voice is kind of like those blues singers on the radio."

"That's a compliment, Vaughan, coming from you. But lately those girls and boys whining on the radio make me tired. Belly-aching about the bum deal they got and how they can't sleep nights, and so on. Seems to me something must be wrong with us all these days, all our songs are complaining. I like a lively song, keeps your spirits up even if you have been kicked around by somebody."

He tapped his foot in its broad-toed shoe and began to sing. The two dogs twitched their ears and cocked an eye at him.

> *Oh, Susanna* [he roared] *don't you cry for me,*
> *I'm goin' to Alabama with my banjo on my knee.*

Pansy chimed in in her true, light, unexpected contralto. "Yes, there! That's what I mean." Like yourself, thought Vaughan. Had your heart broken and never complained. "Cup of coffee, Vaughan? Piece of fresh coffee cake? I baked it last night." Hers was a light and expert hand with pastry. As she ate when she pleased—three in the afternoon, two in the morning if she felt inclined—you sometimes might smell the delicious scent of baking sugary dough drifting out to the street as you drove by at midnight. Dike or Vaughan or even young Mike, driving home from a late meeting or a party, had been known to sniff this tantalizing scent and drop in for fresh coffee cake and hot coffee at one in the morning.

"Had my breakfast not an hour ago."

"I had mine—oh, three, four hours ago. I couldn't wait till daylight to get up and paint. Certain things give you such a feeling of satisfaction. Painting. And scrubbing a real dirty floor. You don't see a really good dirty floor any more, everything's linoleum." She considered this a moment regretfully. "I'm going to have another cup. And maybe a couple of frizzles of bacon." She measured the coffee into the percolator; the frying pan began to sizzle slowly. "Somehow I never can get over coffee and bacon whenever you want it. I guess it's the lovely smell; there's nothing like it, indoors or out."

"Yeh, in the woods, early mornings," he agreed, remembering.

There was a high-backed rocker in the kitchen, an old walnut one with a cane seat, and this she had scraped and painted a bright blue to match the woodwork. She seated herself in it sociably for a moment; she ran a hand over its arms and laughed her warm, soft laugh. "Did you ever see anything so ridiculous? Looks like me when I'm dressed up, really." She looked at him sitting there so quietly in her kitchen. The percolator began to burp, the scent of the sizzling bacon hung in the air. She went to the stove, spread a piece of brown paper at the side of the pan. She lifted a piece or two with a fork and placed them on the paper to drain the fat. She picked up a curl of it in her fingers and nibbled it rather absent-mindedly, her head cocked on one side.

"You ain't sure of yourself," Vaughan observed, as though thinking aloud. "You're a handsome big woman, independent and all. But you ain't sure of yourself. Always belittling yourself to others." Then, with sudden knowledge, "I suppose it's because you never married."

Far from resenting this, she agreed. "That's smart of you, Vaughan. Most men don't figure that. A married woman, even if she's got a drunken bum for a man, why, she's followed the line, she's gone along with the herd. Women like me, we're mavericks, we've got no real set place in what they call the social scheme. Failures, I suppose, no matter what, all the way from Queen Elizabeth to Jane Addams. Say, hear me putting myself alongside of them!"

"Pansy. Pansy."

"What's bothering you, Vaughan? You're upset."

His hand paused in its slow caressing of the dog's smooth head. The animal looked up at him reproachfully; then, sensing the end of a happy mood, jumped down and scampered over to Pansy. "Not upset, exactly. Anyway, no reason for being. I don't know. It's just a feeling."

"Folks all right? Mike?"

"The boy's home."

"Yes, I know." He did not ask her how she knew. "There's nothing wrong up at Madam's?"

"Not a thing. Ma's more lively than I've seen her in years, ever since Reggie came up. She's kind of wonderful, that little girl is."

Pansy pressed down the toaster lever for a second browning. "It's funny she never talks much about her ma or her pa or Germany or what happened. It's as if she couldn't."

"Hurt too deep."

"It's better to talk it out." She poured his coffee, strong and clear and fragrant; she pushed the cream and sugar toward his side of the table. The cream was in the bottle, the spoon was in the sugar bowl; no nonsense about it as at Emmy's table with silver this and china that and hot dish covers and butter fixed to look like roses. She cut a wedge of rich, crumbling coffee cake; she buttered a crisp slice of toast; then she, too, sat at the kitchen table and began to eat. "I got the pink bedroom fixed up for her here and I told her she should think of it as her own room to come to stay in whenever she wanted to, long as she liked."

"That was nice of you, Pansy. She'd appreciate that, Reggie would."

"Well, I thought being up there with Madam, day in and day out."

"No life for a young, pretty girl. Ma's no picnic, even for half an hour."

"Do you know the way I figure, Vaughan? That child's been through so much, nothing can touch her now."

Staring down into his coffee cup, he considered this a moment, then rejected it. "She doesn't strike me that way, Pansy. Nothing hard about her. Soft-spoken and gentle in her ways. Of course she's kind of grown up for her age, when you see the other girls around in those shirt tails and shorts they wear, carefree."

"No, it's more than that. I got the room all fixed up fresh and pink and white, it looked like a dessert you could eat with a spoon. She looked at it, the organdy ruffles and the pink roses, and you can see the bay from the window, and the mountains, of course. I said, 'This is yours, Reggie, long as you want it. A place to come to when you want to be by yourself, no one to say where are you, what're you doing, who's that on the phone?'"

"Mean she didn't like it!"

"She liked it, all right. And then it was as if she kind of braced herself, and she said, shaking her head, 'Thank you, thank you, dear Miss Deleath. But no.' I said, 'Call me Pansy, won't you, like everyone does? And why do you say no to the room?' She went to the window and stared out toward the Cascades and she didn't say a word and we just stood there. Then she turned around and she looked at the room and she said, 'I don't want to get attached to any house or any room or anything or anybody ever again. It's better not to care about anything.'"

Vaughan stared at her, shocked. "My God, she's only eighteen!"

"That's it. Standing there, I felt she was the one who was sixty and I was eighteen."

He got up, pushed back his plate with a gesture of finality, and stamped into the next room and came back, his hands clasped behind his back. "I can't get to them."

"To them?" she echoed inquiringly, though she sensed his meaning.

"Kids now. Mike. It's like he had a glass wall built around him, shuts me out. I can see him but I can't touch him. Mike likes me, not just because I'm his grandfather, but we get along. Can't get at him, though. It's like his mind was up in an airplane alone in the sky and I'm down on the ground, looking at him, miles beyond my reach. It's like the way grown folks feel about children— love 'em and feel kind of sorry for them, they're so helpless and not able to cope with real life. Well, that's about the way smart young kids like Mike and Reggie look at me and you and even Dike and Lina. Compassionate, that's what it is."

Pansy gathered the dishes and brought them to the sink. She stacked the little pile that already lay there and began to wash them. Vaughan Melendy, Seattle's millionaire lumber baron and salmon king (as the newspapers like to phrase it), pulled a clean dish towel from the rack and began to wipe the hot dishes.

"But wasn't Dike like that, Vaughan, time he was Mike's age? Riding around in automobiles, eighty miles an hour?"

"No. You know he wasn't. Dike's face was all kind of scrambled and not set yet when he was Mike's age. Girls, and the right fraternity at college. And then when he went to war it was like a bigger fraternity; he was all excited about it. He came home he was let down as if he'd come out of a fever. But Mike—his face is kind of quiet and waiting. Waiting for what?"

She wiped her hands and began carrying the dishes to the cupboard. "Now, Vaughan, you're just getting yourself upset imagining something that isn't there. The boy's had a kind of odd life." She put a hand lightly on his shoulder as she passed from cupboard to sink. "Lina and Dike, too, gone from home so much when he was a kid. Maybe now that Lina's coming home— maybe she's through with the stage and New York this time."

"Nope. It isn't that." He smiled rather grimly. "Emmy's having everybody for dinner tomorrow. You're invited. She'll phone you."

"Oh no!"

"Oh, come on, Pansy! You'll make it taste better, like salt. Just family, there's no flavor to a meal. Emmy's going over to Lina's now, stick flowers all over the place, and she's stocked up their icebox. Lina won't like it. Lina hates being pawed by the family. I warned Emmy, but no use."

"Emmy means it well."

"Don't be mealy-mouthed, Pansy. It doesn't become you."

She burst into laughter at that, and he joined her rather ruefully. Then, as suddenly, she was serious. She picked up her canvas gloves and slipped into them; she dipped her brush and began to paint again along the baseboard, smoothly and easily, talking to him over her shoulder, her strong, vigorous profile clear against the blue of the panel.

"We're a couple of old folks, Vaughan. We might as well face it. I feel young inside. That's why I color my hair. Time comes when I feel gray inside, why, I'll let my hair go. But we're old, both of us, and kind of ridiculous."

"No such thing! Look at Ma, over ninety and going strong."

"I do look at her. At her and you and me and Emmy and even Dike and Lina. Vaughan, it's like we'd outlived our day, just as Madam has. Time has galloped by in quarter centuries seems, lately. Not just a year at a time."

"You're suffering from paint poison, my opinion," he said, angrily for him.

"No. I'm not complaining—don't you hate people who say they're not complaining and then complain?—but we've kind of made a mess of our lives."

"Why, I've had a fine life, been everywhere, seen everything, done everything, fun and adventure and money."

"Yes. Me, too. That's why I say I'm not complaining. But a mess just the same. Our kind, we've gone hog-wild, like kids in a berry patch, stuffing ourselves. Far as I can see, it's been like that since way back in the early days. Grabbing. Plenty to grab, goodness knows, land and gold and forests and mines and so on. But what've we ever done to pay back—you and me and your ma and pa, for that matter, and Emmy and Dike and Lina and all of us?"

"You're talking like a crazy woman. The Melendys are good, solid American citizens and have been for I don't know how long —oldest settlers and you know it."

"I'm kind of sick of you settlers, you Melendys and all the rest. You came because you wanted land, and you took it free and got rich, the smart ones among you. Why didn't you pay for your dinner by going to Washington when they wanted you to be senator, see that things were done honest?"

"What's come over you, Pansy? Talking like a Communist! All this bellyaching about grabbing and us being old and messes of our lives and so on. What's eating you?"

The brush stopped as she considered this a moment. "I don't rightly know, Vaughan. I suppose the same thing that's bothering you. Dike coming home again with Lina Port, and will it last this time? And the war getting worse all the time and hanging over our heads no matter how we try to dodge it. Everybody jumpy. And Mike's face and Mike kind of floating in the air over our heads like one of his own airplanes. I don't know, I guess I just got to thinking. And when a kind of dumb person like me begins to think, why, it's bad."

"Maybe you need to get away for a spell, go East or something, see some good shows, buy yourself some dresses and stuff."

He prepared to leave now; he was suddenly busy; he took out his watch that was attached to the typical sourdough's watch chain festooned across his vest—twelve solid-gold nuggets strung on a gold chain and matching the single gold nugget that was his scarf pin. Anyone from Butte, Montana, to Vancouver, seeing this, would know him for a sourdough who had made his strike in the Klondike.

"Nope, that won't do it. I don't know, it sounds crazy, it's hard to explain. You've got the same feeling; that's why you stopped in this morning."

He paused at the door. "Maybe. Say, Pansy, what's demi-siècle? Of course demi's half——"

She put down her brush; it made a little spatter which she surveyed unseeing; there was excitement in her face upturned toward him as she sat there on the floor in her smudged apron. "What put you in mind of it?"

"Mike. Something Mike said."

"That's it! We belong to the nineteen hundreds, Vaughan, and Dike and Lina and even Madam, old as she is. But Mike and Reggie and kids like that, why, they're demi-siècle, they're half century, they belong to the two thousands. It scares you, it sounds so far away—but not to them. They'll have the job of fixing up all our mistakes, the demi-siècle boys and girls will. We're tail end of an era."

"Well, God A'mighty, I'm not going to stand here arguing about the next century at eight in the morning!"

"It's nine and after."

"Nine, then. And I'm damned if I see we made so many mistakes. We had guts, if you ask me, and so did Ma's crowd and her folks back of that. Look at the Mercers and the Denny boys, crossing the continent from Illinois to this spot, a wilderness and the jumping-off place. I bet Dike couldn't do it, nor Mike, either. And how about us? Folks read about Jack London and Rex Beach and Tex Rickard up there in Alaska, why, we knew 'em, didn't we? Only we went through ten times what they did; they only kind of looked on. I'll never forget that first day you got hold of a sack of white flour and baked those loaves of white bread up in Lousetown, remember? The smell of those baking loaves kind of wafting out to the street and the crowd running with the gold in their hands and you getting five dollars a loaf as fast as it came out of the oven, hot. I was reading the other day how in Europe white bread is considered like cake, it's so rare. I know just how they feel. The hell with your demi-siècle! I ain't dead yet!"

Her face was sparkling again; she dipped her brush in the paint and slapped it smartly against the smooth, clean woodwork. "No, nor me, either, Vaughan. I've seen one world—two, really—in my lifetime and I'm going to see another, I'll bet. And not only that, I'm going to try to help make it if I can. I may be crowding sixty-five, but I've got my teeth and hair and digestion, and like the song we used to sing, there's life in the old girl yet."

7

When the Emma Ackland Opera Company came to Seattle in *The Bohemian Girl* in 1883 the town was down at the dock to meet them. They helped unload scenery. They followed the troupe to the hotel. Opera! Real Grand Opera! Here was culture for you. The folks back East in Omaha and Kansas City couldn't say, after this, that Washington Territory was a howling wilderness of Indians and cougars and bear and forests and mountains.

Of course Seattle was familiar with the theater. Entertainment of a really formal nature had enlivened the town even before 1866, when the Pixley Sisters in songs, dances, and farce had appeared in a somewhat hastily improvised theater that was the cookhouse of Yesler's sawmill. And Everybody's Favorite, The Little Sunbeam, Charming Katie Putnam, the darling of the mining camps, had crossed the plains to entertain the Northwest Country, traveling up from San Francisco as though that were a mere jaunt. But Grand Opera—that was a different matter. There wasn't a theater large enough to accommodate the scenery. Harry M. Hollister, the manager, had been obliged to engage a warehouse, using hastily improvised benches, a few upholstered seats, and, in the rear of the vast barnlike place, reserved seats that were gang plows and farm implements, priced at two dollars for the evening. Upturned nail kegs far back near the door naturally were a trifle cheaper.

This was very different from the Theater Comique which was a variety house in the basement of a saloon on Washington Street. No box rustlers here, with the women doing their song-and-dance act and then mingling with the customers in the boxes to encourage the liquor sales.

There were fifteen hundred big round silver American dollars in the house when the curtain rose shakily on the Bohemian Girl and the bewhiskered baritone as Count Arnheim, Governor of Presburg, with the tenor as Florestein, came on stage amid the somewhat moth-eaten assemblage of nobles and retainers. In the audience no one in overalls was permitted to be seated farther forward than the nail kegs. Seattle, creaking in corsets and starched shirt fronts, settled back in its seats, a city at last.

If Kitty Deleath as the Gypsy Queen seemed a trifle fragile for a lady so active and blood-thirsty, Seattle was in no mood to carp. Perhaps operatic gypsy queens were supposed to be strangely anemic, given to clutching at convenient tree trunks and the corners of none-too-permanent canvas buildings, and coughing whenever they could manage to turn their backs to the audience. Little Isolde Deleath (Pansy to the Emma Ackland Company because of her amazingly purple-blue eyes) was as undisturbed by the Gypsy Queen's behavior as was the audience itself. She was, by now, accustomed to the cough, the clutchings, the pallor of her mother. She assumed, if she thought about it at all, that this was part of being second soprano in the Emma Ackland Opera Company. Pansy Deleath at seven years had seen more of America and life and good, nourishing, character-building trouble than most females ten times her age. Traveling the continent with a consumptive mother in a third-rate touring opera company had not, perhaps, served to provide Pansy with the rudiments of a formal education, but for life in the rough it had given her a basic training which was to sustain her for the next half century and more. She had learned to sleep quickly and deeply in dressing-room trunks, in boats, trains, wagons, tents. A midnight supper

was often her dinner; a midday meal was likely to be her breakfast. She had learned to thrive on strange food at odd hours, and
by the time she was seven she could even cook various messes over
a spirit lamp with considerable skill.

When Kitty Deleath, looking shrunken and yellow as she removed her make-up in the moldy dressing room of some ramshackle opera house said, "Mama's too tired to eat, darling, or
fix anything. You have a glass of milk and some soda crackers or
maybe Emma or Harry'll have some beer for you. Hm? Then
you'll go to sleep, and tomorrow noon we'll have a great big
breakfast, ham and eggs and coffee and maybe pancakes."

"I'm hungry," Pansy would say stoutly. "I don't want any old
milk." About this sturdy, plain little girl there was nothing of the
angelic Little Eva. "I'm going to fry some eggs and fix some coffee and Harry gave me two bananas." Sometimes they ate in the
dressing room, sometimes in a fly-specked lunchroom or in their
hotel or boardinghouse bedroom or at a railway station counter.

Often Pansy took part in mob scenes, dressed, perhaps, as a
rather astonishingly small musician in The Barber of Seville, or
as a minstrel or a dancer in The Bartered Bride, or mingling with
the sparse group of ill-assorted courtiers, pilgrims, and ladies of
the court in La Favorita. On this night in Seattle she had been a
somewhat dwarfish retainer in the castle scene and, in the street-
fair scene, a child in the group of gypsies. Wearied by this pro-
tean performance, Pansy had then retired for a brief siesta to her
mother's dressing room, her couch being the floor with a satchel
for a pillow and her mother's first-act gypsy costume for a coverlet. She had awakened to the sound of scuffling feet, of shouting,
and a woman's sobs. Dazed, only half awake, she stared with un-
comprehending eyes at the two men—one dressed in his costume
as Thaddeus and the other in the motley gear of Devilshoof—carrying the limp, silent figure of her mother. With a terrible fascina-
tion Pansy saw the bright scarlet stains that soaked the front of
her mother's gypsy bodice. Her eyes were closed and suddenly

sunken in their sockets; her face, in spite of its overlay of paint, a curious putty gray. Staring, the child broke into screams—shrill, calliope screams of utter terror. One of the women rushed to her and put a hand over her mouth. "Sh! Sh! Shsh, darling! They'll hear you out in front!"

"Mama's dead Mama's dead Mama's dead!"

"Shsh! No, she's not dead, Pansy darling. Mama's just sick."

For Kitty Deleath had struggled through that performance to the end, and then, as Devilshoof turns the gun on the Gypsy Queen, killing her instead of Thaddeus, Kitty Deleath had fallen appropriately and expertly. The audience was so fascinated to see the gush of bright crimson that spurted from her mouth that it failed to notice the horror on the faces of the company as the curtain descended. This was opera, they said, applauding vociferously with their hands and hobnailed feet in the nail-keg section and politely but enthusiastically in the modish shirt-front seats. As real as life; you'd think it was real blood; how did she do it?

The Emma Ackland Opera Company raised a purse for her among themselves; they assured the hotel proprietor that the room would be paid for; they huddled in little whispering groups with the doctor, their eyes fixed on his face, their faces stricken as they turned away. There was no time to be with her, to help her, for the Emma Ackland Opera Company must move on as inexorably as fate.

Her face was gray-yellow on the pillow, her eyes were dark pools reflecting such utter despair that the words of false encouragement died on their lips as they stood by her bedside in the grubby little hotel room.

"Only got fifteen minutes, Kitty. We've got to get the boat for Frisco; we'd never leave you like this only you know we've got to——"

"Frisco," she whispered. Hundreds of miles. The end.

They assumed a heartiness whose hollow tones did not deceive even the child who sat perched at the foot of the bed, her plain, square-jawed face looking oddly old and pinched.

"That's no distance at all these days, Kitty. We're playing there a full week; you'll be as good as new in a couple of days resting up here . . . meet us . . . we'll send money . . . uh, any folks of yours we might notify? . . ."

Kitty Deleath's white lips moved again to form two whispered words: "No folks."

Harry Hollister bustled in, his hat pushed back from his forehead, his careworn and perspiring face belying the bluff speech. "Why, Kitty, you look fine! Fine! Just trying to sneak a rest, that's my opinion. Come on now, folks, the bus is waiting. Damn shame to leave you like this, Kitty, but we'll be seeing you in no time, here's our routing; just you send me a telegram collect. Come on now, folks! Late as it is. Well, good-by, Kitty! Good-by, Pansy. Take good care of your——"

Kitty Deleath sat up then; by a superhuman effort of will she pushed the dank black hair back from her forehead with a gesture of utter desperation. "Harry, take Pansy along, won't you? Take Pansy along!"

"Now, Kitty, you know that just can't be done. . . . My God, look at the time! If we miss that boat!"

"Please! For God's sake! You—all of you—for God's sake!"

Pansy jumped from the bed; she stood in the middle of the floor; her sallow square-jawed face was flushed, the purple-blue eyes were black. "I won't go! I'll kill anybody dead that tries to make me! I'll scream and yell! I won't go!"

The distraught Harry snatched at this. "That's right, Pansy. Stay with your ma. Take good care of . . . Come on now, folks! Come on, I tell you! We've got to go. We've got to!"

The women in tears, the men grim-faced. Then the flounces and bustles and bonnets and curls, the Prince Albert coats and the tight trousers vanished from the room. There was the clatter of hurried feet on the stair, voices shrill, voices gruff, horses' hoofs,

and the grinding of wheels. Silence. The shrunken woman on the
bed, the child still standing defiantly in the middle of the room.

Pansy trotted now to the window, peered out on tiptoe, stuck
out her tongue as her parting gesture to them, and then turned
toward her mother, her face radiant.

"Good riddance!"

"Why, Pansy!" murmured the woman.

"I like it here. It's awful pretty. The doctor said milk, much
as you could stuff." She came to the bedside; she smoothed the
lumpy coverlet; she folded her hands at her waist in an absurdly
adult gesture. "I'm going to be the mama and you're going to be
the little girl. You go to sleep now. I'll sing. Tell you what—let's
see—I'll sing the Spinning Song from Faust real low. I'll sing you
to sleep, pretend like you are my baby."

The grubby little Marguerite seated herself cross-legged on
the floor; the woman closed her eyes and the hot tears slid from
beneath her lids and coursed unchecked down the hollow cheeks
as the child began to sing.

Oddly enough, the ten years that followed were not too terrible. A new country. The people of this Northwest region knew
what it meant to be sick and poor and alone. They had under-
gone hardship and privation and even terror. The housewives of
Seattle and their menfolk assumed complete charge of the woman
and the child; they even relished this dramatic touch of life from
a world quite outside their own. Miss Cora Amber, the music
teacher (Amber's Conservatory of Music. Pianoforte. Vocal.
Guitar.) said it was like the Grand Opera called Traviata taken
after that book called Camille that a Frenchman wrote; it was
about a woman that—well, anyway, she had consumption and it
seems his father—but she turned out to be a real noble person
in the end—not that this Mrs. Deleath seems to be anything like
this Camille or Violetta it is in the Grand Opera. Anyway, she
is a real respectable person even if she is a traveling singer, and
the little girl is spunky and smart as can be; takes care of her ma

like a grown-up woman; don't hardly seem natural in a child her age.

A year went by. Two. The Emma Ackland Opera Company had faded into the mists of the Eastern seaboard. No more operatic soprano roles for Kitty Deleath. But she and the child had adapted themselves to this far northwest land; it was like another world. The pine-laden air, the salt winds, the plain, nourishing food, and the majestically paced calm of this vast region effected a healing if not a cure. Kitty Deleath had expected to die, she had prepared to face death, and she had lived. It was as though she had come back from the grave—it gave her an other-world quality.

"You'll have to be careful," the doctor had said. "You'll have to be careful all your life. Rest and good, plain food and lots of sleep. But above all, rest."

"But the life of a traveling opera company isn't very restful," Kitty Deleath said. It was more a question than a statement, really.

"Madam, you won't sing again—not in opera, anyway, or traveling around. Not unless you want to leave your little girl here alone in the world. How about your folks?"

She shook her head.

"Mr.—uh—husband?"

She shook her head.

"Well, rest and plenty of nourishing food and quiet," he repeated rather lamely.

"I can sew. I made all my own costumes and a lot of costumes for the company."

"Mm. I don't think sewing will be so good. Confining work, and sitting bent over so much."

She was a woman of spirit, frail though she was. "Seems a pity I didn't die. It would have saved me and everyone else a great deal of trouble." She looked at the girl. "Except Pansy here."

She had, as she had said, a knack with the needle. She and Pansy found themselves comfortable enough in three rooms down near Yesler Way, close by the water front. It was cheap because it was the wrong neighborhood; though Kitty Deleath did not know this until she found that the wives and daughters of the town's solid citizenry did not come to her for their dressmaking or millinery.

There was a front room, a bedroom, a kitchen. The front room was her workshop and their sitting room, but the kitchen was the cozy room, the restful room, the haven. Kitty made dresses, made hats, did any sort of sewing that came her way from shrouds to topcoats. But the water-front neighborhood with its sailors and lumberjacks and fishermen and Indians and drifting population both male and female was too racy for the staider housewives' trade. Then, too, Kitty's taste in gowns and hats was too sophisticated, too dramatic for these conventional ladies. Like respectable residents of all new communities they wished only to conform; they or their parents still held memories of the small Illinois or Ohio or Indiana towns from which they had come. Kitty's saucy ribbons and feathers and pert flounces were not for their staid heads and ample hips and bosoms.

"Flighty clothes," they said. "I'd like to help her out, poor woman. But Mr. Meakins wouldn't let me wear a dress like that, even"—hastily—"even if I wanted to."

But the quiet, pale woman had a gift with the needle, and the girls down along the Skidroad heard of her bewitching bonnets and dashing gowns. Then, too, the woman's plight touched their sentimental side. The Maudies, the Flossies, the Bellas, the Violas of Seattle's Skidroad became the most modish females in the entire Northwest, and even visiting San Francisco importations admitted that they could get nothing as stylish as this in their own gold-filled and more cosmopolitan city.

Pansy Deleath lived a conventional enough life during most of the day. She was sent properly to the new Sixth Street school which had just been built at the stupendous cost of twenty-eight thousand dollars and which seated eight hundred pupils. It was the largest school in Washington Territory, and Kitty Deleath felt that Pansy, whose formal education until now had been sketchy to the point of non-existence, was on the road to becoming a blue-stocking.

The child did her homework studying at the pine kitchen table. The front room was a web of ravelings, threads, and bright snippets of silk and stuff. Chairs and tables and couch were hidden under the ruffles and widths of gay fabrics and flowers. A violet toque, fresh from Kitty's deft hands, awaiting its purchaser's arrival, was likely to be perched atop the chimney of the unlighted lamp. Pansy at the kitchen table wrestling with a problem in arithmetic or a geographical boundary achieved a double education from the sights and sounds that filled the adjoining room. Brassy bright golden heads, shrill voices or strangely child-like, the strong scent of musk and patchouli, the rustle of silk, the clatter of high heels, shrieks of laughter.

The quiet, sallow-faced woman basted, sewed, fitted. Flutings, prinkings, pleatings formed under her skilled fingers. Quixotically, she refused to combine colors or fashion a style which she herself did not consider in good taste. The Skidroad girls respected her; they were ecstatic about their new chic costumes; they never addressed her except as Mrs. Deleath, but occasionally their exuberant senses found a color combination or a mode too quiet or even flavorless.

"Oh, say, Mrs. Deleath, I want something livelier! I thought pink and then the overdress light green and passementerie down the edges and the neck down to here with a lace ruffle."

"No," Kitty Deleath would say quietly.

"Well, damn it all, who's going to wear this dress and pay for it, you or me?"

"Not me. Nor make it, either."

"Well, good-by! We ain't nuns down at Fat Kate's Place."

But in a day or two they would come back. "I got to thinking it over what you said about having it cream color. I thought cream didn't go good with yellow hair, but Ruby said she saw one in *Harper's Bazaar,* it was cream surah with pale blue——"

"No pale blue."

"Oh my God!"

Cream when finished.

Early, early in the morning she was sewing at the window; late at night she was stitching under the lamplight. Usually she delivered these confections herself, or paid a boy a nickel or a dime to carry the bundles to their destination. But sometimes, hard pressed, she was forced to send the child.

"Now listen to Mama, Pansy. You stand at the door and you ring the bell. Pull it hard so you can hear it ringing. Then when somebody opens the door you hand them this bundle and you turn around and come straight home. The name is on the bundle, here it is, I've written it plain as can be on the top. You hand it and turn around and don't you set foot inside, no matter what."

"Why not?"

"Because I say not."

"But why?"

"Because the people who live there aren't nice. They're noisy and they have bad manners and they don't like little girls."

"Why do you sew dresses for them then?"

"So we can go back East someday and live in a nice house and be happy."

"I don't want to go back East and be happy. I like it here."

"Isolde Deleath, you do as I say!" The Isolde clinched it. When her mother addressed her by that name she meant business. "It'll take you ten minutes to get there, even walking slow, and ten to get back. And maybe a couple of minutes while they answer the door. If you're not back here in twenty-five minutes I'll get Mr. Haney the policeman to go after you."

Strict though the woman was, the child had more freedom

than her schoolmates. Kitty Deleath sat sewing all through the day, and Pansy often roamed the wharves, watched the loading and unloading of the ships, mingled with the motley throng of Yesler Way and Occidental Square. Life was kaleidoscopic; the streets were colorful and exciting in the neighborhood of Yesler Way. Down at the docks a ship manned by a Chinese crew. The Chinese were beginning to drift back to Seattle now. The hideous riots of 1886 had driven them out, pioneers though they were. These strange yellow men had built the railroads of the West— the Northern Pacific, the Union Pacific. Commerce, prosperity, civilization itself had benefited enormously from the presence of these Orientals in the New World. Seattle had driven them out barbarously. Now few remained, and these walked furtively in the streets, keeping to the shadows. Their feet padded softly in strange shoes; their hair was worn in pigtails or wound neatly at the back of their heads. Chinese women one never saw on the streets.

Yesler Way smelled of salt and fish and horses and dock water and strange spices. Drays rumbled heavy laden along the streets. Teamsters shouted. Swinging doors wafted to the sidewalk a rich odor of sawdust and beer and cheese and sauerkraut, and from dingy lace-curtained windows came the sounds of tinny pianos and shrill laughter and guffaws. Men in heavy boots clumped the sidewalk; the store windows held gear foreign to the child's eyes. Unconsciously she was seeing a city in the making.

Sick or well, poor or in funds, the two managed somehow to see such theater or concert entertainments as Seattle afforded. For days they would live in anticipation of an evening in the surroundings which they had known for so many years. For weeks afterward they would talk of it. Good or bad, they saw everything. They saw Katie Putnam and Fanny Janauschek; they laughed at Callender's Colored Minstrels; they heard the Kentucky Jubilee Singers; they even ventured into the Chinese theater though there were no other women present and they soon left.

Kitty Deleath never sang now; her voice was rusty. Once or twice she had tried an aria, had stood in the middle of the room as though she were occupying a stage, and had thrown back her head and had tried to give voice to one of her old familiar roles. But the sound she brought forth was thin, was not even true. She would go back to her sewing; from time to time she would turn her head aside so that the tears would not sully the delicate fabric in her lap.

Pansy sang, but there was nothing of important promise in her voice. It was not soprano like her mother's but contralto, warm in tone and true as to pitch. Kitty skimped and contrived so that the girl could take piano lessons. She taught her something of singing.

"It's no voice," said Kitty Deleath. "That is—voice."

"I know it," Pansy agreed. "Never mind. We'll get rich another way."

When the fire of 1889 swept Seattle they ran for their lives and lost every scrap of their shabby possessions. The girl was ten —twelve—fourteen—sixteen. Kitty had guarded her; she was almost prim. She had learned to cook perforce, for Kitty could not leave her sewing. Her sewing was her medium of exchange. She made dresses in exchange for Pansy's piano lessons, in exchange for meat and fresh eggs and vegetables; sometimes when she was too ill to sit in a chair she sewed sitting up in bed, tiny, fine stitches, tiny drops of her life's blood.

Pretty, fragile Kitty Deleath looked an old woman now. Pansy resembled her almost not at all. A big-boned girl with a strong face and a too-forceful jawline. Kitty's eyes were a warm brown but Pansy's were the purple-blue of her name flower. These, with their long lashes and her chestnut hair very thick and vigorous, were her only good features.

Seventeen. A woman. "Ma, they're getting up companies to go to Alaska to the Klondike. People who can sing and dance."

"People?"

"Girls. Like me. They pay high prices. You get on a boat and pretty soon there you are; they say the gold is just rolling around in the streets."

"Pansy Deleath, have you gone stark, staring crazy? Alaska!"

"No, but Ma! You could make my dresses. I can sing. Everybody's going to the Klondike. We'll be rich! Gold! You won't have to work any more."

8

SEATTLE had sulked for years. And beneath the sulkiness was fear. Seattle, the lusty young town, the cocksure two-fisted giant, was ailing, was sick in its vital life stream. Jim Hill had kept his promise: the Great Northern Railroad actually steamed into Seattle in 1893, but even this injection seemed to have arrived too late. No doubt of it, the patient was dying. The panic of 1893 had struck a fearful blow to this adolescent town that had grown too fast. Its bones and sinews were not yet strong enough, not sufficiently formed to take the crashing punishment. All Puget Sound, the entire Northwest region, reeled, tottered.

Men who had founded the city and invested their all in its future lived now by digging clams along the beaches. New houses went unpainted, old houses went unmended, the salt air and the mists bit their way into wood and brick. The pioneers of the Fifties and the new-rich of the Eighties were alike prostrated.

"I hear old Tom Canby's lost his house."

"Puget Sound Bank's bust."

"The Melendy crowd's lost their shirt. Young Vaughan that just married the Oxland girl, Emmy Oxland, has gone back to logging for a living. Land poor, the Melendy's are."

Men who had invested nothing and risked nothing and saved their money were not so badly off, but others who had built the

97

town from its rough pine-cabin days were again living in shack-town on the bluffs at the edge of the city and grubbing like the Indians for sustenance. Local aristocrats who had had weekly packages of dainties ordered from San Francisco now were glad of the region's salmon and clams and the game in the forests.

In Kitty Deleath's front room down near Yesler Way the silks and the satins, the feathers and the flowers grew scantier; they reached the vanishing point. Pansy earned a dollar when she could, but there was little a woman could do in the way of paid work unless she was a schoolteacher or a boardinghouse keeper. Woman's place was in the home.

Youth had built Seattle; youth had given of its brawn and health and brains and hope and vitality. Now that youth was middle-aged, was old, and new youth stared with lackadaisical eye into a future that seemed to hold no ray of light.

Into the drab and hopeless scene there crashed an event so dramatic, so spectacular, so dazzling in its promise as to make Seattle's citizenry rub its eyes in bewildered unbelief. But not for long. For then it burst into shouts, into yells, into a hysteria of tears and laughter; it danced in the streets, it whooped and threw its shabby hat into the air. Gold! Gold by the ton was pouring into the North country, into Seattle.

Though dozens and scores and hundreds of ships, fit and unfit, were to follow, the first ship worked the miracle. On July 17, 1897, the steamer *Portland* came into Seattle Harbor bearing a ton and a half of gold from the Klondike. Banks gone bust were now bursting again, but with prosperity. Whistles tooted; bells clanged. Women in kitchen aprons thronged the docks; men in worn overalls pounded strangers on the back. They saw gold being lugged off the *Portland* in rough boxes and crates. They saw bearded boys in ragged, dirt-encrusted clothes step off the ship with sacks of gold in either hand as though it were flour or salt. Stories, true or untrue, ran like flames through the town, and the untrue were no more fantastic than the true.

A man panned twenty-four thousand dollars in Bonanza Creek in one day.

Fella from Michigan sold his claim for one million three hundred thousand dollars!

A servant girl cleaned up fifty thousand dollars in gold in one week; just happened to strike it right.

They're only prospectors, these fellows, the stuff on the *Portland's* just a sample; they say the ore in the Klondike's the richest anybody ever heard of.

Pansy Deleath had these tales to tell, and more, as the woman with the hollow cheeks and the wide, weary eyes listened. She listened first in utter rejection, then in terror, then she, too, shook with the excitement of the gold fever; it communicated itself to everyone within reach; no one could withstand it.

"They say it isn't dust, Mama. It's gold in lumps; they call them nuggets. I saw a man in a place on Yesler was weighing it out; they call it assaying. Anyway, that one piece alone was worth hundreds and maybe thousands."

In a kind of panic the woman put her hands over her ears. She was trying to escape the sound of fate's ponderous and inevitable footsteps—it was age attempting to retard eager youth. "I don't want to hear it! It scares me. Anyway, I don't believe it; they're making it up."

"Ask anybody. Ask the Reverend Jackson, ask the mayor, ask Mr. Haney, he's going, he left his beat and he's going on the next ship."

"What's that got to do with you? Women can't go. Decent women."

"They can. They do."

"How?"

"Like I said. Anyway, I can. We, I mean. We can go that way."

"You're crazy. People can't go like that. Just go. People don't know about mining or digging or whatever it is you do. Just everyday people. Alaska! It's bitter cold. A wilderness, and Esquimaux live there and eat blubber—they're like bears."

But Kitty Deleath soon learned for herself. Overnight Seattle became a metropolis. Seattle was the starting point that led to the fields of gold. In Seattle they outfitted you with everything you needed, from dog teams to tinned biscuits. Spindling Midwest bookkeepers and clerks who never had ventured out of doors in a sprinkle without an umbrella and rubbers crowded on little leaky ships to face death in the relentless bitter cold of the Arctic winter. Other cities—San Francisco, Portland, Vancouver, Tacoma—tried to vie with Seattle as a starting point for the Klondike, but word had got round that Seattle was the port from which to shove off—Seattle was the lucky starting place. They came from little shops in Omaha, from farms in Ohio, from New York City basements and Chicago stockyards and New England factories. Clerks, schoolteachers, lawyers, ministers, gamblers, housemaids, butcher boys, policemen, undertakers, doctors, prostitutes. Boys of seventeen, women of seventy.

Seattle was a maelstrom; its streets were torrents. Pale-faced men in fur coats and high rubber boots sweltered in the hot midsummer sun. Ships that had been condemned as unfit to transport cattle and horses to San Francisco or even a few miles down the bay, ships that stank of manure and sweat and bilge, were pressed into the Alaska service. Men slept in horse stalls, women slept on deck.

Names fell glibly from the lips of Seattle's floating, jostling population—Klondike—Nome—Skagway—Chilkoot Pass—but above all, for it had such a merry clinking sound, Klondike, Klondike, Klondike.

"But I can stay here and get all the sewing I want. You can help me now, you sew pretty well—plain sewing, I mean—hems and so on." Kitty Deleath was besieged with orders now; the front room could have been piled like a warehouse with the silks and ribbons.

"Yes, and die of it," the girl said, made cruelly blunt by desperation. "Sit and sew, when we could go to Alaska and in a month pick up enough gold to make us rich the rest of our lives."

"You can't go alone, Pansy. It's no place for a young girl alone. Alaska!"

It was then that Pansy had presented her plan; she blurted it in a barrage of words that seemed to stun the older woman with their force. "They're getting up opera companies. Musical numbers. They pay your fares and everything and wonderful salaries. Once we get there, it's easy. They say all you have to do is scoop it up with a pan."

"Scoop! What?"

"The gold. Like sieving flour for a cake, the gold pebbles stay in the bottom of the pan and the sand and water run through."

"Pansy, Pansy, we can't go to a place like that!"

"I'm going. We'll be rich. You won't ever have to sew another stitch. We'll come back and we'll build a house up on Queen Anne Hill—they say that's going to be the new tony place to live —way up out of town where you can look down and see everything, the mountains and the bay clear to the Straits almost. We're going, Ma. We're going."

Pansy knew the man's name. The very sound of it was dashing and confident. She actually had managed to get one of his cards. She handed it to her mother, a thumbed bit of pasteboard done in very large, very black block letters:

CHET DARE THEATRICAL ENTERPRISES
TIMES SQUARE
NEW YORK
PARIS   LONDON

This entrepreneur had taken the parlor of the Golden Gate Hotel in Occidental Square, together with the use of its battered old piano, and there he was interviewing the talent of the town. There was no time to lose, Pansy said, breathing hard. Six young women wanted—with voices—and already he had engaged four. Mr. Chet Dare even had reservations on a ship sailing a week from today. A man of influence, palpably, for ship space was not to be had even on the smallest and most unseaworthy of hulks. The very name of the ship was enough to assure you and bolster your shaking nerves. *Queen of the Pacific* she was called. Dare . . . *Queen of the Pacific* . . . Golden Gate Hotel. The whole thing added up to perfection. "Well," Kitty Deleath said reluctantly, "well, I suppose it wouldn't do any harm just to see him. Stop your talking, anyway. I think we should wear something quiet but rich-looking. A first interview is always so important." But at the last moment she was a trifle doubtful about Pansy's brown silk. It made the girl's somewhat sallow skin seem darker. Kitty regarded her daughter with a professional eye. "Brown's always nice and ladylike, but it doesn't really suit you as well as—wait a minute—tell you what—I'm going to pick it up with a bit of blue."

As she spoke she had snatched up a length of blue ribbon from the froth of silk and velvet that always strewed the workroom. Needle and thread and thimble seemed to leap to her fingers— her deft hands were fashioning a lover's knot. "Under your chin," she now mumbled through the pins in her mouth. "It's kind of cut-and-dried, brown and blue together, but it's becoming and it'll bring out your eyes. Take off your bodice."

"Ma, for heaven's sake! It's almost eleven! He said eleven. Just tack it on with a couple of stitches."

Kitty stood with the graceful bow in her hand. "Sew it on you! That's bad luck."

"Then I'll do without." She turned away.

"Here. Wait. Just a stitch or two, after all." She caught the blue knot beneath the girl's throat with a flash or two of her needle, patted it, stepped back critically. "That does it. Clears your skin right up and goes in with your eyes. It's becoming, and that's the main thing with men."

The Golden Gate Hotel was not reassuring, but then Seattle was so crowded people probably had to take what they could get. The lobby of the musty little hotel was packed with men—booted, hatted, sweating men, hoarse-voiced with shouting and excitement; the air was stifling with smoke and smells. Outside the hotel it had been even worse. A sledge with a shaggy dog team of six snapping snarling huskies actually was on exhibition there in the broiling midsummer sun. A gaping, shouting crowd milled around it.

Through this masculine maelstrom they edged their way, the fragile woman in her neat black silk, the girl in sedate brown. The men did not even glance at them. The lust in their eyes was for gold, not women.

There were two shirt-sleeved men at the lobby desk, both middle-aged. One had his empty right shirt sleeve pinned by its cuff to his shoulder. A Civil War veteran, probably. Already it was apparent that only the unfit or the timorous were going to be content to stay out of the gold rush. The heartier of the two, red-faced from bawling at the crowd that besieged the desk, heard not a syllable of Kitty Deleath's timid question. He was addressing the multitude.

"Naw, we ain't got a room in the house nor a bed, neither. I tell you we ain't! We got cots in the halls already. Parlor's gone. I'll see if I can git you the billiard table, but that's—— What say, Ed? It is? Ed says that's gone, too."

Kitty Deleath's reedy voice in the midst of this hurly-burly was as lost as the wail of a spirit. Suddenly, in that moment, Pansy became the leader; Pansy's height and Pansy's broader shoulders assumed the burden.

"Here, Ma, let me." Using elbows and even fists she jostled her way to the edge of the desk; she lifted her strong young voice in a shout that cut through the bass growls and hoarse bellows. "Heh, you, Mister! Come here! Listen to me!"

The red-faced bawler and the one-armed man both looked at

her as at a new species. Their gaze was harassed but not unkind. "What say, sister?" the big one yelled.

"Dare!" yelled Pansy in return. "I want to see Mr. Chet Dare."

"Can't hear you."

She gulped once, took a deep breath, turned her head to face the throng behind and all about her. "Be quiet, can't you a minute?" If some did not hear her certainly they all understood the look of outraged dignity which they must have encountered at one time or another on the countenance of their own women-folk. In the second's lull Pansy shouted again, "We want to see Mr. Chet Dare."

"Who?"

The crowd's reply to this was inevitable. "Won't I do, sister?" But the one-armed man came to her rescue. "Dare. Fella's getting up that girl show."

"Oh, him. Checked out, ain't he?"

"No. Parlor floor."

"That's right. I recollect now. Left a call for twelve."

"Twelve!" Pansy gasped. "I've got an appointment with him at eleven. It's past that now."

Again the crowd took it as a cue. "Well, say, that's a dirty trick, pretty girl like you . . . If it was me I wouldn't keep you waiting . . ."

There was plenty of color in the girl's cheeks now, and fire in her eyes; she had no need of the blue bow for brightening. "Where can I find him?"

The one-armed man leaned over the counter; he tried unsuccessfully to drop his voice for her ear alone. "Parlor floor, young lady, like I said. Only I doubt he's up yet. How anybody can sleep in this—— But if I was you . . ." His voice trailed off doubtfully.

"Thank you. I'll manage." Head high. Back to Kitty hovering unhappily now at the fringe of the crowd. "Won't I do, girlie?

How about me?" She put a hand on her mother's thin shoulder. "It's all right, Mama. The whole town's like this."

"Oh, Pansy, do you think——"

"Let's go up. It's on the second floor, the parlor. The man said he might not be up, though."

Mrs. Deleath was not dashed by this; she was on home grounds now. "Professional people always sleep late." Curiously enough, this seemed to reassure her.

The second-story corridor of the Golden Gate Hotel was strewn with cots; there were even rough blankets and uncased pillows to show that sleepers had bedded on the floor. The drab figure of a slatternly chambermaid drifted ineffectually about this murky den of Morpheus, the pail and broom in her hands seeming more symbols than implements of her calling. In answer to their questions she pointed to the closed double doors at the end of the hall. "They ain't up yet, but I'm going to git 'em up. Sleeping all day as if they owned the place." She then grinned horribly at her own unconscious wit. "Say, own! The owner ain't been in a bed over two weeks now, sleeps sitting up in a chair—when they's a chair to sit in."

They had followed her timorously down the hall. Now, before they could stop her, she had banged once on the door, then had thrown it unceremoniously open. "Chambermaid!" she screeched.

Mr. Chet Dare—New York, London, Paris—had not traveled in vain. In trousers, shirt, and dangling suspenders he was standing before the parlor mirror giving himself a cold shave. The mirror did not reflect the doorway; he did not even glance around; he merely brandished the long-handled razor while the other hand pulled taut the stubbly skin of his cheek. "Get the hell out of here, harridan, before I slice off your ears!"

At this the scarecrow bridled and tittered as at the most exquisite flattery. "Parlor's got to be redd-up before noon and you know it. Couple ladies here to see you."

Chet Dare whirled so that his suspenders made quite a little arc in the air before they subsided again meekly against his shanks. One half his face was covered with lather out of which an eye glared with sinister effect. His tousled hair bespoke a restless pillow; he was in stockinged feet, and the great toe of the left foot gaped out. Handicapped thus sartorially, Chet Dare stared for a fraction of a moment only at the two modish and affronted females. Then he proved himself a citizen of the world and, as Kitty Deleath declared afterward, a real gentleman.

"Ladies! Please excuse my-uh-dishabill. This is really——"

Kitty murmured something soothing, the chambermaid cackled contemptuously, Pansy blushed. She blushed but she held her ground. "The man—the other man—said eleven."

"You're right," Chet Dare said affably. To their astonishment he now broke into song with a bit which Kitty immediately recognized as the Merry Maiden song from The Gondoliers, the very latest importation from England. "All is right and nothing's wrong!" he caroled. "From today and ever after, let our tears be tears of laughter."

"Gilbert and Sullivan!" exclaimed Kitty Deleath, enchanted.

Chet Dare beamed so that the drying soap cracked a little, reminding him of his somewhat unconventional garb. "Lady! You know it!"

From a corner of the parlor hidden by the open door there now came a plaintive male voice. "What the hell's going on here middle of the night?"

Mr. Dare leaped nimbly to the door and gracefully for a man of his considerable bulk. "Ladies, just one little moment. My associate—uh—we worked very late last night. Now if I may shut the door for five minutes only—if you'll be kind enough to wait——"

Kitty Deleath bowed, Pansy nodded and smiled, and as she did this the man suddenly regarded her with a sharp professional eye. "Nice smile," he said. And shut the door gently. Almost at once he opened it again. "Pssst! You! There! With the pail!"

He plunged a hand into his pants pocket. "Look, see this bill? If you'll go down and get me a hooker of brandy—about like this, see—and a pot of black coffee I'll give you this for yourself, and tell 'em to charge the stuff on my bill."

"Ho!" scoffed the maiden.

"Well, here, pay for it. Vamoose!" The door closed.

Far from being dashed by the proceedings of the past few minutes, Kitty Deleath was obviously pleased.

"He looks awful!" Pansy breathed. "And brandy in the morning!"

"Nonsense! You don't know about men in the morning." She fanned herself gently with her handkerchief as they stood in the dim, stuffy corridor. "It reminds me of old times. Dear Harry Hollister used to be just like——"

From behind the closed double door came the sounds of muted altercation. "Get up before I boot you up . . . Pour out some water then and put your head in the bowl, you lunk! . . . Here, shove these cots together and throw this over them . . . Come on now, pull the piano forward, everything'll be shipshape . . ."

Plaintive remonstrance met these orders, but even to the two outside the door it was obvious that they were being obeyed. Five minutes. Ten. Fifteen. Down the hall appeared the woman with a tray. At that moment the parlor door was flung open; there was wafted on the heavy, hot air a strong whiff of eau de cologne. Chet Dare, shaved, rosy, correct in a bright brown suit and a stiff white collar and a high-cut vest bowed in formal greeting; one would have gathered that he never before had seen the two waiting women.

"Howdy-do! Good morning. I am Chet Dare, the Chet Dare Theatrical Enterprises. Step in, ladies. May I introduce—uh— Mr. Hap Frazer—Miss——?"

A very tall, very thin, very pale young man with old, tired eyes came forward, raised his hand limply and dropped it seemingly from sheer weight.

Kitty now produced a card which she had miraculously preserved these past ten years. This she handed to Chet Dare. "Deleath," she said with an air. "Madame Kitty Deleath. Late of the Emma Ackland Opera Company."

He stared at the dog-eared card in his hand; his jaw dropped; he looked at Kitty Deleath. Then he took the tray from the tottering chambermaid, placed it on the table with a clatter, and drained the brandy glass with a practiced and perfectly timed toss of glass and head that apparently sent the potion exactly to the spot for which it was intended. "Pardon me, Mrs.—Madame —stomach a little upset last evening. Do you mean you're the one who is applying for the troupe——"

Pansy Deleath knew that this had all gone on quite long enough. She stepped forward. "It's me. I'm the one."

Chet Dare looked at once relieved though doubtful. "Oh. Well. And your name is?"

"P—Isolde."

"How's that again?"

"Isolde Deleath." The pale, limp young man had swallowed a cup of black coffee and had then seated himself at the piano, but sidewise, so that one bony leg was negligently crossed over the other and one elbow rested on the turned-back keyboard cover, a cigarette smoking dimly in his fingers. The elbow now slipped and came down on the keys with a crash of bass notes. "But most people call me Pansy."

"Her eyes," Kitty Deleath explained.

Chet Dare said yes, sure, as one who understood. "What's your voice, Pansy?"

"Kind of contralto."

"Kind——?"

Made voluble by nervousness, Kitty Deleath again interrupted to explain. "She means not like mine. Not exactly professional, you might say, as yet. Of course I am—that is, was—a soprano. Though Harry Hollister, our company manager, always used to say that my temperament was contralto. You probably knew Harry Hollister."

"Harry? Oh, Harry Hollister," drawled the lackadaisical Hap Frazer whose head now rested on the piano. "How is Harry, anyway?"

"Dead," Kitty replied sadly. "Didn't you know? Poor Harry passed away five years ago."

"Shut up, Hap," Mr. Chet Dare commanded out of one corner of his mouth. "Uh, contralto. Well, now, little lady, what would you like to sing?"

Pansy rolled her fine eyes upward a moment in reflection. "Let's see. Well, if you want something new and popular, I know On the Banks of the Wabash. Or perhaps Sweet Marie. If you'd like something more classical, I can do Ulrica's potion song from Giuseppe Verdi's The Masked Ball. If this gentleman isn't familiar with it, I can accompany myself."

"You see," Kitty Deleath now elaborated, "my daughter can play as well as sing, which is a very handy thing in any company. In fact, she's talented at a number of things. She's a real hand at cooking. I've brought her up to cook and even sew, though naturally not as I do; you see I'm a dressmaker now that my voice isn't—— I make all Pansy's clothes; I could outfit your company——"

"Mama! Mama, please!"

Hap Frazer lifted his head wearily from the keyboard. "You actually going on with this, Chet?" he demanded.

Chet Dare ignored him. "Sweet Marie. Let's have that for a starter, Miss Pansy."

9

SOMETIMES, many years later, Pansy would see a motion picture whose background was the Alaska Gold Rush. Pert-faced girls with slim modern figures in spangled knee-length dresses quaffed champagne though no nugget was more golden than their hearts. Stalwart young miners in custom-made shirts floored bearded brutes or outwitted sleek dastards in checked suits and mustaches. In the Big Fight Sequence two hundred extras hurled tables and pianos while the air was thick with chairs, crockery, and lighted lamps.

"I suppose," she said to Vaughan, after one of these encounters with American history, "if they ever did a real Alaska picture—the way it was, I mean—nobody'd come to see it."

"Well, now, there was a lot of kind of real lively goings-on. Romance and adventure and so forth. But folks like us that went through it couldn't see it at the time. Of course you take fellows like Rex Beach and Jack London and so on, why, they saw what we saw, but we were doing it and they were kind of looking at it."

"Maybe so. It's hard to see the stars when your face is in the mud."

"Still, who'd want to see a picture about the awful heat in Alaska, and the mosquitoes? They want to see snow—white snow and a nice bright dance hall about the size of the Seattle Civic Auditorium."

"You boys would've been shocked pink if us girls had come out in these movie girls' getups. Silk tights and no shoulder straps and cut down to here. Why, ankles were considered indelicate."

"Yep, a person forgets. We get to talking about it, old times and so on, down at the Sourdough Club, why, you'd think it had been a picnic. The dirt. And the terrible cold. Wet feet or frozen. The dogs eating you out of house and home. Eight men sleeping in a one-room shack eight feet square."

"Remember that window you rigged up for me, Vaughan, in my first cabin, so Ma could see daylight? A row of old beer bottles stuck together with clay. Lucky thing beer bottles were white those days and not brown like now."

"Mm. Lucky we remember the good things and the funny things that happened and forget the rest."

Only men forget, Pansy thought. Sometimes it was as though he even had forgotten that Dike was her son and not Emmy's—his and Emmy's. Oh well, that's how we agreed it should be.

Pansy had forgotten nothing. Those bitter months, those hard years, were like a tangible thing which she could take out of her memory. She could look at them as clearly as at the dance-hall dress stuck away in the box in the attic together with the old copies of the *Klondike Nugget* with its ads of the Gold Strike Saloon and Dance Hall Presenting Chet Dare's Bevy of Beauties. Those Arctic years passed in parade like living things before her mind's eye. Dark Indian faces; the painted faces of women; her mother's wasted mask; bearded, gaunt faces that had looked on horror and death; the piteous faces of flabby little *cheechakos* who did not know a pick from a shovel; the stricken, defeated faces of gold-greedy men who had risked everything they possessed, and lost. The howling of the gray wolf pack, the answering snarl of the malemutes. *Marchon! Marchon!* the French-Canadian sledgers had yelled to the malemutes. Mush on! it had become then in the language of the American miners. Mush on!

Ma and I were just a couple of babies, Pansy often reflected.

No more sense. But, then, there were lots like that. We were lucky. I had Vaughan. I'd go through it all over again, even if I knew beforehand, so long as Vaughan was in it. If we hadn't been a couple of fools, Ma and me, I'd never have met Vaughan. When she tried to imagine life without him life itself ceased to be.

They had known from that very moment when first they had set eyes on the *Queen of the Pacific* down at the Seattle docks. Their shocked eyes had rejected what they saw. What a travesty on her name, that battered old hulk.

"But that can't be it, Pansy!" Kitty Deleath had cried. "Why, it isn't even a ship, it's a—a—like a cattle boat or something."

"Maybe it's nicer inside, Mama. More painted and fixed up inside. You can't tell about a boat—a ship—just by the outside."

Certainly the *Queen's* aspect belied her royal title. She had for years been a salmon and halibut fishing tub in Alaska waters. She must have fought many a battle with the ice-filled Northern waters, for her sides were deeply gouged and scarred as though giant fingernails had clawed at her in an effort to drag her down into the frozen deep. Paintless, comfortless, dirty. She stank of fish and cattle and bilge and grease and unwashed humanity.

Kitty Deleath and the stout-hearted Pansy shrank back as they saw this filthy crone of a ship. For one moment they contemplated flight. They actually turned to battle their way back through the crowd. The dock surged with the confused and shouting passengers, well-wishers, idlers. Seattle's water front was crowded now from dawn to midnight. The hordes of gold-crazed strangers who stampeded Seattle and who slept in stables, woodsheds, on the floors of public buildings, on the streets, swarmed by day to the water front in hope of somehow boarding a ship or of seeing a boat bound for the golden Alaskan fields or lately returned.

Hoarse shouts or shrill; the frenzied barking and snarling of the malemutes; the stamping and neighing of horses.

"Pansy! Pansy, let's—— Come on, Pansy, let's——" But then Chet Dare had laid a hand on Pansy's shoulder.

"Well, well, girls! Here you are! Ship ahoy and heave ho!" He was purple and perspiring; a smile was pasted slightly awry beneath the hard, unsmiling blue eyes. He talked loud and fast; he linked a compelling arm in Pansy's, another in Kitty's; he whisked them up the gangplank in a sidewise movement that pushed Pansy and pulled Kitty. "Rest of the company's up here on deck. Been looking everywhere for you, you're kind of late, thought you girls were giving me the slip, ha ha!"

Her mother's white face spurred Pansy into spirited speech. "Look, Mr. Dare——"

"Call me Chet."

"Look, we don't like—— Mama and I thought—— This ship looks awful, so little and dirty and kind of—— Phew!" From below, as they passed a companionway, there came a reek that caused them to clap handkerchief to nose.

"Why, Miss Pansy! Why, Madame Deleath! I'm surprised. Girls been around much as you two have, opera and all. You got to be troupers. See that bunch down there?" He pointed to the seething dock. "Why, there's hundreds down there would pay a thousand dollars and more to be in your shoes this minute. Why, say, I heard couple of fellas started out in a rowboat."

"But there isn't room to breathe! Look, they're fixing to sleep right here on the porch."

"Deck," Kitty Deleath interjected hastily, miserably.

"And filthy!"

By now Chet Dare's smile had slipped from the oblique into something almost perpendicular, so that his words seemed to come from the far corner of an up-and-down slit in his round red face. "Why, Pansy, she's as tight a little—uh—craft as you'd find sailing the seven seas. You'll get your—uh—sea limbs, you girls, and you'll be crying because you have to get off." His sharp eyes became suddenly fixed on a spot ashore, then his flabby body seemed to relax, the smile creased his plump cheeks. He pointed toward the dock, and now the two women saw that the dock was moving away from them, the people on it were receding even though they rushed forward to the uttermost edge. "Anyway, too late to squawk. We're off."

Good-by! Good-by! Bring me back a sack of gold nuggets now! Don't forget! They were shouting, they were waving from the wharf. And at the scabrous ship's rail stood little anemic clerks in derby hats and spectacles staring with frightened, myopic eyes at the receding shore. Schoolteachers. Ministers in Prince Albert coats. Bartenders with handle-bar mustaches. Iowa farmers. Texas ranchers burned mahogany by the hot, dry, southwest sun. New York businessmen in polished shoes and starched linen shirts. Good-by! . . . Good-by! . . . By. . . . Gold! . . . Gold! . . . Gold! . . .

A terrible joviality besmeared Chet Dare's features. "Now, girls, now, girls! We're off to the fields of gold! Here. Follow me. Hang on to my coattails, Pansy, and you hang on to her, Madame Deleath, that way we won't get separated. God! It's hot! Come on!"

Vocal director. And chaperon. That was Kitty Deleath's definition of her position in this motley expedition. She had explained it to her clients and to the few Seattle women of her acquaintance. "Naturally I wouldn't allow Pansy to go alone. Besides, I am to coach the vocal numbers and dress the company—make and design the costumes and so forth. I'm taking along the material. Lovely. I'm looking forward to being back in opera again—even though it's through Pansy—and very light opera, of course."

"But it's awful rough out there, isn't it, for a woman? And bitter cold."

"Oh, we'll just be in the cities of course. And to tell you the real truth, as soon as we make a strike we'll come home. Late autumn, at the farthest. I'm sort of planning a trip East this winter."

In the welter of humans, freight, animals, in the clamor and confusion of the tiny deck the three fought their way forward.

The girl's strong hand clasped the older woman's needle-scarred fingers. "It's all right, Ma. Just keep close to me." Long, sweeping skirts; leg-o'-mutton sleeves; high boned collars; big hats laden with flowers, ribbon, tulle perched atop their pompadours. High-buttoned vici kid shoes, cloth-topped, wherewith to walk the mud wallows of Lousetown.

"Here we are! Step this way! This way for the big show!" Chet Dare bellowed like a barker outside a tent show. Oh dear, I do wish he wouldn't, Pansy thought. She jerked his coattail vigorously. A beefy cheek was turned toward her. "Don't do that. Mama doesn't like it."

"Mama——" The red turned to purple. Then he broke into the suety chuckle of a fat man. "Hap!" he bawled. "Hap, remind me to tell you a good one. A lulu!"

And there was Hap leaning negligently against the rail, cool, remote, indifferent, while the sweating crowd milled and jabbered all about him. There was Hap, and there were the other five girls of the company staring at them with shallow, curious eyes. Frightened eyes. Hostile eyes. With squeals and pouts and clutching hands they made a little rush for Chet.

"Chet! Chet! Where you been? We don't know where to go or anything."

He patted a shoulder, he pinched a cheek, he squeezed a waist. "Now, now, girls! You know your uncle Chet wouldn't leave you in the lurch." He threw a glance at the chill figure against the rail. "Don't inconvenience yourself, will you, Hap? Can I bring you a wheel chair or something?"

The cigarette between the thin lips waggled once. "Stretcher," said Mr. Frazer without heat—even amusedly.

Chet Dare pushed his derby hat far back off his forehead; he snatched his handkerchief from his coat pocket and wiped the palms and the backs of his plump hands, the inside of his collar, then the leather hatband of the derby with which he now fanned himself ineffectually. "Phew! Alaska is sure going to look good to me after this. Girlies, this here is Madame Kitty Deleath, the world-famous opera star. She's going to make Adelina Pattis of you, ain't that the truth, madame? And sew your dresses to boot. . . . Miss Pansy Deleath, she can sing, she can cook, she can sew, she——"

"Can cancan," put in Hap lazily. Shrill laughter from the girls, spite in their faces.

"That's right, Hap. Muss it up."

"You, not me, you lug."

"And"—hastily—"so can all these lovely ladies, I'm dead certain."

"Say, wait a minute, you! I didn't hire out to Alaska as no cook!" screamed a girl whose black eyes contradicted her brass-gold hair.

"Now, now. Just my little joke. Madame Deleath—Pansy— meet the other girls in Chet Dare's Bevy of Beauties and Parcel of Posies! Lily. Violet. Daisy. Rose. Bluebell."

"De Flower Girls," murmured Hap. But this doubtful mot was lost in the screech of protest that arose from the blossoms themselves. "What do you mean—Lily? . . . Violet? . . . Rose? . . . What the . . ."

"Ladies! Ladies! I got the idea from this young lady here calling herself Pansy. It's a catchy name. There's nothing catchy about Sophy and Min and Jessie and Gert and Cora, see."

Rebellion smoldered in their faces as they looked at Pansy. The girl designated as Bluebell flamed into anger. "I can't see where Pansy's such a cute name. What's there to it makes us all have to be called out of our names?"

Hap Frazer detached himself from the rail. "I'd take it up downstairs if I were you, Chet. Might be trouble."

But now Pansy stepped forward a little; she smiled her warm, friendly smile. "Oh, you girls thought—— Why, Pansy isn't my real name, you know, either. It's just kind of a nickname."

The girl Lily spoke up in a curiously childlike treble: "What is your real name, then?"

"Isolde." They stared. "Isolde. *You* know."

At that their anger, their resentment melted into shrill laughter. "What's it mean? . . . Well, who ever heard . . . Say, I don't blame you for changing it . . . Outlandish . . . Soldy! That's a good one."

Chet Dare circled the group, shooing them with a little gesture of his hands as though they were feathered things. "Come on, dearies. Can't hear yourself think in all this ruckus up here. Hap, you lead the way with Madame Deleath. Let's all go down where it's cozy and comfortable."

Even after almost half a century had gone by Pansy could smell the stench of that dark hole into which they were herded. It was more than an odor. It was like a physical blow assailing them. Dimly they saw a row of cots close-packed, gray-blanketed. A kerosene lamp cast a sickly light. A few hooks on the wall. No porthole. Mrs. Deleath's face suddenly yellow, old. The girls' shrill yammer. Something inside Pansy's head saying over and over and over, "Oh God, what'll we do now? Oh God, what'll we do now?"

Chet Dare's unctuous voice, his hollow heartiness would not have convinced a child. There was even a note of fright in it. "Off!" he bawled, catching the word from the girls' yells of sheer panic. "You're crazy! You can't get off; we're in the middle of the bay. Sh-sh-sh-sh! They'll think you're being murdered. Shut up, will you, while I tell you! It's only two, three nights and we'll be in Alaska you'll have more room and air than you ever saw in your life. Ain't that the truth, Hap? I done the best I could; this is the best they got."

Hap had escorted Kitty Deleath to this noisome hole as though it were a throne room. Now he lounged dreamily in the low doorway. "That's right. Compared to what Chet and I've got this is the bridal suite." He contemplated the ceiling. "I'm going to sleep on the deck if the horses'll move over."

There came an odd little sound from Kitty Deleath. It was less than a cry, it was more than a sigh; she became a huddled heap of clothes on the dirty bare floor.

If one could put a finger on a moment in life to say this was exactly when I became that, Pansy Deleath could then have said, I ceased to be a young girl and became a woman. Certainly as they lifted the limp bundle off the floor Pansy Deleath became the head of the family, the leader, the source of courage and sustenance.

"No, Mama isn't sick. She's just tired. I've got spirits of ammonia here. If you'll just open a win—— No, there isn't one. If you'll all go away—— No, I forgot, you can't do that. Look, I'll give her something'll make her sleep; tomorrow she'll be——"

She felt suddenly strong, reliant. Gently, swiftly, while the chattering girls looked on wide-eyed, she removed the sick woman's bodice and skirt; she hung the absurd hat on a hook and skewered it there with a long hatpin jabbed through a stiffly starched embroidered white petticoat.

"You go away," she said crisply to Chet and Hap. "She's all right, I tell you. Just tired out. Here," to one of the girls, "you help me turn her."

A bedraggled parcel of posies, their faces wet, their eyes swollen with tears. Abovedeck, in the gritty little bar to which they had fled, Chet and Hap were going over the old argument, over and over, for the hundredth time. Somewhere in his murky past Hap Frazer had sprung from gentle people, had known a college education, was familiar with the usages of a formal society. The ruined mind, the dissolute body found the solace of revenge in taunting the fat, slow-witted fellow who was his partner. He delighted in using terms which the duller mind could not grasp.

"Well, *boule de suif*, I trust you are content. You great pachyderm! Mass of blubber without a brain! New York wasn't good enough for you, nor Chicago. No! This Columbus, this searcher for the golden treasures of Cibola, had to set sail in a stinking tub with a clutch of squawking hen-headed wenches bound for destruction in a wilderness——"

"It's going to be good, I tell you. What's the East got? The whole country's flat broke; you ain't seen a yellowback since Ninety-three."

Scorn flickered palely in Hap Frazer's cold gray eyes as he regarded the suety face opposite him. "You'll be wonderful with a pick and shovel."

"Pick and shovel hell!"

"You'll come to that, with this seraglio on your hands."

"Tex Rickard got away with it, didn't he? And what's good enough for Tex is good enough for me. They don't come smarter than Tex."

"That's the catch in it, my fat friend."

"All right. I never set up to be brainy. I got personality. Brains, that's where you come in—or was to. Far as I can see yours are the kind they used to serve in the good old days with black butter down at the Holland House. God, I wish I was back there!"

"*Touché*," said Hap.

"How's that?"

"Just an expression of my admiration for you, Chubby. Every now and then you surprise and delight me. And while you're being so bright, how about the old cow that's sick, and the girl with the sensible face? My God, that good, sensible face is going to look fine in a Klondike saloon."

"That's just how I figured."

"Oh, you figured, hm? And may I ask——"

"Don't need to. I'll tell you. That Pansy, she looks like everybody's sister, see. Or wife. She looks genuine; she looks like you could tell her what was eating into you and she'd understand."

Hap Frazer let his eyes travel slowly around the room, the smoke-choked reeking room, the floor strewn with spittle, mud, tobacco, wads of crumpled paper. Bearded faces; rapacious, worried, eager, wild faces; meek, defeated faces. They sat or stood in little clusters, their heads close together, their eyes agleam. Puny or great-muscled, ragged or diamond-studded, the look in their eyes was the same. Greed shone through the smoky room like the eyes of a monster in a cave. The red-brown of whisky filled the glasses in front of them, but they drank absently, the taste of the stuff was lost on their tongues; they drank and did not seem to feel the hot bite of the liquor.

"So you think these gentlemen are going to want to sit with their head in the lap of somebody who looks like their mama, eh?"

"I didn't say mama. I said sister——"

"Oh, sister! My mistake."

"Or wife or girl. She does, too. They will, I mean. Maybe not just at first. But after a while."

"That'll be nice. We'll pay her and the old woman while we wait for the boys to find out that they're lonesome for their ugly-mugged wives and sisters."

Decision stiffened the flabby lines of Chet Dare's face. He twisted his soft bulk in his chair so that he faced the men crowded close beside him. He and Hap Frazer had been talking in an undertone, heads almost touching. Now Chet raised his unctuous fat man's voice.

"Have a drink on me, boys!"

The men at the next table seemed none too eager. It was as if he had called them back from a far place. Slowly their eyes focused on his round red smiling face. "Uh, don't care if I do," one or two said cautiously. Others, keen-eyed, shook their heads. In the Broadway clothes, the flashy linen, the hard eyes, the soft hands, they recognized the type against which they had been warned.

"What'll it be, gentlemen?"

Among them a young fellow stood up now and shook himself and clapped on his head a broad-brimmed hat that he had been turning over and over in his great hands. He was a giant of a boy in his twenties—blue-eyed, pink-cheeked.

"Thanks," he said now. His manner was easy, assured. His hand came up in a gesture of friendliness. "I'm choked up for air. A little Puget Sound fog in my throat's what I need. See you later, gentlemen." He put a hand on the shoulder of a sandy-haired young fellow of about his own age. "Want to come along out, Dave? Breath of air?" These two were garbed much alike in the sort of clothes a lumberjack might wear after he has washed up for supper. Palpably friends and perhaps even partners in this venture, their similarity ended there. The first young fellow, in spite of his rough clothes and offhand manner, had a look of background, of breeding. The other might have been a teamster, a shoveler. But his eyes had a certain shrewdness which sometimes went unnoticed because the eyebrows were so light as to be nearly white, making no accent for the important features beneath them.

"No," said the man called Dave. "You know me, Vaughan. Rather choke to death talking than live forever lonesome. Anyway, I got enough fresh air falling trees last winter to last me rest of my life."

In the laugh that followed the young fellow called Vaughan moved to go. Chet stood up, shoving his chair a little so that it blocked the young stranger's way. "You boys all headed for the gold fields?" he chirruped.

The sandy-haired Dave sneered an answer. "Why, no, bub, we're just out on the bay for a moonlight ride and clambake."

Politely Chet sniggered amid the guffaws. "Say, you're kind of a comic, I can see that. I could use you in my business when I get back to New York." He whipped out a card, he tossed it to the table. The genial young giant picked it up. He read it aloud, idly, for the benefit of the others. "Chet Dare, Theatrical Enterprises. Times Square, New York, Paris, London."

A skyrocket whistle from the group. "Say, you the fella's got the troupe of girls on board?"

"That's right. Chet Dare's Parcel of Posies."

The pink-cheeked giant returned the card to the table lightly, politely. "Kind of rough for girls up there."

"Oh, they'll help cheer things up for you boys. Dance and sing, cute as a basket of kittens."

"A poke of gold is the only thing'll look cute to me up there in the Klondike," said the young stranger.

"You bet your life! . . . Me, too." From the others.

A little humming, whirring sound from Hap Frazer—a deadly sound like that of a snake coiled to strike.

Hurriedly, ignoring this, Chet beamed on the wary-eyed group. "Where you boys bound for? I'm headed for Dawson, myself— me and Mr. Hap Frazer, my partner—uh, pardner—and the ladies of our troupe."

Skagway. Whitehorse. Running Creek. Dawson. Lousetown. Fairbanks. Nome, Nome!

"Nome! Holy smoke! That's end of the world, ain't it? Jumping-off place to Russia."

"Well, I'm headed for the deck," said the big fellow. Gently he set Chet aside as though he had been a child; again that little friendly gesture of his hand, open-palmed. "See you all."

Chet looked after him. "That's a strapping young fella. I bet he'll get what he's going after, come out with a ton of gold. I didn't catch his name."

Dave swallowed his drink, wiped his mustache this way and that with the back of his hand. "Seems to me you ask an awful lot of questions for a stranger, cheechako."

"How's that again?" He didn't know the meaning of the word, he wanted everything friendly and hail-fellow-well-met; but maybe this was a fighting word. God, he hoped not! "Uh—how's that again, brother?"

Out of a corner of his mouth, cigarette waggling, Hap Frazer was snarling words that came fragmentarily to Chet's ear. The intent of these words, at least, could not be mistaken. Chet ignored them.

"Cheechako, fat boy, that means tenderfoot. It's Indian talk," one of the bearded men explained contemptuously.

Relieved, Chet Dare bubbled with laughter. "That's me! I wouldn't know a gold nugget even if it was big enough to trip me up. No offense meant, gents. Chet Dare is my name and Do or Dare is my motto. Hap Frazer, my pardner. Everything open and aboveboard, and I've always been told the West was the same. Didn't mean to be nosy, and that's a fact."

Slightly shamefaced, the man said, "That's fair enough. General thing in a crowd, why, it's a good idea not to ask too many questions, somebody might give you the wrong answer. But long's you ask, why, I don't mind telling you my name's Dreen— Dave Dreen. And that fella's name just went out is Melendy, Vaughan Melendy; you'd of heard it many's a time if you was from these parts. The Melendys owned half of Seattle before hard times hit."

10

It was cool on deck; it was actually cold. Passengers who, on sailing, had fought for a sleeping place in the open now huddled wretchedly in sheltered corners. Hats pulled down, coat collars turned up, shoulders hunched, they sought the odorous warmth of the open companionways. Blanket-rolled cocoons were everywhere underfoot.

Vaughan Melendy knew ships. He had piloted these waters. Warily he stepped over dark figures huddled thick as beetles. Up. Far forward. Here the wind tried to lift the hair off your scalp. This was more like it; this was good. He breathed deep, pulling the clean moist air into his very stomach and sending out the stale with the bellows that were his lungs. His great chest came up until it threatened to bump his chin. He felt free and alive and able to think clearly. The stink of that room down there, he thought, was worse than a logging shanty in midwinter. Those two men with the show troupe. The Klondike would finish them up soon enough, cloth-top buttoned shoes and hands like women's hands. Sure would hate to think of any womenfolk he knew mixed up with a pair of skunks like that.

In the dark he grinned. He thought of his mother, that iron woman Exact Melendy. Emmy, his wife. Emmy with her little white hands that she was so vain of, and her little pink-and-white face. What would she say to a pair like that? Mama was a

Mercer Girl. Well, golly, they had spunk, those girls; they had roughed it all right and chased halfway round the world for their husbands. Well, that was all right. Funny Emmy hadn't inherited any of that from her ma. Three years now he and Emmy had been married. No child. No son. It was kind of like being married to a real good little girl. Wasn't that he was so crazy about children, or like that. But married maybe you didn't really feel married unless you had kids. Maybe Emmy's ma had had it on her mind that she had kind of gone out and caught her husband with her bare hands, you might say, and had brought Emmy up to be overnice and ladylike. Emmy's ma and his mother had kind of fixed it up between them though he hadn't realized it at the time. Emmy was always there, pink and white and gold and blue and looking up at him, such a little thing. And the two women going on as if she was a princess like in Europe, and he a king or something; it was a joke to him but they had meant it. People had to be stuck up about something, and they seemed to think that getting to Seattle first was something to be stuck up about. His mother had got there in Fifty-one, a baby, and Emmy's ma had come in Sixty-five, a young lady with the Mercer crowd, so Exact Melendy figured she was tonier than Abbie Oxland, who had been a Griggs from Massachusetts. Funny way to figure in a democratic country. Oh well, married and done for, so what the—— Done for! That was no way to talk. Emmy was a pretty little thing. But somehow——

Girls he had known—big, lusty Swede waitresses and girls down on the Skidroad. For some of these he had felt more warmth and a kind of gratitude than he had ever felt for—— Gosh, he mustn't think that way about Emmy. Why, he was a low skunk to be thinking of his wife Emmy in the same breath with girls like that. That bunch on deck when they were casting off at the Seattle dock—that show troupe. A hard-faced lot, all except that one, kind of plain and rawboned, but her eyes and the way she looked, different from the rest, almost ladylike. How did she get mixed up with a bunch of mavericks like that? Probably just like the rest of them.

What was that? Standing there, very still, very still, leaning against the rail, face to the wind, he had been conscious of a sound, a sound of agony, a sound of a human being in desperate sorrow, half stifled but wrenched free by its very depth and force.

He stood there, scarcely breathing, waiting for the sound again. It was the way a man cries, but it didn't seem exactly like the sound of a man's sobs. Must be, though.

There it was again. He hesitated a moment. Whoever it was had thought himself alone. He could make out a dark huddle crouched against a lifeboat. The sound of his own footsteps had been carried back and away by the wind that rushed past. That same wind had brought the sound of the sobs to him here. Well, better not monkey in other people's business. Let him bawl and get it over with. Some poor little rat from the city somewhere scared and lonesome and wishing he hadn't started out for gold, wishing he was safe back there in the ice-cream parlor in Illinois or Kansas. Or maybe it was a farm boy from Nebraska or Idaho thinking of the farm kitchen and the warm critters in the barn and the ham and fried potatoes for breakfast. Heh, wait a minute! The stifled sobs had now broken free into a boo-hoo-hoo starting high and diminishing in an unmistakably feminine wail of woe.

Utterly without thinking he strode over to the huddled figure; he stooped over it. "What's wrong, sister?"

A little stifled scream. A sob choked halfway. A deep catching of the breath. She stood up, her hand at her throat, her hat hanging crazily over one ear; she was sniffling; she was in utter fright. It was the plain, big-boned girl of the show troupe. She said, "Go away! Go away! Don't you lay a hand on me!"

"Don't talk so foolish. I heard you bawling. Way you cried, so kind of deep and still, I thought it was a man, or leastways a boy, scared. I didn't go to scare you further."

There was no mistaking his sincerity, his decent kindliness even in the dark. His voice was gentle, there was in it nothing light or amused. "Oh, I thought—— You scared me so—— I didn't hear a sound till you——" A belated sob now rushed up, surprising her, on its way to join the others. There was about it something touchingly childlike. But her next words belied it. "I don't know what's the matter with me. I never cry."

"It sounded like somebody who didn't cry much. Most women like to cry. But this—— That's why I thought it was a man."

She straightened her absurd hat and the wind twisted it again impishly. "Well, I guess I'll be going," she said primly, as though they had met on a city street.

"Melendy's my name, Miss. Vaughan Melendy. Seattle. I didn't mean to—— If I can help any, why, just say so."

"Well, thank you, Mr. Melendy. That's very—— Uh—— My name is Deleath—Pansy Deleath. That is, it's really not Pansy but Mama and everybody calls me Pansy."

Well, for God's sake! he thought. She isn't making believe; she's a decent girl; something's wrong here. Now keep out of it you'll only get yourself into trouble. But against his judgment he heard himself saying aloud, "Look, Miss Pansy, I know you're with this show troupe. I'd kind of figure anybody with a show troupe could take care of herself. No offense. I mean. But if somebody said something or did something, or if you're in trouble and I can help——"

From below deck a door must have been opened; there came up to them a roar, a shout, hoarse laughter. Her hand came to her throat; she looked up at him; she was tall but he was much taller; her eyes were wide and glowing in the dark. "Their faces are so terrible. All of them. Not like human beings. Their eyes."

He understood. "Gold. That's the way men look when they're after gold."

"It's like they were hungry," she went on. "Their eyes glitter and you can see their teeth way back, like an animal's." He was silent. "Oh, I hope I haven't hurt your feelings. I didn't mean you. I haven't even seen you. You sound good."

"What're you doing, anyway, with a bunch like that?"

"We thought—Mama and I thought—you know, she was an opera singer, a famous singer. Maybe you've even heard. She took sick in Seattle when I was a little girl—and now here she is sick again—oh—awfully sick———"

"Where?"

"Here. Right here."

"You mean your ma's on this boat with you!"

"Yes. Yes. And she's terribly sick. Maybe she's just tired, oh, I hope it's just tired. And those men—maybe it's just their way —that Chet Dare and that other scarey one——— But it's all——— And those girls. Don't let me cry again. I don't want to cry. I don't want to cry!"

"Just you cry, honey. Just you go ahead and cry. It'll do you good. It ain't natural for a woman to hold back crying like a man." And her head was on his shoulder and her ridiculous floppy hat was tickling his chin; his arm was about her and he was saying, "There, there! There, there, Pansy." His cheek against her wet one.

From the lovely warmth of his shoulder she was sniffling a little even while she said, "I don't know what's got into me, behaving like this; I don't know what you'll think of me." But she did not move.

"I think you're a nice good girl. What I can't figure is how you come to be traveling with an outfit like that."

Gently she removed herself from his arms; he could see her plain honest face, her lovely guileless eyes in the clear northern light. "That's what he said."

"Who said?"

"The thin one. The mean one—not mean, but he scares you, he's so kind of quiet and sneery. The one they call Hap Frazer. He said I wasn't the type for a girl show, but Mr. Dare he kept

saying I was wholesome, and it takes flour to make a cake, not
only sugar and spice."

"Oh, he did, did he!" Vaughan Melendy said truculently.

But she went on in the lovely soft voice that matched her eyes
and that made her a beauty in the dark, "And now I think he was
right—that Mr. Frazer, I mean. He was right and Mr. Dare was
wrong."

Three weeks later it was plain enough that Chet Dare had
been wrong and Hap Frazer right. If the prospectors were indeed
lonely for their wives and sisters and mothers and sweethearts
they did not go to see Chet Dare's Bevy of Beauties and Parcel
of Posies in the hope of being reminded of them.

In their modish dresses and their stiffly starched embroidered
white petticoats and their big hats and their gloves the Chet
Dare troupe had stepped off the filthy boat into the mud and
heat and squalor of a gold-rush mining town. Miraculously, Kitty
Deleath had seemed to recover from the threat of complete collapse. On board ship Vaughan Melendy had somehow managed
to have her brought up into almost comfortable quarters. The
Queen of the Pacific had been built to accommodate perhaps
forty passengers. Six hundred were jammed into her decks, cabins,
saloon. But this young Melendy seemed to be a power; he suggested a thing and it was done. After six days and nights on a wallowing tub with a gale driving in from the Pacific they were grate-
ful enough now for the comparative stability of Skagway's false-
front wooden shack whose sign proclaimed it the Broadway Hotel.
But even this was not their destination. The *Queen of the Pacific,* filthy, close-packed, a pandemonium of wild sights and
sounds, now seemed in retrospect a conveyance of almost effete
luxury. Certainly Chet Dare and his cadaverous partner had
been completely ignorant of the fantastic hardships which now
lay ahead of them. These girls and this ailing middle-aged woman
must be hauled somehow over the Pass on muleback and on foot.

In their flounces and their high-heeled shoes and their flower-laden hats this shrill company actually started out, then; and once started there was no turning back. The thing was so monstrous, so nightmarish that their minds recoiled from it. Almost hysterically they went on, and when at the end of this hideous excursion the benumbed cavalcade beheld their next vehicle they burst into calliope screams of mirthless laughter. A ramshackle river boat now received this incongruous freight. It was like a flimsy aquatic birdcage. Again, fortunately, they were ignorant of the distance they were to travel in this floating crate.

"Tomorrow," the purple-faced Chet said, over and over, as they plunged through river rapids, skirted whirlpools, careened away from outjutting rocks. "Tomorrow we'll be there, sure." Curiously enough, Hap Frazer stood it better than he. Frazer took it in grim sardonic bitterness. He permitted himself an occasional venomous sneer.

"New York wasn't good enough, h'm? Too tough. Easy money in the Klondike. Lumps of gold in the streets. You pot-bellied chowderhead!"

The sublime idiocy of the whole undertaking, the vastness of this wild country, the fantastic sights and sounds they encountered, worked a kind of magic madness in the girls and even in the frail Kitty Deleath. Numbed, perhaps, in their deeper emotions by fright, weariness, and an inability to comprehend what they were undergoing gave them a sort of lightheaded gaiety.

"Oo, looka!" they screeched, surveying the vast hills. They saw moose and bear. Once a herd of caribou plunged into the river far ahead of the boat. "Lookit! Cows!"

When, days later, they swept round an outjutting bend and beheld a huddle of shanties and cabins in the shadow of a dark-timbered hillside, Chet essayed a feeble cheer. "Uh—hooray! Here we are, girls!"

Again, as they stared at this cluster of crazy huts, the five girls broke into shrieks of hysterical laughter that rose to a wail, a scream, and ended in tears. Kitty Deleath, looking yellow and old, shut her eyes as though this might blot out the sight forever. Then she, too, began to weep, the tears slipping out from beneath her closed lids and coursing unchecked down her waxen cheeks.

Only Pansy did not laugh, she did not cry. Dry-eyed, mirthless, she gazed at the sordid little settlement toward whose shore the crazy river boat was nosing its way. She looked down at the shrinking woman beside her, she put a protecting arm about her mother's meager shoulders. She said in that reassuring voice of hers that was so quiet and yet so strong, "Well, Ma, here we are, troupers together, just like we always wanted to be."

"Oh, Pansy," quavered the older woman.

"After this we can stand anything. It's kind of wonderful to know you never have to be afraid again."

A one-street town and that street a mud wallow. A boom camp. Ten saloons to every dwelling. A kind of craziness in the air, in men's faces. Chilkoot Pass, they yelled in their ignorance and greed. White Pass is easy. Come on. All you need is a shovel and a pan. They were like children let loose in a candy store. Hundreds of them were to die; thousands of them were to return broken in health and spirits, penniless.

Certainly the saloons and dance halls were the most imposing buildings in the town. They were situated back a little distance from the water front and a few feet above it so that they looked down like vultures on the huddle of shacks and tents below. They were the clubhouses of the town, those saloons; they meant warmth, sociability, relaxation. Here they heard such news of the outside world as leaked into this remote region; tales of adventure from inside; here they met their friends, played their games, drank, boasted, danced, laughed, forgot hardship, disappointment, and terror. The grim streets below had little to offer; they were not in fact actual streets but mere gaps in the lines of shacks and tents.

Toward the fantastic life of this nightmarish town the other girls of the company behaved with cheerful acceptance. They were like tough, carefree children, good-natured enough if they were not crossed in their simple demands. But Pansy and her mother looked about them with horror and dismay. They saw men ravenous for bread but able to buy caviar. Eggs were two dollars each. Milk brought sixty dollars a gallon and the lone local cow was a sacred cow. A long-handled shovel cost twenty dollars.

"It's—it's so topsy-turvy," Mrs. Deleath said inadequately. "Gold in everybody's pockets and you can't buy a loaf of bread."

In two weeks Kitty Deleath turned out six dancing dresses, all ruffles and ribbons and flounces. They were devised to show the ankle and even a glimpse of calf. She essayed to teach these pretty imbeciles the art of singing. Their songs were sentimental ballads or the rakish ditties of the day. There'll Be a Hot Time in the Old Town Tonight. Just Tell Them That You Saw Me. I Don't Want to Play in Your Yard. On the Banks of the Wabash. Little Annie Rooney. Where Did You Get That Hat?

"Round!" said Kitty Deleath, making a circle with her thumb and second finger and holding it up for them to see as they stood huddled like sulky sheep on the creaky stage of the Gold Strike Theater Dance Hall and Saloon. "Round! Let the tone out round and full. Bring it up. From here." She put a hand on her diaphragm.

"I'll bring it up all right," one of the blossoms would snarl, "if she don't quit that stuff."

Hap Frazer directed the dancing, if their untrained cavortings could be dignified by the name of this art. Though the rest of the Klondike's male world went arrayed in boots, overalls, or rough shirts with trousers tucked into boot tops, Hap and Chet were attired exactly as they had been when they had leaned daily against the doorway of the Palace Theater idly watching New York's Broadway crowd sifting by: diamond ring, derby hat, razor-toed shoes, creased trousers, pointed silk coat lapels.

"Watch me, you cows," Hap would say wearily. "Lift those piano legs of yours, will you! This isn't an elephant quadrille. It's supposed to be dancing." He would raise his long leg; he would point his slim foot in its patent-leather cloth-topped shoe. "Watch me." Incredibly graceful and light he would twirl, pirouette, leap. In spite of the shirt sleeves and suspenders and the yellow hawklike face, he somehow managed to suggest the seductive poses, the audacious steps that these untalented coryphees never could imitate.

Of them all, Pansy alone had an authentic voice, limited though it was. When the other flowers in Chet Dare's Parcel of Posies lifted their voices in song there issued from their pretty throats such a shrill and nasal cacophony as to smite the ear with horror.

"Who'll listen to that screeching?" Hap Frazer demanded. "Damned if they don't sound like the zoo at feeding time."

"The boys ain't coming to hear the singing," Chet reminded him mildly. "It isn't what they hear, it's what they see. Anyway, she's going to sing for 'em, isn't she—Pansy? Give her a good patriotic number and follow it up with a tear-jerker. The lunks'll love it."

True, warm, Pansy's voice lent itself ideally to the song that Chet Dare thought best suited to her. "The war. Song about the war with a good swing to it and then the girls on with flags and so on."

Hap, the cynic, did not agree. "If these grizzlies up here were interested in the Spanish-American War they'd be in it and not up here scratching for gold."

"Nah-ah-ah-ah, they don't belong to a regiment or a Company G, or like that, what'd they want to be fighting a war? That's for soldiers. They'd like a flag-waving song, though."

Years afterward, though she was to endure many hardships and terrors, Pansy Deleath's nightmare, from which she awoke wet and shaking, was always the same. She was standing on the stage of the Gold Strike Theater and Dance Hall and men with wolf faces were snarling at her, their teeth bared like fangs, their hands like claws, their eyes blazing yellow.

Actually, they were, for the most part, bearded boys who had come to the saloon for entertainment and a bit of fun, for liquor and company and a glimpse of a pretty face, a plump bosom, and a not too knuckly knee. These boons they received, in a measure, from Lily and Daisy and Violet and Rose and Bluebell. Surrounded by these floral offerings, Pansy's face was startlingly—almost comically—real and wholesome and unromantic. Chet had been right in this—she did remind them of their wives, their sisters, their mothers, even their sweethearts. But this was not what the Gold Strike Theater and Dance Hall had promised them. These they had left safely at home. Unconsciously they resented a dance-hall girl who reminded them of their own proper and sheltered females.

Pansy's song, too, was unfortunately chosen. The martial note, since she was tall, sturdy, and equipped with a strong—or strong enough—voice, fell to her. But these men were not dying on San Juan Hill; they were not with Dewey in Manila Bay, nor with Sampson or Schley at Santiago. They were not particularly comfortable or happy, but they were not eating decayed beef nor writhing with dysentery. They were out for gold and gold and gold. They did not object to news of the war, for it came rarely enough in this far-off arctic wilderness. But they did not want it rubbed under their noses.

Chet Dare had selected Saturday night as the most favorable time on which to open his show.

Hap remonstrated. "You're crazy. Tex Rickard's got a fight fixed up between Slavin and Cassidy. He gave 'em a workout last week and the boys have got all their money up for Saturday night."

"We'll put our show on at eleven. Fight'll be over by that time, and the money circulating."

"Uh-huh. That's a lovely idea. Dreamy. Of course Tex, being the bartender over at the Monte Carlo, won't like the boys to stay and spend their money right there. He'd want them to save it up and bring it over here to the Gold Strike and pile it up in your fat lap."

But Chet's round red face remained amiable and even serene. "There's enough for all. You're getting grasping, Hap. Next thing you'll be mushing up the Pass with a shovel like the rest of these fools, looking for gold and freezing to death on the way."

Hap studied his long, delicate fingers. "We may come to it, at that, both of us. One good thing, it would peel some of that lard off you."

"What's eating you, Hap? You always had the disposition of a rattlesnake. But now there's no getting along with you. Things are shaping up good. The girls get along. The old hen and the girl sewing and cooking their heads off for 'em. Say, anybody would be a real bitch couldn't get along with Kitty and Pansy. Like cooing doves, the lot of 'em."

Hap, slumping in his chair, now uncoiled lazily. He sat up almost straight. "Yeh. Doves. Doves are just what we want to get out and rustle drinks after the show. And Horse Face, I suppose———"

"They're crazy about her. Pansy's been cooking for the girls, rigged up a stove up there in the room. I bet she could get ten dollars a plate for what she serves the girls. Says she's going to try to get hold of some white flour and maybe a couple of eggs, make some———"

"Look, Chet. We've come thousands of miles. We stand to make our pile or lose our shirts. And you talk about flour and eggs. For a man that's been in show business all his life, you sound like a hop head."

"Now what have I said?"

"That girl. And her mama! Say, what is this? A female seminary!"

"Old lady's done what she was hired for, sick as she is. I never saw strikinger costumes, let me tell you, even in a Weber and Fields show, or at the Palace, or anywhere. Sensational, that's what. The girls look cute; they can sing and dance good enough —nothing extra, but good enough—and Pansy's voice in that song——"

Hap rose now and flicked away his cigarette without lighting a fresh one at its butt—a sure indication of deep disturbance. "You're stuck on that big, ugly-mugged Statue of Liberty, damned if I don't think you are."

And over Chet's already roseate features spread the telltale purple of accelerated heartbeats.

"Well, my God!" said Hap Frazer, and groped his way blindly toward the bar.

Only once during these days of rehearsal in the hot, fly-infested dance hall had Pansy seen the man on whose shoulder she had cried with such abandon. He seemed to have vanished. Sometimes she found herself wondering if the romantic incident of the boat deck actually had happened. Her eyes searched for him though she walked demurely enough and rarely enough on these mud-wallow streets that were thronged with bearded, booted men of every age and condition.

"Where's that nice young man?" Kitty Deleath would say. "The one that was so polite and kind when I was sick on the boat?"

"I don't know I'm sure," Pansy would reply, regal indifference in her tone. A group of men lounging outside a saloon or an assayer's shack. Her eyes searched their faces as she approached them, dropped demurely as she passed them, and her downcast lids hid her sick disappointment.

She came down the thin wooden stairs of the rooming house on her way to the dance hall and there he stood, waiting. The shock of seeing him made her a little faint, so that she went white instead of red.

He said almost roughly, "You look funny. Not good. Are you sick?"

"Oh, it's you, Mr. Melendy! My, how you frightened me!"

"How are you?"

"I'm fine." Brightly. "I'm——" Somehow her breath was gone. She could not go on.

"Look at me."

She breathed deeply then; she raised her eyes; she looked at him. They stood a moment. Then he said quietly, "I've been up the Pass."

"I thought that was it."

"I'll be there for your show, Pansy. Pansy." He took her chin in his big hand; he tilted her face as though to kiss her; he dropped his arm suddenly; he was gone. She leaned against the doorway, her eyes shut.

Though he had failed to make articulate his vague fears and premonitions, Hap Frazer proved himself right. To the men who made up her audience Pansy Deleath was a double reproach. She was the accusing, tender eyes of all the women waiting for them in the respectable and conventional homes and farms and flats from Seattle to New York. She was Uncle Sam and the Constitution and Dewey and young Colonel Roosevelt at San Juan Hill, all accusing them of loving gold more than country.

She came out with a broad swathe of red, white, and blue draped over one shoulder, brought across her bosom, and tied in a sash on one hip. On her head was a miraculously contrived imitation of Uncle Sam's high hat, and this was patterned with the Stars and Stripes. Daisy, Rose, Violet, Bluebell, and Lily bounced out of the wings for the chorus, similarly sashed but minus the top hat, since one of these had been difficult enough to contrive. Theirs were Rough Rider hats, cocked. At their waists, suspended by colored ribbons, were tiny drums made of stretched native walrus hide, and on these they beat a martial and spirited, though slightly ragged, rat-a-tat-tat-ta-roo.

Hap Frazer had rehearsed her, Kitty had coached her until between them she was numb with repetition. Over and over Pansy has stood up before the sallow-faced woman with the burning eyes and had sung her verse and chorus. "More spirit!" Kitty said. "It's about war and your country. Make it sound like marching."

"I'm getting stale. It doesn't sound like anything to me any more."

But the audience was a good one that first night; they had seen Rickard's fight; they were full of whisky and arctic air and hunger for the sight of fresh, pretty females. So far the show had gone over, no doubt of that. Big girl. Not pretty. Sings good. Flags, huh?

She came to the chorus and sang it alone the first time. The girls were to follow with chorus effect for its second rendition. Full voice. Her eyes alight. Strong and loud and straight and patriotic.

> "You don't belong to the Regulars
> You're just a Volunteer.
> You're only one of the rank-and file,
> But someone holds you dear.
> Many a mother's heart will break,
> But in the coming year,
> Uncle Sam will take off his hat,
> To you, Mister Volunteer."*

They did not like it. By the time she had reached the chorus the second time they began to stamp out the rhythm with their great boots.

> "You stamp belong to the stamp, stamp, stamp
> You're stamp a stamp stamp stamp.
> You're stamp . . ."

*Copyright, 1901, by Howley, Hairland & Dresser. Copyright renewed and assigned 1928 to Paull-Pioneer Music Corp., New York City.

Now her voice was lost in the noise. They began to clap it:

> *"Many a clap stamp stamp clap clap clap*
> *But stamp stamp clap clap clap*
>
> .   .   .   ."

You could see she was singing, for her lips formed words. The beat of the drums came through, throb, throb, with the muffled sound of a death march.

"Come off, you fool!" shrieked Hap Frazer from the piano in the pit.

"Stay on! Finish it. God damn 'em, finish it! That's the girl! Stick!" Chet Dare bellowed from the wings right.

The drummer girls were pasty white beneath their make-up; they stared left, they stared right, mouths open, eyes round. Pansy, bedecked in flags and bunting, stood her ground, her lips stiffly obeying her will. She looked big and awkward and very plain and terribly frightened. Beyond the wretched smoky lamps that were the footlights she saw a gigantic figure rise and clamber roughshod over the others seated in his row. He strode down the aisle; he leaped catlike to the stage as though propelled by a springboard. He did not approach Pansy. She went on with her song to the end, like an automaton that is wound and that must go until it runs its course. Words. Words. And sounds coming from the back of her throat.

> *"Uncle Sam will take* off *his hat*
> [She took off her wretched headgear]
> *To you, Mister Volunteer."*

She stood there a moment. Her great eyes stared into the audience like those of one hypnotized. Then she covered her face with her hands.

There was a clatter of high heels behind her. They had scurried off, the drummer girls—Daisy, Violet, Bluebell, Rose, Lily.

You could hear their high-pitched, hysterical voices babbling in the wings, and Chet's frantic sh-sh-sh! Hap Frazer had long ago fled the orchestra pit and his lone piano.

Vaughan Melendy's huge frame leaned over the proscenium into the footlights so that he threatened to pitch headfirst into the orchestra pit. One great arm with its clenched fist was outstretched so that it seemed to threaten every bearded jaw in the close-packed rows.

"Come on, you big baboons! Come on up here and tackle somebody your own size! What's the matter? Scared! Fight a woman, huh?"

There was silence for a moment. Then, "Hero!" a man yelled from the back of the hall. "A goddamn hero, that's what!" The voice was affectedly mincing and high-pitched. The audience found relief in a thundering guffaw.

Pansy's hands came down. She stood there. She heard Kitty's voice from the wings. "Pansy! Pansy! Come off. They're going to fight!" But the girl did not move.

Another voice, strong and masculine, bellowed above the clamor of the hall: "Why ain't you in Cuba if you're so stuck on it?"

"Yeah. Rough Rider! . . . Melendy! Melendys are rich as all hell. . . . What you doing up here? Whyn't you fighting out there you're so stuck on it? . . . Johnny, git your gun, git your sword, git your pistol . . ."

They caught this up now, stamping. "Johnny, git your gun, git your sword, git your pistol. Johnny, git your gun . . ."

With a completely unpremeditated movement as swift as it was thoughtless Pansy hurled her hat into the audience. If she had had a rock she would have thrown that. The crowd was surging forward now. Someone caught the hat. There was a wild scuffle and scramble for it.

"Stop it!" she yelled. "I don't want anybody to fight. I'll go. I'll go. Only stop!"

But now Chet Dare had managed at last to bring down the shaky curtain in a series of jerks, but not before Vaughan Melendy had ducked under it and leaped over the footlights and down into the melee. Stiffly Pansy turned and walked to the wings. Chet's scarlet face like a balloon about to burst. Hap Frazer's clammy mask, dough-colored. Her mother's sunken eyes. The girls huddled crying. Shouts, yells, scuffling from the other side of the curtain.

She went straight to her mother. Her voice was hard and clear. "Don't you do any collapsing, Ma. Hear me! If anybody's going to collapse, it's me, and I ain't going to." She turned to the men. "What did I do? Was it my fault?"

"Yes!" snarled Hap. "They didn't like that ugly mug of yours."

"Oh!" The girl's head jerked aside, as though she had been slapped in the face.

"No!" wheezed Chet, his voice suety and smothered by emotion. "It just hit 'em wrong. That song. God, what'll we——"

Hap pointed one bony finger toward the rickety steps that led down to the floor. "Get down there, you girls, and circulate. Break it up."

Whimpering, they shrank back. I won't. You can't make me. I'm through. I'm quitting.

Pansy walked toward the steps; she turned and beckoned them, smiling. "Oh, come on, girls."

Her mother shrieked: "Pansy. Pansy, don't you——"

"You going into that?" Chet squeaked weakly.

"Come on, girls. Here, I'll take my sash off, see, and wave it like they do in war, a flag of truce. It's my fault. They didn't like me. Come on, they can't kill you. Or anyway they'll kill me first." She beckoned again with her eyes and her head and her hand. "They're not mad at me," she said surprisingly, in an unaccountable flash of inner knowledge. "They're mad at themselves and took it out on me. Come on!"

Serenely, with a calm that would have been absurd if it had not been sublime, she walked into the midst of the brawling, heaving mass of men. Her head was high; her eyes were blazing; she held the scarf aloft like a banner; and where the senseless fighting was thickest there she walked, smiling, and they must perforce stop or their fists and feet would find a target in her. One glancing blow did indeed strike her, and she reeled, and the reluctant girls, cowering far behind her, screamed shrilly. As suddenly as they had begun the brawl the men sobered, ceased, stood shamefaced. Their shoulders heaving, their faces sweating, they made a sorry sight. And as she saw them a quick, courageous anger rose in the girl. In the middle of the littered floor she stood; she threw back her head; she began defiantly to sing, and she sang the song they had rejected; and as she sang they joined in almost shyly at first, and then with gusto. And Hap Frazer leaped to his piano and now the flimsy wooden building rang with the beat of the song.

" .   .   .   .   .   .

You're only one of the rank and file,
But someone holds you dear.
Many a mother's heart will break,
But in the coming year
Uncle Sam will take off his hat
To you, Mister Volunteer."

Oddly enough—or perhaps quite naturally—she became something of a favorite now in the Gold Strike Theater and Dance Hall. The ill-fated patriotic number was never repeated. Instead Pansy broke them down nightly with sentimental ditties. She sang Mighty Lak a Rose and Only a Bird in a Gilded Cage. They listened. They loved it. They wept as they gulped their whisky straight. The other Posies in this bouquet were beginning to feel the stir of jealous resentment. But now Kitty Deleath took to her

bed. The melodramatic shock of that opening night had proved
too much for her. In the weeks that followed the Bevy of Beauties
numbered five oftener than six. Pansy was alternately nurse and
dance-hall girl. It was plain that Kitty Deleath was not merely
a sick woman now; she was dying.

"I can't play tonight, Chet. I've got to stay with Ma. She's
worse."

"That's all right, Pansy. We'll miss you but we'll make out."

"You're awful good, Chet."

A fatuous look besmeared the round red face. "I could be a
whole lot better if you'd only let me, Pansy. Know what I mean?"

"No, Chet. I mean I know, but no, Chet."

"I could turn ugly and you'd be stranded here, you and your
ma, if I wanted to."

"Yes, you could. But you won't."

"Yeh. You're right. Look, Pansy, you holding out for marriage?"

"Oh no! No."

"I always said I wouldn't ever get caught that way again. Last
two times was enough for me. But hell, I——"

Hap Frazer was not so amiable.

"Hap, I can't work tonight. She's talking wild and burning
up with fever."

"Yeh, well, no workee no monee. What do you think this is—
a charitable institution?"

August was gone. September. October was the beginning of
winter in this arctic land. Soon they would be landlocked up
there in the North.

"Uh, Pansy," Chet stammered huskily, like a lubberly boy.
"Uh, look, Pansy, when your ma—if your ma—if anything should
happen to her, why, I'll take care of you. Don't you worry. I'll
take care of you."

"That's nice of you, Chet, the way I haven't been over to the
hall half the time."

"Well, no, I mean I'd take care of you. I mean."

The sick woman was keeping the girls awake nights—or mornings, after their late night's work—by her hard, dry coughing.

Pansy had seen Vaughan Melendy only twice since the opening night's fracas. He was off now for weeks at a time, prospecting. Between these two the magnetic current flowed strong and stronger. It united them; it separated them. If they stood talking, however casually, each could feel it a powerful force drawing them together. He did not touch her. Her marvelous eyes looked up at him, shadows under them now in spite of her strength and youth. From his height the young giant looked down into them and felt himself drowning.

"Old married man like me," he would say casually, lightly, when he felt himself going down; it was a straw toward which he reached in the vain hope of saving them both. This was not a lonely man infatuated by a pretty face. Pansy was not pretty. He was not lonely. He loved her. "Got to strike it rich for my wife and kids—only I've got no kids. . . . Guess I'd better settle down when I get out. Look, gray hairs. I'm a son of a gun if I'm not getting gray and not near thirty."

Calmly and evenly and carefully she took it up. "Maybe it runs in your family, gray hair early."

"Nope. Ma, she's near fifty; not a gray hair in her head. Pa died couple of years ago, but his beard was black as a Turk's."

He had been gone weeks. "How's your ma?"

"No better. Worse."

They were sitting at a table in the dance hall. He reached into his coat pocket; he tossed a sack into her lap, very small, rather heavy for its size. She had seen hundreds of these in the past weeks. A little leather-thonged sack, made of moose hide or caribou. Gold dust. That was the medium of exchange in the Klondike—gold dust or whisky, and gold dust came easier. She looked up at him, startled, shock in her eyes.

"For luck," he said. "A little poke of gold for luck. It's the first handful; if you take it, it'll bring us luck sure."

"Us?"

He looked at her. "It's only a couple of hundred; that's about all it'll bring, assayed."

"Where?"

"Up there. Up over the Pass and beyond. I'm going back up. I'll be gone till spring—maybe summer. It looks big. If it turns out to be what I think it is—— Look, Pansy, you'd better get out of here, you and your ma."

"I can't."

"I think I can get you passage if you go right now."

"She won't go."

"But that's crazy. I didn't go to say that. I mean you can't let anybody sick as your ma decide a thing like that. You've got to take hold and decide for her and for yourself, and then do it."

"I know. I did. A month ago. More. Dr. Moriarty says she can't be moved, it's too far, she'll die; she says she'll die on the ship and they'll throw her into the sea; she screams and goes kind of out of her mind. I can't. I can't. She made me promise not to take her on a ship. She made me promise to let her die here. I promised. I have to stay."

He sat silent, drumming the table top with his fingers. He nodded once in assent. "Tough," he said grimly. He drew his chair closer now; he laid his plan before her; he was instructing her as a fond husband provides for a young and inexperienced wife so that she may be safe and comfortable in his absence. His tone was matter-of-fact.

"You've got to get her out of this place. The hotel, I mean. You, too. I know where I can lay hands on some lumber and a bit of this and that. I'll build you a shack—now wait a minute, I'm doing the talking—two rooms, leastway one decent room and a lean-to; you oughtn't to sleep same room as her; I heard it wasn't healthy. I'll leave you what I've got."

"No."

"It isn't much. You'll need it. Doctors. And if anything happens to your ma."

"I'm working. Of course I have to be with Mama half the time, nights, when she's bad. But Chet understands; he's been good about it; he lets me work when I can."

"Chet." He looked at her.

She shook her head. She put a hand out toward his and then withdrew it hastily. "You know such a thing couldn't be, Vaughan."

"I'll be halfway out of my mind, up there, thinking about you."

"I'll be all right."

"Wait for me, Pansy." Then he covered his eyes with his hand. "I haven't even got any right to say that to you." He laughed shortly; his hand came down; he looked around the room with hard, bright eyes; then his eyes came back to hers and held them. "It's like you were my wife, not her."

Her plain face took on a radiance that gave her momentary beauty; her eyes were sapphire stars.

Vaughan pressed into service a score of men he knew and they built her a house in three days, a weatherproof, two-room shack. Into its making had gone everything from driftwood to muskeg and peat moss. Precious tar paper insulated it. There were shelves of milled lumber, very grand. One window was of canvas rubbed over with bacon rind, the other of beer bottles chinked together with clay. A two-hole stove provided heat and a cooking surface. Pansy's bed in the tiny lean-to was of walrus hide stretched between posts driven into the floor, but the sick woman lay in luxury on an iron bedstead whose mattress Vaughan had bought, begged, bullied, or browbeaten the captain of the ship *Sophy of Seattle* into giving him. There was a green baize table, too, evidently filched from the ship's saloon, and a collection of chairs, tables, pots, pans, and stools that embraced several countries and innumerable professions and periods. A battered samovar spoke of the Alaska which had been Russia a hundred years before; there were glasses and a pitcher donated by the bartender of the Mud in Your Eye Saloon; there was a tiny gilt French chair as absurdly out of place as a satin slipper on a miner; there was even an ikon perched on one of the shelves among the pots and pans.

"Bring you luck," Vaughan said, surveying this incongruous addition to the warm, bright room. The two women had been installed. Kitty Deleath lay like a waxen figure in her bed in a corner. "Somebody must have swiped it from one of the old Russian churches around Kodiak or some place."

"I don't know about ikons. But anyway I'll make a prayer for you in front of it every morning and every night while you're gone."

"Will you, Pansy?" He had eaten with them the first meal in their new house. By some miracle of influence or persuasion he had managed to buy a barrel of white flour off the last steamer in. In a sourdough country, where bread was a leaden mixture that looked and tasted like unleavened clay, a barrel of white flour was worth four hundred dollars. Pansy had baked, not biscuits but bread, fragrant, light, hot, and they had eaten it with gravy, with honey, with tea, and just as it was cut from the loaf, without butter. No cake ever tasted sweeter or more delicate.

"Bread," Vaughan said, and held a last slice of it in his hand. Wholesome, nourishing, sustaining. "It's like you, Pansy."

"I don't know's I take that as a compliment."

"It's so meant." He looked at her. "I'm leaving you tomorrow. Anyway, coquetting doesn't become you."

Her heart was hammering. "I was hired up here, wasn't I, to sing and dance and be coquettish?"

"Not by me you weren't."

Together they washed the dishes, she washing, he wiping; he

placed them neatly on the shelf. "I'll have this to remember and get warm by up there."

"What are you taking with you? Food, I mean." Primly.

"Bacon, beans, flour, tea, sugar."

"Oh."

"Course it's the dogs and the dogs' food that costs. They took my roll, or just about. Three huskies and three malemutes. All the way from two hundred to five hundred dollars apiece. And eat! It's ferocious. Costs five dollars a day apiece to feed 'em. But there's nothing to this mushing but keeping yourself and your dogs fed and healthy."

Nothing to this mushing but keeping yourself and your dogs fed and healthy. She was to think of this a thousand times in the winter to come, and he was to laugh a rueful laugh when he recalled it all the rest of his long life.

Up the Pass, thousands of feet tramping a trench in the frozen earth and snow. Their tiny figures against the snow as they filed up the Pass were like ants on sugar. Higher and higher, their eyes bulging; their breath coming in gasps from bursting lungs; their hearts breaking with the effort. Gold, gold, gold. They were black specks against the snow and sky, hunched figures moving like the buckets of a dredge in an endless human train. Sprays of needles drawn into the lungs with every breath. A hundred thousand booted feet sludging through the snow and mud and slush. There's nothing to this mushing but keeping yourself and your dogs fed and healthy.

"Vaughan, you're so good. So good. I didn't think anybody could ever be so wonderful and good to me as you have been."

"Nobody ever loved you like I do."

At her next prim, matter-of-fact words he burst into a shout of laughter, then remembered the sick woman and contented himself with shaking his head in wordless wondering amusement.

"Vaughan, all that flour—a whole barrelful; nobody's got that much. I can't take it from you." He was not amused that she should think flour too lavish a gift. It was her effort to turn aside his frank declaration that had caused his fond laughter.

"It's like money in the bank. Better. That's why I gave it to you. It's a lot more valuable than gold dust."

"I know. I know."

Suddenly from the bed in the corner came a thin, reedy voice raised in song. Melendy jumped to his feet, startled. He stared at the white mask on the pillow; he saw the wasted throat swell in song. "Pansy, for God's sake! What's she——"

"It's all right. She often does that now. Times she's a little lightheaded. It's Traviata she's singing. You know. Camille. She's singing the part where Alfred comes to ask her forgiveness."

"Pansy, I can't leave you alone with her like this all the winter."

"Sh-sh! She'll fall asleep in a minute. She'll sing awhile, and she wants me to sing the opposite part, and then she smiles and is asleep. But first I must sing with her—Alfred's part—it soothes her." She went to the couch; her warm, deep voice took up the singing; it was Alfred telling her that they would go away together and be happy. The two voices—the one cracked and weak, the other fresh and clear—rose and rang in the crude little cabin; the sound went forth into the blackness of the squalid arctic town. The woman on the bed sat up; she held out her wasted arms; her face was alight; she smiled blissfully; she sank back on the pillow then, still smiling.

Vaughan looked at Pansy, a fearful questioning in his eyes. She shook her head, whispering. "It's all right. She'll sleep now. It's been a hard day for her, moving here and all. She'll sleep now."

She walked lightly to the table, turned down the lamp a little. The woman on the bed was breathing evenly, peacefully.

"Well," Vaughan said woodenly. "Well, I guess I'll be going."

"Yes."

They stood there a moment, the length of the room separating them. On the clear night air they heard the thump and jingle of the piano and the high, thin voices of the Parcel of Posies in the Gold Strike Saloon and Dance Hall far down the street. The sounds were muted by distance and came softly and even musically, like an accompaniment to a scene of love. The little shack seemed to rock and sway as he walked toward her with his arms outstretched. She, too, seemed to sway a little, but her lips were serene and half smiling and her eyes were a wonder to see.

Perhaps during that autumn and winter it was the comparative comfort of the little cabin that kept the sick woman alive. It may have been Pansy's cooking, miraculously contrived. The clean, bitter arctic air may have stayed the ravages of the deadly disease. When spring came to Alaska she was still there, and in June when Pansy Deleath's son was born.

Hap Frazer's cold mackerel eye had been the first to note her condition. Even her mother, the girls in the company, Chet had not guessed it. The change in her was evidenced by a blooming, a kind of radiance. Her skin took on a glow; her eyes were brighter, softer; her mouth was ripe and curved in lovely smiles.

Hap Frazer had decided that a cakewalk would provide a refreshing dance number for the Gold Strike's program. To the tune of A Georgia Camp Meeting the Posies were rehearsing the simple prancing step. Hap was both pianist and dance director; he dashed from keyboard to stage; he achieved the incredible feat of playing the tune with one hand, standing, while he demonstrated cakewalk steps. "Higher! Bring your knees up higher. Prance it! Throw your body back from the waist. Back! Nah-ah-ah-ah! This isn't a wand drill." He left the piano; he leaped to the middle of the stage; he accompanied himself with his own dee-da-*dee*-da—dee-*da* as his long legs jerked up and down in the high-stepping figure of the dance. "Now then, you animated broomsticks, if you'll just take the pokers out of your spine——" His eye fell on Pansy. She was clutching the back of a chair; her parted lips and stricken eyes and ashen face made plain that the room and all the figures in it were whirling and dipping in nauseating motion.

"Sit down, all you belles!" he snarled. "On the floor or wherever you are. Yeh, you, Pansy, flop down on that chair. You certainly are in swell shape, nursing your mama all day and night and dragging your carcass over here so tired you can't tell your left foot from your right ear."

"I'm sorry. I just—— I guess throwing my head so far back made me a little dizzy."

"Uh-huh." The girls were chattering, pouting. Daisy sprang up and went through the paces of the dance for the benefit of the others and in defiance of Hap.

"Looka! Who says I can't cakewalk? Old scarecrow!"

Hap stood in front of Pansy; she looked up at him; he spoke out of the corner of his mouth, the cigarette as always wagging tauntingly.

"Kid, eh?" She said nothing. "Boy or girl? H'm?"

"Boy, I hope," she said spiritedly.

"That'll be nice," he drawled, still under his breath. "Chet'll be pleased to hear this. Yeah." His tone grew menacing. "You can't stay with this show, shape you're going to be in."

"I know."

Curiously enough she was not distressed. She felt serene, secure, cared for. After this she left the frowzy little company. Almost automatically, as though heeding the instructions of a dear voice, she dipped into her precious barrel of flour and baked her first batch of that winter's bread. No more of that pretense of sociable drinking, no more forced smiles and labored dancing. No more din and raucous laughter and leering eyes.

By the end of that first week she was selling tickets for the day's baking; you bought your ticket before you were entitled to stand in line for your loaf of bread. The scent of those baking

loaves floated out to the men who for months had lived on sourdough biscuits. They stood sniffing in the doorway as it came from
the oven hot and fragrant. Some of them ate it there as they
stood, like greedy little boys stuffing on cake. She had got hold of
a jar of summer clover honey. She sold slices of hot bread spread
with honey for two dollars a slice.

It was a terrible winter, ice-locked, desperately cold. She felt
well and strong and curiously lighthearted. The shadows on the
snow and on the hills were a wonder to see—deep shadows, yellow and blue and pink.

When she saw that she was scraping the bottom of the flour
barrel she announced hot baths to be had in a wooden laundry
tub, five minutes allowed for each bath at two dollars and the
water to be emptied by the departing client. Her lean-to off the
main room was the bathhouse.

The sick woman on the bed sometimes raised a wasted hand
in greeting as the men passed through. Sometimes the glazed
eyes saw nothing. As the men clumped through in their great
boots which they had scraped outside the door before entering,
they would say with paradoxical formality, "How-do, Miz Deleath! How are you, ma'am? Excuse me, Miz Deleath." Tiptoeing. They sat soaking in the next room for their luxurious five
minutes and thought it all cheap at the price.

Pansy did not use the gold dust Vaughan had left her. Her
own needs were few, her mother's less. Life flickered feebly in
the sick woman but it did not die. When Pansy's son was born,
Kitty Deleath accepted the child without question. She was living in the past now; sometimes she called him by names out of
her young years. Once, surprisingly, she said, "What's his name,
Pansy?"

"I haven't named him yet, Mama. I thought I'd—wait."

It was Vaughan Melendy who named his son that spring of
his return, it was Vaughan who held him in his great arms and
said, "We'll call him Klondike. Eh, Pansy? Klondike that's

brought us luck and gold and a son. Klondike Melendy. Dike for short."

The first bed the boy Dike knew was a handmade cradle that had been a rocker used for rocking the gold found on the beach when the Bering Sea surf rolled in. It had traveled far. Here it had been used by a prospector on the Klondike River. The first printed word the infant's eye beheld was the word "saloon," which was painted in large gaudy letters on building after building lining the muddy street as Vaughan carried him, a month old, down to the boat bound for Seattle.

"Let me have the boy, Pansy," he had pleaded. "Let me have him."

"I can't. I can't. How can I? He's mine."

"Yours and mine. I'll adopt him. He'll be my own son. That way we both can see and have him. I promise. I can't lose you now—you and him. I'm going to build up on Queen Anne Hill, like I promised Emmy and Ma. I'll build a house for you, too, the same time. You're a rich woman now, Pansy; you're partner in the mine. I told you I didn't come up here for any piddling little pay-dirt mining. We're going to be rich again, I tell you. You and me and our son. It'll be best for him, best for all of us. Let me take him back with me, Pansy."

"Mrs. Melendy. Your—your wife."

"We'll work it out, Pansy. You'll see. When he's a grown man you'll be glad you saw it my way."

She looked down at the child in her arms; she looked at the dying woman in the bed. "It's no place for him here, I know. But when Ma's gone—then what? He's mine. Then what?"

"I saw Doc this morning. He said your ma might live another month, she might go any day; she'll never last out another winter. Even so, I wouldn't let you stay, no matter what she said or cried against it. You'll come out before September or I'll come up and get you if I have to use force."

"How do I know she'll be good to him? How do I know? It isn't right or natural."

"It's right and good. You'll see. I'll bring him up for what he is—my own son. I'll adopt him; it'll be legal; he'll have my name. He'll be a Melendy."

They were down at the dock to meet him as he came off the boat in Seattle Harbor. There stood the towering figure of his mother, Exact Melendy, and beside her Emmy, pink and gold, her nearsighted, pale-blue eyes looking up at him. He looked down at them. He waved. They waved. He saw the smiles freeze on their faces; he saw Emmy's mouth drop open, her eyes grew round and staring. He had the child under his arm like a sack.

With his feeling for the dramatic he had a poke of gold in either great hand because it was expected of returned Klondike prospectors. He was bearded and roughly dressed as were the other men, but he had washed and tidied himself as neatly as possible. As he stepped off the boat he dropped a poke of gold into the hand of each woman—a bag of gold for his mother, a bag of gold for his wife, just as he had promised. "And plenty more where that came from, Ma. A million like it, Emmy."

But they held the little sacks in their palms as though they were dried leaves.

"What baby's that," demanded Exact, "you're lugging like a sack of meal?"

"Whose young one is that?" said the more literal Emmy.

"Yours," Vaughan replied.

"Stop talking foolishness, Vaughan. We don't feel like joking, a time like this. Your ma and I've been standing here hours, waiting for your boat. Give that baby back to whoever it belongs to and come on home."

"Emmy's fixed everything you like for supper," Exact said. She regarded the infant with a critical eye. "Nice-looking young one. Whose is it?"

Emmy was saying, " . . . and rock crab and steak and new peas . . ."

"Mine, I tell you. Mine and Emmy's. I'm adopting him. I—I found him up in—up there, and I took to him and I'm adopting him. His name is Klondike. Klondike Melendy. We'll call him Dike for short. Come on home, Emmy. We've got us a son at last."

11

Dike melendy sat in his transcontinental train compartment and watched the United States of America slide past his window. It was a thing he always had loved to do. The train was the crack Streamliner and he still thought streamliners wonderful, no matter how many stratoliners glinted and flaunted their silver sides against the blue sky. The Streamliner had shining aluminum sides, too, and the chair he now sat in was a movable chair, all bright metal and peach-colored upholstery. The walls of the little room were heaven blue with silver tracing. A gay cubicle; trains had had their faces lifted, leaving the Victorian wrinkles in the discard.

Half-past twelve. Almost lunchtime. There was no sound from the adjoining room. Lina always traveled like royalty. She had the drawing room; Dike had his compartment; Lina's maid Hagar had what the railroad company kittenishly called a roomette. Lina wasn't up but he knew she soon would be. Then she would have breakfast in her room, and he would have the porter open the panel between the two compartments and he would sit and talk to her while she ate.

Lina was not interested in seeing America go by her thick plate-glass window. She had refused even to glance out since leaving Chicago. When they pulled out of Chicago after the transfer from the New York to the Western train had been made ("And a bloody bore, too!" Lina had stormed. "It's only a racket. Why don't they run their silly train under a tunnel? They could. It would cut a day off the trip." And she was right.), she had glanced up as her baggage was being disposed, and there on a building had been a large sign which said HILKER & BLETCH. FOOD SPECIALISTS. She had hastily pulled down the shade and announced that she was a dead pigeon and that she would not be up until next noonday. Hagar had then made up Lina's bed with pink silk sheets and little lacy pillows, and now it was next noonday and she had proved herself a woman of her word.

Dike had suggested that they fly back to Seattle in one of the great new stratoliners, but Lina had said no, too sick-making and no rest, really, even if they did make it in a third of the time or less. Always swooping down and zooming up, leaving your stomach behind you in the air. On the Streamliner you could rest the old bones, she said, and boy, did they need it! They were clattering like castanets.

Dike had risen at eight; he had managed to shave and even to bathe in the ingeniously contrived washbowl. He had sprinkled into the water a little of that pine-and-leather-smelling toilet water that Lina had given him. "Very male," she had said. "For gents only."

"What's masculine about pine and leather?" he had wanted to know. "That's for sissies who're afraid they might be suspect. I like that sweet, spicy stuff smells like my old man used to when he came home from the barbershop."

He had breakfasted well at half-past eight, weaving through the long train, car after car, and bumping into utter strangers in every stage of intimate disarray. There were women with babies; unshaven men with suspenders dangling; girls in metal curlers. In the dining car there were as many women as men; they were women like his mother, he thought, they were like Emmy, not like Lina. Well, once she was awake and in circulation he preferred the Lina type; she was later but she certainly was easier to look at. He wished these early risers wouldn't drink tomato juice for breakfast, tomatoes were never intended as a breakfast drink.

Certain foods, he reflected, were dining-car provender. Chicken potpie and buckwheat cakes and ham with sweet potatoes. He wondered why. Coffee was always good on these trains, that was the main thing. And oceans of cream. God, the coffee they used to give you on European trains! Poor devils over there—France and England and Holland and Belgium—as good as gone. Well, let 'em fight it out; the thing to do was to keep out of it. He'd had his war. No, thank you, I'm not having any more.

They had taken on some newspapers at Cheyenne, Wyoming. One of these had been handed him at breakfast. War. War. War. All the headlines. Not so bad as the New York papers, but bad enough. Baffling, trying to read an unfamiliar newspaper. Seattle papers made sense, he thought, and a couple of New York sheets. But these in-between towns. They all had those columns—Eleanor and Pyle and Pegler and those political stuffed-shirt writers—but when it came to news there wasn't anything you could get your teeth into. A.P., too, but it didn't sound the same. Maybe they didn't have the smart desk men to dress it up.

The porter would be making up his room. Hope he wouldn't make a lot of racket, wake Lina up. He walked back to the luxurious lounge car to while away an hour or two, smoking and reading. The passengers who glanced at him had unemotional approval in their gaze. Dike Melendy was not handsome. He hadn't Vaughan's ruddy color. Rather he had inherited Pansy Deleath's somewhat sallow skin but not her redeeming deep-blue eyes to offset it. His eyes were brown—Kitty Deleath's brown— and in them there lurked the unserene and questing look of a man who is not sure of himself. Yet you saw a tall, broad-shouldered fellow who definitely had had a childhood full of lamb chops and spinach and oranges and milk and light, airy rooms and fine, soft clothing. Here, you saw at a glance, were American luxury items such as golf and Harvard and good scotch and French lisle socks and third-row seats and four-rib roasts and sixteen-cylinder cars and *Fortune* in a neat stack on the library table.

Funny thing about a cross-country train trip such as this, he thought. It lulled and relaxed you and exhilarated you at the same time, if such a paradox could be. He did not often travel by train now, but he never failed to be moved by the sight of his country seen from a train window. Illinois, Nebraska, Wyoming, Idaho, Oregon, Washington. It was the damnedest thrillingest country in the world, he thought. The thing to do was to keep out of that mess over there; everything here we need, practically.

The man next him in a good gray suit and spectacles whose lenses were octagonal now broke into long-pent conversation.

"Quite a train."

"Yes."

"Yessir, quite a covered wagon. I always get a kick out of traveling on it. Gosh! Barber, valet, buffet, soda fountain, radio——"

"I could dispense with the radio." It was braying boogie-woogie.

"Oh yeah, well, it had the news on a while back—European war news."

"That's all I heard in New York."

"You a Westerner, too?"

"Seattle."

"I'm from Tacoma myself. Orpe is my name—with an E." He flipped open a billfold, handed Dike a card.

"My name's Melendy."

"Well! Melendy! I guess everybody in the Northwest knows that name."

The war. "Nothing but war talk in New York; you'd think the Nazis were right on Staten Island."

"That's the Easterners for you," the man agreed. "Scared out of their didies because they live on the Atlantic seaboard. Nothing to protect them the way we West coast folks have. We've got the Hawaiian Islands and good old Pearl Harbor. We don't take any chances with those yellow monkeys—not that they'd ever dare take a shot at the United States. But why don't the Easterners do something about it if they're so scared, the big sissies!"

"Well, that's the difference between the East and the West, I suppose. Back there they talk and up here we do it."

"Old Franklin D. been doing plenty of talking lately. Somebody doesn't shut him up he'll talk us right into it. Calling names over the radio, Mussolini and all that knife-in-the-back stuff about France. What's it our business?"

Dike laughed a little self-consciously. "Maybe I oughtn't to say anything about a Harvard man—I'm Harvard myself—but——"

Dike heard himself talking as though it were someone else. Perhaps he was unconsciously repeating what he had heard many other men say. "Well, sir, glad to have had this chance to talk to you. Guess I'll have to go back and see if my wife's up."

"Oh, the wife traveling with you, eh?"

"My wife is Lina Port—the actress, you know."

"Oh. That so! Well." It was plain he had never heard of her. The fathead! Wasting time talking to a lunk like that. My wife, Lina Port. Oh, Lina Port the actress! Really! That was what he wanted to hear and frequently did hear—but not often enough.

Back in his own room he found it neat and shining as well it might be after the size of the bill—and the promise of another at the end of the journey—given the porter last night. But still there was no sound from the adjoining room. Dike moved his chair to face the window directly. Wyoming. Funny, there always seemed to be more sky in Wyoming than any other place in the world. Bluer and higher and more like a dome. And those big puff clouds, white and cottony, like the kind Lunt sat on when he played in that Frenchman's play, uh, Amphitryon. Now if Lina were awake he could have said that to her and she'd have understood.

East. West. Lina was definitely an Easterner in her tastes and thinking and manner and appearance and accent, even though all these had been applied as carefully and delicately as she applied that red stuff to her lips with a miniature brush when she was making up. You'd never know she came from Michigan except that now and then unconsciously she rolled out a Midwestern *r*. In all the twenty years of their married life she never had seemed really at home in Seattle. She gave the effect of a very temporary visitor with whom the climate and the people and the food did not agree. Well, he thought now, they didn't, and that's a fact. Sunshine! Sunshine! she kept saying longingly. These damned everlasting fogs and mists depress me. But he loved the fogs; he wouldn't give you a cent for that New York climate, boiling like the tropics in the summer and cold and windy in the winter; and when it snowed they hustled around and dumped it into carts and buried it or something, as if it were pestilential and unclean.

Twenty years. In twenty years he'd hardly had a chance to talk to Lina. Really talk, that is. That's crazy, he said to himself. Crazy, but true. Weaving back and forth between the Pacific and the Atlantic. In the air, on planes, back and forth, back and forth, he and she. And the boy, too. Somewhere he had read of an insect —some kind of bee or spider or butterfly or something—that had its courtship and mating high up in the air, and after the mating the female destroyed the male. Ate him up or something pretty like that. More like a mistress than a wife, Lina. He grinned as he pictured his mother's horror if ever he voiced this. Emmy the prim, the conventional. His mother . . . He shut the door on that, the little secret door in his mind, the door that hid the thing that caused the unsure look in his eyes.

New York hotels, New York furnished apartments, apartments of their own while Lina was playing in this or that production. And Mike carried back and forth. Nanas and fräuleins and governesses in his babyhood, private schools in New York in the winter, private schools in Seattle when Lina came West. The house

in Seattle always was staffed with Japanese servants. This irked
Emmy; she never ceased to harp about it.

"There they sit," she fumed, "month after month with nothing
to do. It sets the most awful example for my couple. They see
those Japs being paid for just sitting and doing nothing. Not a
thing!"

"They're there when we need them."

"That's more than you can say of your wife," Emmy retorted
rather brightly for her. "She's so crazy about New York too bad
she didn't marry an Easterner."

"My dear Mrs. M.," Dike had said rather elaborately, "Lina
happens to be an actress and New York is the center of play production." Emmy snorted, the sound being meant to convey that
the center of play production could dispense with Lina Port's
services without damage to its prestige. "You know, Mother, you
and Dad talk about New York as if it were a foreign country."

"It is." Fantastic, the way Emmy and Vaughan resented the
East. Mike said they were jealous as well as resentful. Mike said
all Northwesterners had an inferiority about the Atlantic seaboard. Mike had no such feeling. Mike was at home East or West
or Northwest. Mike was the true cosmopolite of the Melendy
family. Mike and Pansy. Pansy! Pansy wasn't the family. He
slammed the little secret door again. Stirred restlessly in his seat.
Funny marriage, his and Lina's. Modern, I suppose, but damned
funny. Not any odder, though, than his father's had been, married
to Emmy all these years, when he really . . .

He heard Lina's laugh from the next room, her high, clear,
carrying voice, and Hagar's melodious measured tones. He looked
at his watch. Almost one o'clock. Due in Green River, Wyoming,
at one fifty-eight Mountain time. He'd like to get out and stretch
his legs there if they stopped a couple of minutes. He tapped at
the door that separated the two rooms. "Hi!"

"Hi yourself!"

"Can I come in?"

"About twenty minutes, dolling. I've only got one eye open. Where are we?—Not that it matters."

Twenty minutes. Well, that means at least three quarters of an hour Lina time. Joke. He thought he'd try it through the door and above the roar of the train. "Heh, I suppose that means about three quarters of an hour Lina time."

"What? Can't hear you."

"Central time—Mountain time—Pacific time—Lina time—you know——"

"What?"

Oh, the hell with it!

All those morning toilette rites would be meticulously observed, train or no train. Hagar performed them like a priestess. Hagar herself was a good deal of the priestess type, come to think of it. Nothing of the comedy-stage maid about Hagar. A stately, imposing Negress, middle-aged, low-voiced; she looked and moved like an Egyptian queen in eyeglasses.

"I must be quite a nice person, really," Lina said, "or Hagar wouldn't have stayed with me all these years. If Hagar ever leaves me I'll fall to pieces like the one-hoss shay."

Lina never had been a beauty, or even pretty. She never would be. But she had a quality of pride or drive or ambition or electricity or some damned wonderful thing, he thought, that might prove better than beauty in the long run, for an actress anyway, because it grew and became stronger while mere beauty faded with the years. Lina, plain, rather undersized, her head a fine head but somewhat large for her body, Middle Western, no family to speak of, decent folks but no money, no position, had set to work on herself, Pygmalion and Galatea in one. As a sculptor works on clay, she had pinched off a bit there, she had added a bit here; she had dieted, exercised, danced; studied herself with a hard, cold, critical eye. There had been something ruthless and almost frightening in her determination to re-create herself.

Her laugh—light, lilting, girlish—she had made that, too, until

now it had actually become her real—or almost real—expression
of mirth. Hers was a gash of a mouth, almost a clown's mouth,
and this she had brazenly emphasized. She had learned not to
smile too broadly; she remembered to curl her lips at the corners
and to hold her lips a little taut against her white even teeth
(straightened and jacketed where needed), and now audiences
found her smile one of her most engaging features, and press
agents and interviewers wrote in trite terms of Lina Port's wide,
generous mouth.

A knock at his outer door which stood open. He turned to see
Hagar and just behind her the porter. Hagar was in correct black
with a white apron. Hagar said good morning and I hope you
slept and it's a lovely day and Miss Port thought it would be nice
to fold back the partition Miss Port is just having her breakfast.

Miss Port. Sometimes this Miss Port stuff infuriated him and
sometimes it made him feel very gay-doggy and illicit and romantic. Now the porter made various magic passes involving the bits
of metal that had seemed to ornament the wall nearest Lina's
room. The wall melted, folded back on itself, disappeared, and
the two rooms became one, spacious, luxurious. And there sat
Lina in bed against a background of pale-pink silk. And "Thank
you, porter," she said. "That's wonderful!" And smiled her second best smile. A solemn, responsible man, a family man, a man
whose bearing reminded you that those stripes on the sleeve and
portership on a crack streamliner were things not lightly achieved.
Now you heard him in consultation with the dignified Hagar in
the passageway outside the room.

A tray on her knees: orange juice, coffee, toast. Clean, delicate
scent in the air. Skin, eyes, hair, nails burnished bright perfect.
Tiny ermine bed jacket with a little rounded neckline, a great
clump of sapphires and rubies smoldering insolently against the
baby white, and a slightly smaller matching clump on her left
hand.

She leaned forward an inch or two; she presented a smooth,

fragrant cheek for his kiss. "How are you, Rat Boy? And what were you doing this morning at crack of dawn, bumping and crashing around in there?"

"What do you mean—crashing around?"

"Doors, suitcases—and for all I could gather from the sound—trunks and pianos and portable houses. You were throwing them."

"Not true. I was tiptoeing around like a burglar. I suppose that anyone accustomed to the rural peace of New York———"

"That's a different kind of noise. I'm used to that."

There was a familiarity about this conversation. They had had it a dozen, a score of times. The fog-smothered hoots of the distant ships in Seattle's Harbor bothered her, but when they had had an apartment on the East River in New York she had slept like an infant through the tooting of river traffic just beneath her bedroom window. Taxi horns, rumbling busses, grinding gearshifts were her lullaby.

She sipped her coffee black. She nibbled her toast butterless.

"Why don't you eat some breakfast? I mean breakfast."

She snuggled into the pillows; she closed her eyes luxuriously and opened them. "Mmmmmmmmm." It was a sort of descending whinny of sheer sensual delight. "I'm putting it off. It's going to be so wonderful. I can't bear to begin, it is going to be so rapturous. Darling, I'm going to let myself go. You're going to have a great butterfat hulking wife. I haven't had enough to eat in twenty years."

He pointed toward the Spartan tray. "Just teasing yourself?"

"I may get up for lunch like a nice, dutiful wife."

"In the diner you mean?"

"Well—maybe not exactly that far. But I might. And from now on I'm going to have sugar and cream in my coffee—but clotted—and rice pudding and pork chops and chicken fricassee with dumplings and chocolate ice cream and fresh cocoanut cake."

He had heard this, too, before. "I'll divorce you, of course."

"Promise!"

"Why don't you crawl out of that pink silk cocoon and shake a leg? We'll pull into Green River, Wyoming, in a few minutes. Maybe they'll stop long enough for a little stretch on the platform."

But somehow when they reached Green River she was still nested among her cushions, and she said it was just as well because they scarcely paused there and Green River, Wyoming, turned out to be mostly shale mountains, bleak and barren, though Dike said they were rich with coal and iron.

"Like a barren old maid with a warm, rich, human heart," Lina said. "But anyway it's nice to know the Green River really is green. Look." Up and up the engine climbed and panted, up and up, five thousand feet, six thousand. "You know the blue Danube really is brown. So dishonest of Strauss, I think."

"Yes." Absently, gazing out of the window. Cottonwood trees and a gray horse. Little dusty towns whose one street was stopped by a dustier mountain. The wistful defiance of a white-painted cottage with a white picket fence and a trellis meant for pink roses. A Westerner now whose New England blood still stirred nostalgically in his veins.

"Look, Lina, this is such a chance to talk about things—Mike and the house and whether you want to take a trip to Honolulu this winter——"

"Oh, darling, did I tell you what happened last night?" She laughed her lovely chiming laugh; her grin was mischievous and engaging. Things were always happening to Lina and she told them so entertainingly that they took on the importance of drama. These were Cinderella stories, usually, the joke was somehow on Lina, but from these tales she emerged a charming elfin figure, touching but gallant. She seemed always to be extricating herself from monstrous situations; adventure waylaid her at every turn; she could not slip out to mail a letter at the corner box but something exciting and wryly humorous happened to her.

"I woke up at two o'clock last night just raving, tearing hungry —you know I was too tired to eat any dinner, that's why, I suppose. Anyway, I tried to sleep and couldn't, and then I began to think of that champagne you'd had the porter put on the ice when we left Chicago, and the caviar that Ben had farewelled me with. I didn't want to wake you and I didn't want to wake Hagar, poor dear, and finally I couldn't stand it any longer. I rang for the porter——"

It was fairly amusing and had to do with the thermos being filled with Pommery Sec '32 and it turned out to be flat and the caviar was that red horror stuff, wasn't that just like Ben . . .

He listened; he laughed; he forgot about the war talk which had assailed his ears and eyes in New York. He forgot about Europe and business and Lend-Lease and taxes and the family and the Board of Directors' meeting day after tomorrow.

When she was up and dressed, finally, it was evening, and they had their cocktails cozily, waited on by Hagar. Lina had donned a black dress that was all line, and her tiny, girlish body and the unlined face were like those of an impish little twelve-year-old. But not the eyes. Lina carried her head high—she said it was the result of being shorter than almost anyone outside a circus. She always had to look up at men, her face tilted tantalizingly. It was a great advantage in her career, this looking up at producers and playwrights and leading men. Towering below you, Dike called it.

Dike, the somewhat ineffectual product of the strong Melendy background—Vaughan, Emmy, the powerful Exact—with Pansy Deleath's maternal blood in his veins, had belonged in his twenties to that somewhat sniveling tribe known as the lost generation. Certainly a much stronger man than he would have been hard put to it to stand up against the phalanx of robust women, tall and small, young and old, ranging from his grandmother Exact Melendy to his wife Lina Port, who had surrounded and outnumbered him from babyhood to today. Difference in method, he told himself ruefully. That was all. Old Exact bellowed, Emmy com-

plained, Lina cajoled, Pansy Deleath stood afar off watching him
with those tender, unfathomable eyes.

"And Dike dolling," Lina was saying, "We're going to get out
of that house, aren't we? And that neighborhood that has nothing
but View. No, dear, I don't mean to be rude. But it's like living in
a stockade or a concentration camp or something. We might as
well be behind barbed wire. Family, family, family. Honestly, you
can't go to the john without Madam knowing it, or your mother."

"Look, Lina, I'm not going to yelp about my folks and how
good they are or aren't. After all, my family——"

"But I'm not objecting to your family. I think they're rather
wonderful—all that pioneer stuff and everything. I just object to
living in a house whose windows and doors and chimneys and
bureau drawers and bathrooms can be looked into through the
windows of your mother's house and your grandmother's house."

"Good God, to hear you a person would think they do nothing
all day but peer through windows to see what you're up to."

"That's exactly what I mean. That's exactly what they do. Ah,
don't be cross, dolling. Besides, the house itself."

"What's the matter with it? Good, solid, comfortable house."

"You never said a truer word. Good and solid as bread pudding. Your father built it, and I know everything that went into
it is genu-wine A-No. 1 first-class expensive building contractor's
dream stuff and it's ugly as mud."

"What do you want me to do? Burn it down?"

"No. Let's build at Highlands, simple and modern, just a huge
circular living room, all glass, and perhaps only four bedrooms or
five at the most, and a sun deck and a heated pool."

"Seattle isn't southern California—and neither is southern California a good deal of the time."

"But when the sun does shine at least we'll be able to catch it
and coax it and use it."

He sat looking at the frosty sides of his cocktail glass—he had
mixed the drink himself out of the choice bottles in his luggage;

the iced, dry, stimulating liquid suddenly seemed to become impotent as water. This was a bargain she was making. She had made others. Her face was alight with purpose; her tiny feet in the filmy stockings and the mere scrap of velvety black suède were moving a little restlessly; the hand that held her glass was steady; it was a larger hand than one would expect in so small a person—it was the big-knuckled hand of the purposeful woman.

"This is a crazy time to build. I'm talking about the practical side of it."

"Oh, let's not. Let's not be practical. It's bad enough to be middle-aged without being practical as well."

"You've been living the life of an actress. You've been going from the apartment to the theater and from the theater to supper, a fitting at Hattie's and a hat at Fred's. You just don't know. All these carpenters and stonemasons and so on—they're out at Boeing's or at the navy yards making planes and ships for the British."

She began to hum a little tune—always a bad sign. "Dinner in here would be sort of stuffy, don't you think?" she said chattily. "What's it like out there? Awful?"

"Oh, it isn't exactly slumming—a streamliner dining car." He got up rather to his own surprise and went over to the window and pushed up the shade. "Idaho. Remember how cross it always makes you because we pull into Huntington after midnight Mountain time of the next day and two minutes later when we pull out it's eleven-thirty of the day before."

"Dike dearie, we sound like the dialogue in a Chekhov play. Now it's my turn to jump. Mike. Do you think it's good for him to be brought up with so many petticoats hovering over him? Grandmas and great-grandmas and—uh—Aunt Pansy."

"Brought up! It's a little late to be thinking about Mike's bringing up."

"Why? He's a kid at school."

"That's what you think—or what you'd like to think. Listen, Lina. Mike's a man at college. When I was his age—or only a little more—I was driving an ambulance over in France———"

"Don't don't don't don't! Once you begin to say when-I-was-his-age you're old."

"Why won't you face things?"

"Why, here am I, an itsy-bitsy dirl, trapped in a droring room on a speeding train with a ferocious old grouch if I ever saw one. Help! Help! Save me!"

"Oh well. I'm sorry. I'm just trying to give you an idea of what the world's coming to———"

A little scream of delight from her. "Well! Fancy your knowing! What *is* the world coming to, Mr. Bones? And here you've been walking around with this secret when everybody—Hitler and Roosevelt and Churchill and Stalin and that smart Chinese couple and everybody—would give their shirts and their right eye to know what the world is coming to—or even what's coming to the world."

She was at her worst. She would be like this until she got what she wanted. He turned his back to her; he stood at the window; it was dusk; it was dark; a little white muscle ridge showed at the side of his jaw. That doctor in New York had said no, it isn't a stomach ulcer; I'd say it's a warning, though. Something been troubling you for a long time? Well, people don't get ulcers, you know, from being happy. Have you a hobby? Nothing more relaxing than a hobby when you're the tense type.

Dike pressed a button at the side of the wall. Chimes sounded faintly in the outer passage. "What time do you want dinner, Lina? We'll have them bring us a menu. If we order ahead we won't have to sit and stew—that is, if you really want to eat in the diner."

"Don't be like that, Dike sweet!" She ran to him; she nestled under his arm; she patted his chest with a distracted hand. "I'm horrid. I know. It's just that I've been so upset about the play closing. We thought it would run all winter."

"Do you know why it closed, Lina?"

"Why, I don't know—Ben and Cliff thought that last act wasn't——"

"Money. Money and taxes and people scared and the war in Europe. Of course the theater's shot to hell. The theater and the stock market. They'll barometer every time."

But she must talk of herself. "Dike dolling, do you think I'm a failure? As an actress and as a wife and a mother and everything?"

Actress first. "Look, Lina. If a new house would make you more content with Seattle, why, perhaps it could be managed. It's just—uh—it isn't only labor shortage, it's a funny time to build a luxury house; money is tight."

"D'you mean we're poor?" Real fear leaped into her eyes. With a quite unconscious gesture she clutched the great whorl of jewels clipped on her gown.

"Don't be silly!"

A great deep breath of relief, half real, half exaggerated. The hand that had grasped the glittering stones now went to her breast. It was the classic gesture of the overburdened heart made lighter. She laughed her tinkling little laugh; she got up and walked about the little room with a sort of swagger; her head was high, her hands were on her hips; it was triumph; it was the exhilaration of one who has momentarily doubted her power and been reassured. The room grew big, she became tall, and he somehow diminished as they swelled.

He wanted to say, look, Lina, would you have married me if I hadn't been rich? Would you have stayed all these years? He wanted terribly to know; he shrank from knowing. Sometimes it was wiser not to demand the truth. . . . His mother . . . Solicitous hovering. . . . Eat your spinach. . . . Put your rubbers on. . . . But Dorothy's a perfectly lovely girl and the Gorsens are perfectly lovely people; a girl like that would make a perfectly lovely wife for any man. . . . Don't drive so fast; you must be going eighty miles an hour at least. I wish you . . . I'll speak to your father. . . . Your father. . . . Your father. . . . She had been a loving and careful mother. She had nourished a grudge, a resentment, deep, deep down somewhere, and now and then it leaped out vixenishly. There had been times when she had looked at him with hate in her eyes. Maybe that was it; maybe that was why he never felt quite sure of himself; maybe that was why his marriage was a kind of mess. Not a mess exactly. But sometimes he fancied he saw that same look on Lina's eyes. What was the matter with him? What . . .

"I'll have another cocktail, dolling. Don't let me fall on my face on the way to the diner. Dike, do you know what? I'll bet anything I can get Cliff Garnett to come up and help plan the house."

"Cliff! All the way from New York!"

"He isn't in New York. He's in Hollywood. We were a flop in New York, all right, but he sold the play in pictures and he's out there doing the treatment and getting a billion for it. He'll be through by December, and he's simply marvelous about houses and colors and fabrics and dimensions and all those things. He never has seen Seattle; he says he's crazy to; he says he doesn't believe there is any such place or any state called Washington that has a town named Walla Walla."

"Oh, you've already arranged to have him come, then."

"No. No, I don't think he'd even———"

"Why, listen, he's queer, isn't he? Garnett."

"Why do you frightened he-men sort of people always think that any male who doesn't behave like Tarzan is effeminate? Cliff's wonderful. He's understanding and sympathetic and talented and sweet."

"Why, that's dandy. It's just too damned bad you didn't marry him."

"Cliff doesn't want to marry," she said. And wished she hadn't.

"Is that right! Why, that's too bad, too. Have you tried everything? I mean everything."

She came over to him; she linked her arm through his; she twisted about and looked up at him, rapt. "Dike dolling, no one flatters me the way you do. I was feeling so low and doddering and washed up and then you say a thing like that that makes me feel young and dazzling and dangerous. Oh, Dike! Lamb pie! You *are* sweet!"

Defeated, he said, "Let's go in to dinner. I'm cockeyed. So are you, my good woman—or good enough."

12

Lina had been home four days and the telephone rang practically all day, and it never was for her, it always was for Mike and Mike always was out. The Japanese houseman or the cook would answer it as she had carefully taught them to do. But then they, just as carefully, would turn the telephone over to her. She would say, "Is it long-distance? Is it California?" This question they appeared unable to cope with, so she would go to the telephone and a high, clear, girlish voice would come over the wire.

"Mike?"

"No, this isn't Mike." Good God, had her voice gone bass or something?

"Oh. Sorry. I want to speak to Mike, please."

"He's out."

"Oh. Do you know where I can get him?"

"No. Airfield, I think."

"When'll he be home?"

"Heavens! I don't know."

"Will you tell him to call me? Tell him Jennifer." Or Susan or Kit or Puffy or Midge. "Tell him it's a matter of life and death —or anyway death."

Sometimes they would come to the house in quest of him. They would wander in casually; you found them at the door or whistling shrilly or tooting the horn from their car at the curb. "Hi, Mike!"

174

They turned up in the garage or in Mike's workshop. Lina said she expected any day to wake up and find one of them sitting on her bed like a spider in the tropics. They all looked quite a lot alike, their hair was worn shoulder length, their clothes were casual to the point of being almost non-existent. Sometimes they appeared in blue jeans rolled to the knees and a man's old shirt with the shirttail out and their hair sticking out in little braided tails Topsy fashion. There was something insolent about their indifference to clothes and appearance. This offended Lina. Their extreme youth made it still harder to bear. This new role of stay-at-home mother and telephone operator was not, Lina said, her dish.

One in particular seemed indefatigable and quite shameless. She was the Jennifer one. Tiny, almost childlike, with black hair falling to her shoulders one day and twisted into eye-pulling pigtails the next. Sometimes she wore slacks or knee-length pants; once she came to the door at dinnertime in a long tulle dress and a little fur jacket and flowers in her hair and too much make-up like most of the Western belles, Lina thought, and she had demanded in her deep, hard young voice: "Has Mike gone to the party? Tell him he's going to take me. I'll wait." She had the tenacity of a bulldog, the voraciousness of a Ganges crocodile.

"Oh no, you don't!" Mike had yelled down to her from upstairs. "Go on home, brat."

Astonishingly the tulle-and-flower miss then said, "I'm coming up," and actually had made for the stairway. Mike then had appeared over the banister in shorts, socks, and garters and had hurled a wet washcloth at the fairylike figure below, catching her with a squish on the chest. Lina and Dike rushed forward utterly dismayed. Jennifer had merely pouted, "Mike, you disgusting swine!" after which she had put out her hard little hand and had said with the most beautiful manners, "How do you do. I'm Jennifer Burkett. Mother says you're having dinner at our house next week. Oh, Miss Port—Mrs. Melendy, I should say I suppose, but I always—— I saw you in New York when I went there with Mother last September and you were simply heaven! But heaven!"

Lamely they said, "Won't you come in and sit down? We're just finishing dinner. Would you care for a cup of coffee?"

"No, thanks, I'll wait in Mike's car. Tell him, will you? He's cross with me. But I'll wait."

They were forever down at the airfield begging to go up with him; he had to brush them off the plane like flies.

Lina spoke of this to Dike crisply. "Who're all these girls? Prowling the place like hungry wolves! Looking for Mike."

"They're just nice kids live in the neighborhood and so on."

"They look like tramps."

He stared, startled. "How do you mean—tramps?"

"Their clothes. And the way they act."

"You don't mean they're rude to you!"

"Oh, they're polite enough, in a way. They say thank you and all that, but you'd think I was a piece of wood that could talk. They look at me as if I weren't there except to answer their idiotic questions."

"Oh, they're shy because you're Lina Port."

"Shy hell! They're after Mike like ravening wolves, I tell you! Mike isn't a kid any more. Don't they know he's grown up?"

"They do. They do indeed, ma'am."

"Don't be silly. Those children! Why, they can't be more than seventeen or eighteen at the most."

"Well, old lady, you might as well realize that Mike is fair game."

"For what?"

"Marriage."

"You're crazy! Mike isn't twenty."

"They catch 'em young and eat 'em quick these days."

Marriage! The sequence ran through her brain like a hot needle. Son, marriage, babies, grandmother. Lina Port's a grandmother, you know. Oh no. No! She would put in a long-distance call to California. This is a person-to-person call. I want to speak to Mr. Cliff Garnett, Los Angeles, the number is Granite five-one-one-one. C as in California, l as in loony, i as in idiot, f as in fool . . .

In New York she had gone out to supper with Mike; they had danced at the Stork or El Morocco. Mike had seemed suddenly very grown up, but that was different, that was somehow cute in New York and not at all to her disadvantage. People seeing them moving so expertly on the little close-packed night-club dance floor said, "Her son! That! But it can't be! Why, she looks as young as he does—younger!" She was young; she was chic; she was a name in the theater; she was rich; she could produce a son like this—and never lose a spangle. In New York she had worn Mike like an ornament. But this—this was different; this was serious; this wasn't Mike in long pants isn't he cute? This was Michael Melendy, a man.

She was frightened; she was frantic. As she waited for the call she would stare around the big, bright, luxurious room; she would look out through the great glaring plate-glass window to the bay and the mountains and the sky, and her fingers curled with the impulse to pick up a lamp or a heavy silver cigarette box and hurl it through the glass and right into the big howling wilderness of view view view! You ought to see the view from Queen Anne Hill. She didn't want to see the view from Queen Anne Hill. She wanted a view, half blinded by the footlights and a pink spot, of an audience of nice white moons that were faces row on row downstairs to the very last row and upstairs in the balcony to the back wall. That was the only view a real actress wanted.

The theater's shot to hell, Dike had said. It wasn't true. It always was like that, down this season, up the next. That was one of the things that made it fascinating. You never could be sure. The Melendy money, you could be sure of that. Here it was in the great big house, and Emmy and Vaughan's house next door and

Madam's house up there and I wish they'd burn down to cinders to ashes to dust. Ashes to ashes, dust to dust.

"Where's that call, operator? . . . But I know he's there. Did you remember to say Extension 297? No! No, not Barnett! G! As in goof!"

Forty. Forty, she told herself, looking in the mirror and talking to herself like someone in a bad melodrama. Forty, and she hadn't made it. All those years of training and self-denial and work. All those sheer stockings to make her legs look slim and shoes by Edouard to make her feet look small, and that low velvet note in her voice, and not being seen around too much because of the gossip columns, and telling the producers to send her the script and she'd read it and let them know, and not calling up when she thought there was a part for her but finding out about it in devious ways so as not to appear too eager. Beautiful clothes but quiet, so that they wouldn't say she was a rich amateur. Why, damn it, she was good. But she was an actors' actress; she was clever and technically right and dramatically sound, and audiences just didn't love her as they did Helen Hayes and Kit Cornell and Lynn Fontanne. She wasn't beautiful, but neither were they. What was it? Warmth. Feeling. Love. People.

She had to talk to somebody. Well, who? Emmy was furiously offended because she had refused to come to that awful midday Sunday dinner the day after she and Dike had come home. Anyway, you couldn't talk to Emmy. Pansy. Pansy had said she wanted to see her New York clothes. Nice old bum, Pansy. What time was it? Only half-past ten. Ten-thirty in the morning and nothing to do all day. No wonder Cliff hadn't answered. Middle of the night, practically, for a late riser. Here you couldn't be a late riser. Somehow the damned bracing climate woke you up early.

There was something warming and reassuring about Pansy Deleath. You felt it the moment she entered the room, Lina thought. A paradoxical person adding up to something heart-warming and sustaining. Raffish, battered, eager as a child, strangely sympathetic; interested in you. Once, in talking of her, Dike had said, "Pansy's more interested in everyone else than in herself. That's the thing that makes people so fond of her—or one of the things."

Doesn't he know? Lina had thought. He must. Everyone knows. But perhaps everyone knows but Dike. Sometimes it's like that.

She telephoned Pansy. "Come on over. Look at my rags. Style show. Lina Port modeling." Now Pansy came in, bright-eyed and alert. Pansy loved to look at clothes though she herself was something of a frump. Out of some battered trunk, relic of the Nineties, she still was quite likely to fish out—and wear—heavy white silk stockings ivory now in tint and embellished with sprays of clocking up the sides. She rouged her ear lobes; she touched her chin with color; she applied it under her eyes and high up on the temples as she had been taught to do by the Parcel of Posies in the old Klondike days. This dated make-up, together with her bright golden hair, gave somewhat the effect of a *fin-de-siècle* professional madam—until one noticed the lovely, honest eyes.

Being fond of her, Lina would sometimes say, "Pansy dear, let me make you up, will you? That red, white, and blue make-up of yours is simply naïve. You must have been scared by a picture of Lillian Russell when you were a little girl."

"Why, I thought I looked grand. I made up specially to impress you. Isn't it all right?"

"It's fine if you want to go on just as you are as one of the original sextette in a revival of Florodora. Tie this around your head and slap this cleansing on your face. Here. See? Start your rouge on the cheekbone near the nose—not too near—let me do it—three dabs here and here and here in an arrow shape—and then work it back and up a little with the tips of your fingers. Not too high, it makes the eyes look glassy; not too low, it makes your cheeks look hollow. Dolling, you really can't use a pencil in the corner of your eyes—it's frightening. . . . If you must go in for eye shadow, blue isn't right for you. Beige brown with your skin."

"Where's that fashion show you promised me?" Pansy demanded.

Lina shrugged her shoulders; she spread her hands in a gesture of defeat. "Thanks for your interest. It's probably the only chance they'll have for an airing in this town."

"Why, there's lots going on, Lina."

"Mm. Bridge luncheons with chicken patties and green peas and vanilla ice cream. Or maybe lunch on Mondays at the Olympic Hotel. Why on Mondays? I never could understand it. Every day here is like Sunday in August in New York. . . . Hagar! Hagar! My farthingale! My pelisse! My cashmere shawl! My bombazine! My sarcenet! My mantle!"

The bed, the chairs, the chaise longue were hidden under crepes, silks, furs, woolens. Hats perched atop lampshades.

"What's that?" Pansy would demand. "That fancy sweater thing."

"Dinner dress."

"Why, it's a sweater!"

"Mainbocher. He kids the girls and they don't know it. Black sweaters with gold sequins sewed on them. For evening."

"It's like the old Klondike days, boots with pink satin dresses."

A tall, thin figure in coveralls appeared in the doorway. Mike, a grease-stained mechanic. He leaned against the doorjamb; he sniffed dreamily. "Smells elegant."

"Your shoes!" Lina cried. "Keep off my white carpet! I thought you were out at the airfield."

"I was. Hello, Pansy! Look. I want Reggie to take a day off and go up with me. She says she can't leave Madam."

Lina, in a pale-blue dressing gown and a very smart fur hat, stared at him. "Reggie? You mean that maid over at Madam's?"

"She isn't a maid," Mike said quietly. "Not that it matters."

"Who is she, anyway?"

"She's a wonderful girl," Pansy said. "She's the kind it wouldn't make a bit of difference what she was doing."

"All right, all right, she's a wonderful girl. But who is she?"

"Why, Emmy engaged her for Madam as companion when Birch broke her leg."

Still wearing the incongruous fur hat, Lina whirled on the boy, all the pent-up fears and frustrations of the past few days surging now to her throat. "Really, Mike, all these little insects that have been creeping out of the woodwork are bad enough, swarming all over you ever since I got home. Those brassy little brats. But you don't have to take out the hired help, do you?"

But Mike did not rise to these histrionics. He only grinned and said, "Lina, you ol' reactionary you, you're talking just the way I've been told Grandma talked when Pappy fell for you."

"Do you mean you're comparing me to this little upstairs maid or whatever she is—this—do you mean you've been seeing her!"

"Not enough. But whenever I could. She's hard to see. Not to look at though."

"I'll speak to your father about this!" Suddenly, oh my God, she thought, I'm talking exactly like Emmy. He's right.

Mike shifted in the doorway; the quizzical eyebrow went up in a V. "I'll try to get you her family tree, Maw, though I understand it's slightly bloodstained because her father and mother were murdered by the Nazis. That kid hasn't had a day off since she came up three months ago. She didn't tell me. I found it out."

"And why," inquired Lina, "in the words of the old melodramas, why are you telling me all this?"

"Because I thought maybe you'd go over and spend the day with Madam and let Reggie get a breath."

Lina plucked the hat from her head; she tossed it on the bed. "In the first place, Madam doesn't like me and wouldn't sit in the same room with me for a day even—no, that's the second place—in the first place, would you mind telling me why I should encourage my son to entertain a maid on her day off? I'm all for being democratic and brotherhood-of-man stuff, but this is just too broad-minded. Now listen, Mike——"

Pansy stood up. "It's been lovely seeing your pretty things, Lina. My, imagine being a size twelve! The Duchess of Windsor certainly started something. Mike, I'd love to go and sit with Exact. She thinks I'm real good company. We play gin rummy and I let her cheat and win. You aren't taking a girl out in those greasy overalls though, are you?"

He reached out with long, strong arms; he snatched her to him; he dipped her down in the manner of motion-picture lovers; he kissed her. "Pansy, I love you. Will you marry me?"

"And be an old man's darling! Not me!" said Pansy. "Tip me up straight, you libertine, and I'll go over and get Madam all buttered up so she won't think she's being neglected."

He was off down the stairs trailing words behind him. "Tell Reggie be ready, will you? Gosh, hope she isn't the kind of gal gets sick in a plane."

Lina stood a moment staring about the room that was heaped with furs and silks and bright woolens. Then she ran to the telephone; she snatched an armful of dresses off the chair and threw them to the floor. The office. "Mr. Melendy—Mr. Dike Melendy. This is Mrs. Melendy. It's important. Tell him it's important."

Dike's voice. "Hello! Hello, darling! Coming down to lunch with me?"

"No. No. Listen. Mike's going out with that girl at Madam's. He's taking her up in the plane."

"Oh. Well, that's all right. Don't worry about it."

"But he's taking her up now, I tell you. He's planning to spend the day——"

"Lina, they called me out of a meeting. Glad to talk to you, but look, dear, Mike's been flying for I don't know how long; he's done hundreds of hours—thousands—he's a real flier—don't you bother your little curly head——"

"Dike, you're talking like an idiot! I don't mean flying——"

"Oh, I thought you said flying."

"I did. I did. But it isn't flying that bothers me——"

"Look, honey, this connection is bad or something, or maybe it's the noise down here. I can't hear you very well. I'll be home around five; you can tell me all——"

She clashed the receiver down on its cradle; she sat there breathing fast. I'm being dramatic. No, I'm not. This is ridiculous. If I were in New York, working, I'd think it was unimportant. It's this place. Now pull yourself together. Emmy. I'll call Emmy and talk it over. No. Exact. God, no! Dike. Pansy. Vaughan. Nobody. Cliff. Cliff. "Long-distance. Long-distance. Look, I want a California number. Los Angeles. . . . Granite five-one-one-one. . . ."

13

THEY HAD FLOWN OVER the vast fir forests; they had swooped over the bay; they had flirted with Lake Washington; they had taunted the mountains from the blue above them. Conversation had been impossible through the roar of the engine. Dip and swoop as he would, Reggie had not been sick. The moist, cool air had brought the color to her cheeks. Her hair and skin were sweet with the pine and salt and sun. Down below were the geometrically tidy little squares of the Japanese market gardens. The formal contours of the houses on the smart new estates at Highlands. Ravines and hills. Black masses of pines. The docks. Water. Water. Water. The wilderness of the Cascade Mountains. Ranches. Orchards. The Olympics. Reggie thought Olympia—Olympics—you see the words everywhere here; they're right, it is a place of the gods.

He brought down his plane, a little red-and-yellow bug. He lifted her out. "You're a good kid," he said.

"So that is what America is like. That is exactly what I thought America was. And it is." She drew a deep breath.

"Then it's a sale?" She looked up at him. He grinned. "I forget. Sometimes you talk like an American, and I think you know our double talk. Sometimes you're kind of Oxford English, and then it gets a German sound—not German accent, but sentence arrangement—words—kind of stiff, see what I mean?"

The little locked silent look came over her vivid face. Then she said with an effort, her voice quite lifeless, "My father was German. My mother was an American. I had an English nana. That's why."

He did not pursue this. He took her hand easily in his in the way of silent companionship, boy and girl, and hand in hand thus they walked toward the airport lunchroom. "Hungry?"

"Oh yes!"

"We can get a sandwich or something here. Isn't very good. You know. Where'd you like to go?"

She threw her free hand wide in a gesture of careless happiness. "Anywhere! Nowhere! Wherever you say! That's what makes it wonderful."

"All kinds of dumps. Look. We'll get a bite here just to stay the pangs. What d'you say? Have you ever been down at the Farmers' Market? Or maybe that wouldn't—— It's just a market."

"What is there?"

"Just a kind of shed thing down on the water front. At First and Pike. Japs and Italians and Slavs. Stalls, and you can buy anything from smoked salmon to diamond rings. Look, let's not eat here. Let's go down there and kind of eat our way through it. What do you say?" Then, doubtfully, "I don't know. Most girls wouldn't call that a treat exactly. Galumphing around the Farmers' Market."

"Oh, Michael, yes!"

He drove the car as he had piloted the plane, effortlessly, with the relaxed expertness of his generation born and bred to engines and motored things. They talked little as the car whipped through the outlying roads and the city streets. "Just a market," he said again. "But it's alive down there."

"Markets are like that, alive. Everywhere. Like a fair. That's why I love them."

"That's right. There used to be joints down there, sailors' rooming houses, and some of them are still there. Flights of rickety wooden stairs and little black halls and they say trapdoors and stuff where they used to shanghai sailors in the old days, for the ships going to the Orient. Seattle's a kind of new town, you know. It's still sort of raw around the edges, though it pretends to be oh so ripe."

"I am so happy!" she said with apparent irrelevance. Then, "It's very odd. Americans apologize for their country when there's no need at all. Or they boast about it. I can't imagine why. It's the most wonderful country in the world. One needs only to be of it, and that is enough. Like a great, great lady who can be serene and confident and sure. When they let me have my papers and I am really an American citizen I never shall apologize and I never shall boast. People in Europe are really so envious of Americans that they try to make them feel inferior."

"Oh, you're kidding!"

"Really not. When we used to travel, Mother and Father and I, and we would come to the border of Italy or France or Belgium—or our own country, Germany, for that matter—the officials in their uniforms and their gold braid and their shiny buttons would look at Mother's passport and they would say, 'Where were you born?' though there it was for anyone to read. And Mother would say proudly, 'I was born in the United States of America.' And they would look at her. It was a look of envy. And I always thought how wonderful it must be to be able to say that."

"You're a funny kid."

"Is that nice?"

"It's very nice."

He parked the car opposite a long, shedlike structure high above docks and buildings on the water front. Together they walked into a world of color and sound and motion. Teamsters and produce men and housewives and market gardeners. Japanese girls, Japanese women, Japanese men quick and expert in their stalls banked and brilliant with the scarlet and green and gold and purple of fruits and vegetables. Scandinavians. Slavs. Irish. Italians. Fish, flesh, fowl, cheeses. The tantalizing scent of coffee. Rock crabs huge and fantastic. Great Alaska king salmon. Columbia River sturgeon six feet long. Red snappers bright orange and Indian red. Prawns. Herring. Smelts glinting silver and blue. Oregon apples. Rome Beauties that were vast globes of pink and green. Everything seemed bigger and greener and redder and heavier and more lavish than the species could be in real life. A sign read: Palace Fish Market. If It Swims We Have It.

And, "Oh!" said Reggie. And, "Mm!" she said. "I can't believe it. So much food. In one place. I can't get used to it. Everywhere in America. It is not even to be dreamed of."

"Sack of shrimps?" Mike suggested. "As an appetizer." They stopped at a stall and bought tiny coral shrimps and ate them like popcorn out of the little paper sacks as they strolled through the throng, and the miniature crustaceans were sweet and salt and delicious. On every side the stallkeepers called their wares, and above all you heard the dry, brittle bark of the Japanese. Their wares were more brilliant than any others—every leaf and branch and stalk glistened with crystal drops from their water sprays. "And they weigh in all that lovely water right with your stuff," Mike remarked cynically. "How about lunch?"

So they sat perched on high stools at a lunch counter whose windows faced the water front, and the gay, colorful life of the market eddied about them. The blue and gold and silver of sky and water and mountain lay before them. A dingy little lunchroom with big-fisted men in leather jackets and women with string shopping bags drinking coffee and eating stew. Mike and Reggie ate rock crabs and drank the coffee for which the place was famous—hot, strong, rich.

Mike waved a hand toward the windows. "I had the sun turned on especially for you. It doesn't happen very often, this time of year."

"And I just took it for granted, like all these other lovely things."

"Not in Seattle you don't. Usually the fogs and the Jap Current and the mountains all combine to—— Would you care to hear about all that?"

"No, thank you. And could I have a piece of that lovely apple pie with a ball of vanilla ice cream on top like the one that man is eating? That man in the brown sweater who looks like a truck driver!"

"What a girl! Wouldn't it be just my luck to get stuck with a girl who eats like a truck driver!"

"What a country! Where truck drivers eat apple pie with ice cream on top for dessert at lunch!"

He caught the waitress with his eye. "Apple pie. Two, please. And two portions of ice cream on top. On top of each, I mean."

"You mean apple pie à la mode." Plainly she was outraged at his ignorance. "Double ice creams is extra."

"I was afraid of that." His right eyebrow went up in the little quirk. "But I'm stuck with this young lady."

The waitress brought the colossal sweet. Reggie Dresden looked at it a moment. Then she picked up her fork and neatly arranged a little mound of ice cream on a small triangle of the pastry; solemnly she ate it; she looked up at him and smiled like an enraptured child.

"Imagine!" she exclaimed.

"Dear little Miss Dresden," Mike said, and just lightly touched her hand with his forefinger. He had called her Reggie casually the first time they had met. Wordlessly now she understood that the formal-sounding Miss Dresden was a fondly humorous term of affection.

"I am a greedy girl. But there were so many years when I never had enough to eat——" She stopped abruptly.

Mike turned full face and looked at her in the merciless glare of the afternoon sun that poured through the windows facing

Elliott Bay. The fine skin beneath her eyes was young and tender as an infant's. Her clear golden hair, too, was fine and soft; she did not wear it brushed and shining loose about her shoulders as the American girls did. It was parted and brought into a knot at the nape of her neck. He hadn't seen a girl wearing her hair like that in years. He thought suddenly that it would be wonderful if he could just run his finger tips lightly down her firm little chin to her throat and the tender little hollow at its base. She was eighteen. She must have seen death and agony and fear and brutality and starvation and cruelty. Her eyes were clear and compassionate and they seemed to see far beyond the human eye. She was eighteen. She was older than his great-grandmother Exact Melendy.

He saw the warm color creep into her cheeks under his ardent gaze. "You're sweet."

Like a schoolgirl she said, "Thank you." She laid down her fork and sighed blissfully. "That was a lovely dish. Too much—the waitress was right—but lovely. I do hope I shan't have a stomach-ache."

"Nice little girls don't mention stomach-aches."

Suddenly she pointed a dramatic finger toward the panorama of sky and water and mountain. "If that were in Europe—that glorious thing out there—then here where we are sitting there would be, instead of a market for farmers and vegetables and lunch counters and Japanese gardeners and women with shopping bags, there would be a splendid restaurant called the Grand Restaurant des Etrangers et de l'Europe et Deux Mondes. And there would be terraces. And waiters in tail coats streaming out behind them as they run, and red plush and gold chairs and crystal chandeliers and an orchestra——"

"And Nazis."

"And Nazis." She sat silent a moment.

"Uh, sorry, Reggie. I didn't mean to bring that up."

She shook her head. "Oh no. I just meant it's so amazing. Here everything is big and free. You throw it away. Like that!"

"Yup. We throw it away. Anyway, we did. That's where I came in. My crowd, we've got no place left to go but up. My great-grandpappy and Grandpa Vaughan Melendy and all that gang just came along in covered wagons and grabbed the stuff with their bare hands, and then they hitched machinery to it, and so now we just sit on our cans and our job is to get up every now and then and oil the machinery. So I get in a plane and go up in the sky."

She stared at him in shocked surprise. "But Michael! It can't be like that! In school at home we learned about the American pioneers and how they could have land—millions of acres—just for the asking. And everything was here—mines and forests and rivers. They had only to take."

"And did they take! My family's been taking with both hands since way back in eighteen fifty-one."

"Why, I think your family is wonderful! Madam Melendy, a miracle. And your grandfather. And your father so young and clever. And Pansy, she's like those pioneer women in the history —— Oh, I forgot. She isn't your family."

They had forgotten the lunch counter and the view and the market. Each was leaning on an elbow facing the other. And the waitress said, "You want something else, another cup of coffee or something?" And Mike said, "Oh yes, sure. And check, please." Without really having heard her. "Only there's no more land to conquer. No more gold to dig. No more forests to snatch, see. Grandpappy Vaughan went up to Alaska and snared him a couple of million. Old Jotham, Madam's husband—well, you know—my great-grandfather of course he was—he had the seeing eye. He owned practically every Seattle corner that any bank or office building wanted to build on. He got it for peanuts and sold it for millions."

"But that was all right, wasn't it? I mean it was honest business, that's the way it's done."

"Oh, sure, honest. Smart, but honest. Only we Melendys have been taking out of America now for about a century. What've we ever put in?"

"Surely work—and—and money—and business. Work for other people is made by your grandfather's business and your father's. Lumber business and the big canneries in Alaska he has told me about."

He paid his check; he tipped the girl. Reggie, horrified, wanted to say, oh, that is too much! But didn't. He swung clear around on the high stool as though to dispel the mood into which he had fallen. "Oh, we're talking like one of those radio forums. Let's get out of here."

"But I like it. I want to hear about this. Why do you talk like that?"

"Listen. Did you ever hear of old Chief Seattle?" She shook her head. "This town was named after him. They say he was a wonderful old coot. A Siwash Indian. When my folks shoved up on the beach here in 1851 old Seattle was about sixty-five, and they say he was over six feet and not bowlegged like the other Siwashes from squatting in canoes all their lives fishing for salmon and so on. Gray hair down to his shoulders, loose like the prophets in the Bible, not braided, and looked like a philosopher. We learned about him at school. He must have been quite a guy —not only for an Indian, but I mean something really big. Well, along came the white people and it was all up with the Indians. They'd had a fine time until then, fishing and hunting and so on. This place must have been a paradise."

"But it is now! It is still!"

"For them, I mean. Well, the poor lunks, along came the white brother and hit them over the head and took the land and shoved them off it and herded them on a reservation—you know—kind of like a concentration camp."

"No! It isn't possible!"

"They did, though. And this old Seattle, he was the white man's friend, God knows why. Look, do you want to hear the rest of this?"

"Yes. Please. I want to hear."

"Well, I'll make a quickie of it. I don't know what started me on this. Sitting here middle of the day giving you a thumbnail history of my folks and a lecture on Seattle—well, anyway, they called the whole bunch of the Elliott Bay Indians together because the new governor of Washington Territory, Governor Isaac Stevens, had come to talk to them. It must have been quite a sight. The shore black with hundreds of canoes drawn up on the beach, and Indians pouring out of the forest trails, thousands of them. So this Governor Stevens stands up and gives them the old eyewash. They say he was a short little guy, Stevens. The Great White Chief in Washington loves them like his own children and so he's going to buy their lands from them———"

"But if they bought it they didn't just take it."

"For peanuts. And he's going to put them on fine reservations with everything dandy like schools and blacksmith shops, just like the white man, civilized. And they'd live happily ever after and never have to bother about going out in canoes for salmon and so on. Gosh, it makes me mad just to think about that guy."

"Did they go?"

"Well, sure. What could they do? But here's the pay-off. Up stands old Chief Seattle. He was about a foot taller than little Governor Stevens and he's got a blanket on him wrapped like a Roman senator's toga, though he'd never heard of a Roman senator. He was just made of the same kind of stuff, I suppose. They say you could hear his voice for half a mile. He talked in Duwamish, and old Doc Smith had learned the language and he wrote it down. Look, this is no place to say it. We learned it in school. Every kid in Seattle learns it in school. It didn't mean much to me then. But in the last year or two I kind of remembered it and I began to think, gosh! Wow! Gives you chills."

"Say it. Say it now!"

"I wish I hadn't started this. I like talking to you, Reggie. Regina. Regina. Why did they call you Regina? Queen, isn't it?"

Almost angrily she shook her head. "Don't be like that. A little boy, self-conscious. Say it!"

"All right. I feel foolish, though. I'll say it low. It's good. Good and scarey. Well, uh—let's see—uh——" He leaned toward her, his elbow on the counter. Her head was close to his; they were gazing at the breath-taking sight beyond the window. To see them one would have said that here was a boy whispering his love to a girl. She listened raptly. His face was earnest, passionate. " '. . . Why should I mourn at the untimely fate of my people? Tribe follows tribe, and nation follows nation, like the waves of the sea. It is the order of nature, and regret is useless. Your time of decay may be distant, but it will surely come, for even the White Man, whose God walked and talked with him as friend with friend, cannot be exempt from the common destiny. We may be brothers after all. Let the White Man be just and deal kindly with my people, for the dead are not powerless. Dead, did I say? There is no death, only a change of worlds!' "

The two sat silent a moment then. From the stalls beyond came the cajoling cries of the vendors. Lettuce! Carrots! Beets! Get your Rome Beauties! How about a nice mess of smelts fresh caught? Herrings! Crab!

The girl shivered a little. "The old boy said a mouthful," Mike commented rather grimly. They slid off the stools; he took her arm. "Come on down to the level below. There's a woman down there has old phonograph records, like The Cowboy's Lament and Scandinavian records. There's one I want called Den Norske Fiskermann; she promised she'd try to get one for me. Maybe she's got it now."

But to reach the phonograph stall downstairs they must first pass a score of tempting wares. Jewelers' cases on whose dusty glass shelves zircons glittered up at you with their hard, shallow blue eyes. Like Mrs. Vaughan Melendy's eyes, Reggie thought. Smoky diamonds set with turquoise. The kind of jewelry, she said to herself, that the Parcel of Posies might have worn in the old Alaska days that Pansy had described to her with such gusto. Neither of these things she might say to Mike.

"Buy you a zircon?" Mike suggested grandly. "It ain't considered binding."

"Let me see—what is the thing to say to that? Oh yes. Diamonds or nothing."

"Might be—if you play your cards right."

"I'm unlucky at games."

"That's all right. You know the old saying. And I guess all us Melendys must have been lucky at cards."

Past the little stalls and counters. Hardware. Smoked fish. Fresh loaves. Chickens and eggs. Secondhand furniture. Old silver. Lace fans with yellowed ivory sticks. Licorice candy. Faces drifting by; a panorama of the world; oriental faces, Scandinavian, Latin, Slavic, English.

"Why do you talk like that, Michael? As though you were hurt by something deep inside? Everything here is so marvelous. You can't realize. But I don't know you well enough to say this."

"You know me better than they do. Look, I didn't mean I don't like my family and my—uh—country. Stuff like that is hard to say. I mean I think they're top flight. The family's full of guts and brawn and talent and brains and they're just screwy enough to be interesting. That goes for the country, too, like a bigger family. But something's gone wrong. Maybe it's them or they or whatever it is. Maybe it's me. What d'you say?"

"You've had a curious childhood—very rich and self-sufficient and a little spoiled and alone a great deal and never having to be afraid."

"Me or the country?"

"Both."

"How do you mean—spoiled?"

"You've got everything. There's nothing to fight for. Here's space for everyone. Land and sunshine and oranges and motorcars and shoes and movies and food and fun and books and magazines and newspapers where you write what you please, and free schools and lovely clothes all made for you every size, every color, every style to choose from in the shops, and baseball games where someone else even does your playing for you, and refrigerators and radios and airplanes like yours for toys——"

"Heh! Now wait a minute, wait—a—minute! It isn't as slick as that, it isn't so easy——"

"You see, you take it for granted. You've always had it. Perhaps someday you may have to fight to keep it. Then you'll know."

But his chest came out and his eyebrow went up and he swaggered a little without being aware of it. "Not a chance! They know better than to tackle an outfit like ours."

"You don't know them, Michael. You don't know."

"Oh well, let's not go gloomy. Here. Do you like China tea? Let's get a box each for Pansy and Madam." They stopped at the stall of a Chinese merchant, a wizened yellow man with a charming manner and no high-powered salesmanship. Surrounded by gay little paper boxes and covered glass bowls containing strangely shaped seeds, and by bits of brass and china and ivory and silk, he smiled and nodded and made soft answer. Evidently he and Mike were acquaintances of long standing. It was Pansy Deleath for whose well-being he inquired, and old Madam Exact. Evidently Emmy Melendy and Lina were not Farmers' Market habitués.

Soy-bean flour, a sign read. Sesame seed. "Sesame seed!" Reggie exclaimed. "Is it magic?"

They wandered like children, happily. They tasted. They listened to old phonograph records. They bought odds and ends; they were hung with little parcels and boxes. They peered up dark stairways; they wandered down to the docks. They dumped their bundles into Mike's car. "Tell you what. Let's amble down the Skidroad."

"What is that?"

"Nothing much now. Just a street, a district. Long ago it was the logging road. First Avenue, really, and Yesler. It used to be tough. But tough! It isn't exactly Fifth Avenue even now. I wouldn't advise you to go down there alone. It's our local Seattle version—or was—of the Marseilles water front. Sailors in off their ships—pawnshops—flophouses—fishermen in from Alaska—lumberjacks in town to spend their money—Indians, beggars, soapbox orators, Salvation Army, beer parlors, dance halls."

"It sounds lovely." After the labyrinth of the Farmers' Market the broad street seemed quiet, moribund, the decrepit end of a shabby old business street. As they walked along she said, "Tell me when we reach it."

"Honey, you're in it."

"Where?"

"Here. Now don't sulk. I told you not to expect a knife in your ribs, didn't I?"

"But I thought it would be dramatic."

"It was. Not so long ago, at that. This town got self-conscious about its rip-roaring days and cleaned up. It tried to be the New York of the Northwest. Very cosmopolitan. But lately it's begun to be fashionable again to brag about the old hell-raising times. Look at Madam, she's the belle of the village because she's a living monument to the old days and smokes a pipe and yells about pioneer stuff. I think she makes it up."

Bleary men with whisky-blotched skin; sailors, narrow of hip, their tough young faces incongruously framed by the babyish collars of their uniforms; a sign outside a shop window—Stoneham Sailmaker; loggers' boots in the windows, their soles an inch thick; woodsmen's knives and saws; seamen's kits; Indian faces, Japanese, Hawaiian, even the broad flat features of an occasional Esquimau; lodging houses; mission hotels; cheap movies flaunting posters of lurid Westerns; a gigantic totem pole in Pioneer Square, carved by the Thlinget Indians, its minks and whales and seals and frogs leering out in crude reds and greens and blues and yellows to tell the folktale of the woman who married a frog.

"Pansy says Seattle has swept its past under the rug but it keeps blowing out."

"Pansy's wonderful."

"Stop saying everything's wonderful!" Mike suddenly snarled. "Ever since we started out. Gramp's wonderful and Madam's wonderful and Pansy and the shrimps and the view and the lousy pie à la mode and the Skidroad and Seattle."

"But it is! It *is* wonderful!" She faced him spiritedly, and the two stood there on the sidewalk outside a beer parlor glaring at each other. From the doorway came the mechanical rhythm of a juke box. "You are like children! All of you! Don't you know what's happening in the world? Here you have everything. Everything! Forests and mines and rivers and orchards and farms. And freedom and riches and happiness. I tell you it is wonderful. This city is wonderful and this state and this country and the pioneers who made it and you and your grandfather and your great-grandmother all, all are wonderful. But in this you are like children picking flowers in a forest of wolves. Don't you know what they are planning to do to you? Don't you know those devils? Don't you know that you will have to fight to keep what you have made here in this wonderful country? You are children here. Children!"

"Oh, so that's what you think of us, huh!" Suddenly the two were no older than their actual age.

"Yes! No! Oh, Michael, today has been so——"

"Don't say wonderful." He took her arm. "Come on in this dump; let's have a coke and dance."

The place was dim with a sickly pink light. Sailors and their girls sat with their hats on; they drank beer or they filled their glasses from bottles they themselves had brought in. The juke box was a massive thing lighted like a cathedral at Christmas; it had some special organ attachment which gave it a thundering tremolo that penetrated your vitals. Except for this there was little sound in the room. These boys and girls were strangely quiet, with a trance-like quality.

They sat a long moment in silence. He lighted a cigarette. She broke a match into small pieces and arranged them in a pattern on the table. "You're kind of damned wonderful yourself," Mike said sheepishly.

She did not look up at him; she went on making a little pattern with the pieces of match stick and wrecking it and forming it again.

"Let's dance." He pushed back his chair. They stood up. Except for the throbbing, sentimental music the place was quiet. Almost every table was taken; now they all rose and moved to the dance floor. They were all young, very young and serious; they talked little. Now and then a couple broke into the whirls and clutchings and convulsive jerks of the jitterbug. But for the most part they moved dreamily, their young faces grave and almost sad.

Reggie was light in his arms. Quickly he perceived that she knew nothing of intricate steps or recent ones; he confined himself to simple dance patterns and she followed him easily, naturally; she had perfect rhythm sense and motion. They did not speak. The music sent out vibrations that flowed into them like hot, strong drink.

He felt something—a tense, convulsive movement that came from her diaphragm. He looked down at her. She was weeping quietly, her eyes closed, her face distorted into a grimace of anguish. A sudden nostalgic memory swept over him—a feeling that he had experienced this before, or had dreamt it. He bent his head so that his cheek met hers and was wet by her tears; his lips moved against hers; he felt for the first time a protective tenderness for a woman, he who all his life had been surrounded by strong, capable, self-sufficient women, managing women. There was something terrible about this young girl's silent tears.

She said in a small choked voice, "I'm sorry—forgive me—I never cry—I haven't cried in a long, long time . . ."

"Cry if you want to, darling. Go ahead and cry. Dear. Reggie dear."

She smiled gratefully up at him; he reached into his pocket and took out his handkerchief and wiped her face gently and said, "Blow," and they laughed; and he kissed her as they laughed and they stopped laughing.

They went back to their table. "I shouldn't have brought you to a dump like this."

"I like it. It's——"

"—wonderful!" he finished for her. Then they laughed again as at something exquisitely witty.

"Suppose," he said, "you stop being a brave little woman for ten minutes and give with this stuff that's getting you down."

"Refugee stories come a penny a dozen. Who wants to hear them?"

"I do. Yours, anyway. I don't know anything about you except that your name is Regina Dresden. Refugee. I never thought of you as a refugee."

"It's a horrid word—refugee. It gives a picture of people scuttling into holes, down the road, hiding, running—well, so we did. So we do. Some of the societies call us *émigrés*. Much nicer, they say. They are charming about it and very careful."

He sat twirling his glass round and round in those thin, strong brown fingers that had been so expert with the plane, so sure at the wheel, so gentle with the big white handkerchief. "I'm glad to hear you say something isn't wonderful and lovely. For a girl who had an American mama you certainly are low on American adjectives. And stop wincing, will you, every time I mention anything that isn't Seattle scenery or something remote like that. You don't want to grow up to be a wincer, do you?"

"It's that music. That cheap, treacly music. It made me cry and made you kiss me and now it makes us want to talk about ourselves. Let's go, shall we?"

He hitched his chair around so that they sat next each other, side by side, shoulder to shoulder. He covered her hand with his. "We're staying. And I like juke-box music. I may have one in that three-room shack I'm going to live in someday."

"Oh, you're planning to live in a three-room shack?"

"Yup. And to clean it you turn the hose on it, inside and out. No Queen Anne Hill. No Highlands. No monogrammed silver and silk spreads and old French gips. None of those dusty possessions. Lots of window and floor space and fireplaces and sprawl seats." He pressed her hand hard. "Come on. So they named you Regina."

"I can't."

"All right. Look. I know a lot of girls. I've never talked to any of them the way you and I talk. You know. Out with it."

"Oh, Michael! Ever since you've been home I've seen them, they come by, they come in, they call you from their cars. I wish I were like that; they are direct and sure and American. So sure and so wise."

"And I've known them all my life. And I've known you less than a week. And I've never talked to any of them the way I'm talking to you now."

"I'm an old, old lady. No, don't be frightened. I'm not going to cry again."

Disconnectedly he said, "Funny. I just thought of something kind of funny. People hardly ever talk about themselves—I mean, people hardly ever care enough about each other to talk about themselves or listen to somebody else talking about themselves—I mean—I suppose that's what people do when they first are married—talk and talk to each other about things they couldn't talk about to their families. Just spill the works. It must be kind of wonderful. If it's somebody your own age that loves you a lot—I mean—free and clear. That's what it says in those real-estate papers they're always wanting me to muck around with up in Dad's office. Free and clear."

Gently she said, "I think I know something of the things you —you have never talked about in your family. But do you think you want to say them to me?"

"Maybe you don't want to hear."

"Yes. I want to hear."

He took a deep breath, like a diver about to make the plunge. "Uh—you know—Pansy is Dad's real mother."

"I know."

"The family all pretend they don't know, see. Especially Dad. Well, that kind of bitches up your life inside. A thing like that, being cagey and dishonest about it."

"What could they have done?"

"I don't know. But it's so silly. They haven't fooled anyone but themselves, and it might have been a lot better all around if they had come out with it—if Pansy had just brought up her son open and aboveboard. Maybe not in Seattle. Away from Vaughan and the family."

She smiled up at him. "Then you wouldn't be here talking to me."

"Gee, that's so! But what a mess. All these years and years Grandma's had a poisonous feeling against Gramp, of course. Dad never has been sure of himself. Dad was in the World War —World War—well, anyway, that's what they called it—the one before this one—I suppose this will be known as the World-and-All-Points-West War. He hardly ever talks about it, but when he does it's as if it had been the only time in his life when he really felt free and sure. Confident. Well, that's a funny way to feel about war. Then when he got back—I've asked him about it a little—everything was all snarled and he was, too; people just wanted to forget about the war and the hell with it. So they just shoved it into a closet and slammed the door on it. Anyway, he never did anything about it and Gramp never did anything about it and nobody did anything about it. And that, my dears, is the story of why your uncle Mike will probably be going around someday with one leg—if he's lucky. Gosh, I sound like a swine!"

"Now you're the one who is being self-conscious."

"All right. And Mother——"

"There's nothing anyone can do about people like that, Michael. She has a husband and a son and a career and a great deal of money. But she wants the world."

"And she can't have it, so she takes a bite out of Dad every now and then."

"Yes. But Michael, in her own way—in her own ruthless way —she is rather—forgive me—wonderful, too. Like a self-painted portrait."

"Reggie, do you think I'm talking like a stinker?"

"You know I don't, Michael." Soberly they sat silent a moment. Suddenly she was laughing. "Madam Melendy," she said. "Now there is one!"

He grinned, agreeing. "No repressions in that little curly head. That's why she's lived about a hundred years. She's pleased with herself and the Melendy tribe and she thinks Seattle is heaven ——" He threw out an arm as though the whole city lay spread before them in that murky little Skidroad beer parlor. "Look at it! They certainly bitched up this town. It could have been the most beautiful city in America."

She said gently, "Perhaps it will be, someday. Rome wasn't beautiful when it was less than one hundred years old."

On his face was an expression at once puzzled and relieved. "You mean Rome wasn't—— Say, I never took that old saw literally before. And what's this I've been bellyaching about! I thought I had something terrific to say. Now it's out I feel silly— good but silly." He turned and looked at her. "This is a funny way to spend a day with a girl."

"How do you mean, funny?"

"Not very plush—for you, I mean. A whirl in the plane—lunch at a counter—a coke in a beer joint. Look, do you want to go to dinner at the Olympic? Or out at the club, or——"

"Michael, can we drive somewhere? And then I must go home. Dear Pansy. All day with Madam Melendy. It isn't easy."

"How about you? All day every day."

"But I'm fond of her. It's like living with a miracle."

"Hell of a job for a kid."

"Hell of a world—but I like it. I thought I never would again. But I like it."

Dusk had come on. The fog was rolling in. "Let's go over to Alki Point. That's where Madam landed, you know, when she was a baby. Can you imagine her a baby!"

In the mind of each there rose up a picture of a six-foot stentorian infant in satin and diamonds squalling in her mother's arms, and they started off in a gale of young laughter.

"Alki? Is that a name? A pioneer's name?"

"Alki's a Chinook word. Indian. It means by-and-by."

"By-and-by."

"Move closer to me. That's better."

"Do you always drive like this, so fast?"

"Yes."

"In the plane, too. I suppose it is your substitute. It gives you a feeling of adventure. You feel powerful and free, driving fast like this. Toward the horizon."

"The horizon always ends in a hamburger joint." Shoulder to shoulder, swaying with the motion of the car. "So you won't talk, eh!"

She was silent for so long a time that the boy thought, well, it doesn't matter now. Someday she'll want to tell me. She was clasping and unclasping her hands like one trying to free them of shackles. Then suddenly she was quiet again. Now she began to talk in a hard, dry voice unlike her own.

"To hear the stories they tell, one would think everyone who escaped from Germany was a famous scientist or a great banker or a brilliant writer or a noted actor. Well, we were nice, middle-class people who lived in a big pleasant flat full of beautiful things, in Charlottenburg. That is a part of Berlin. Father had a big linen shop in Berlin, with branches in other places. There is nothing very grand or distinguished about that, is there? Not like most of them. Mother was an American; she had a voice, not a big voice but good; she had come to Germany to study singing. Father loved music; that is how they met. Father was a Jew, but Mother was not. I say 'was' because they are probably dead. I wish I knew. But of course they are. By now they must be. When I read the newspapers I hope so. Safely dead. When things became quite bad they sent me to France. They were going to come as soon as their affidavits were in order, and their visas. I was only twelve then. I was still at home when the men came to the apartment for the first time; they searched everything and knocked Father about but Mother kept saying to him in English, over and over, very low, 'Do nothing. They will go soon. There is nothing here. For my sake and Reggie's do nothing.' So he suffered them to shove him about—Father was a slim man and rather delicate with a fine, long head and merry brown eyes. Not merry. Humorous. When I was a little girl I thought merry was the word. One of the men slapped my father's face. No reason. He slapped his face hard and laughed and spat at him. You see these things in the movies and you think they are made up and ridiculous, but they are true. Father's face was terrible to see—my father was a proud man. I was frightened and I began to cry, but I cried without making any noise; I knew I must not make a noise. Mother put her hand very quietly on his arm and he shut his eyes a moment and his face looked dead. Quite dead. In a way I suppose he really did die in that moment. In a way. . . . This isn't very . . . Do you want to hear the rest?"

"Yes, if you can. Not if it hurts you too much, Reggie."

"I thought it would. It doesn't. That's queer, isn't it? It feels good in a queer way. That's the way you felt a while ago, isn't it? There were six of the men. They were stupid louts, very young, eighteen or twenty years old, not more. They were like the boys you read about here, sometimes, in gangs, roving the streets destroying things and hurting people and killing them sometimes only out of frustration or a longing for power. They are ignorant, and angry at the world, and they feel better when they can smash something. Things or people, it doesn't matter. Their faces are silly and mean and little. I can see them as clearly as though they were before me now. They took the silver from the cupboards and the dining-room side tables. It was rather beautiful old silver that had belonged to my grandmother, Father's mother. A tea service and a coffee service and all sorts of beautiful old plates and goblets and pitchers. Well, they took these fragile things and they threw them on the floor and they jumped on them with their great heavy boots. Jumped and jumped, and their lips drawn back from their teeth. The pieces lay on the floor broken and twisted and smashed flat like tin. They had belonged to my grandmother and to my great-grandmother. In Europe people care a great deal about such things. If they had taken them and run off with them there would have been some sense in it. This was just love of destruction. Then Father said '*Schweine hunde!*'"

"What's that mean?"

"Literally, pig dogs. Swine. One of them—a very young boy— hit Father on the face very hard with his fist and he fell. Then the one in command—the eldest—said, '*Hör auf! Noch nicht. 's nächste mal—und' fertig.*' Stop. Not now. Next time we'll finish it. So they ran down the hall and were gone. Mother and Father knew then that we must leave Germany. Mother might have gone without too much trouble because of her American birth, but she wouldn't go without Father. So they sent me ahead—there were societies that were very kind and helpful for children—the Quakers and others. But even then it was too late for them. Or perhaps Father did something or said something in rebellion, They vanished. Both."

"What d'you mean—vanished?"

"My father and mother are gone. Swallowed up. No letters, no sign, no word—nothing. It's rather an old story now, you've heard it and read it and seen it in pictures, people scarcely listen to it any more. It went on all the time in Germany, and I saw enough of it in France, so now it's an old story. All that running down the road and hiding in ditches and living behind barbed wire and dying horribly or existing horribly——"

She stopped as the car came to a halt. They sat facing the Sound and the Olympics in the dusk, and the lighthouse whose great godlike eye searched their young faces, their young serious faces, and swerved away quickly and returned as though hoping to find them transformed into happy young lovers' faces of the sort on which it always had winked on Alki Point.

"You're here now. You're safe here, Reggie." She laughed shortly. He said sharply, "Don't do that."

"We should go home now."

"How did you get here? Across the ocean and across this whole continent. You've got to tell me."

"Oh, that is a long, long story full of not nice things. And by that time I was quite an elderly person, as you see. I arrived in New York after days and days on the ocean in a ship that was like a floating hell, only we were not lost souls, we were saved. In New York I got a job as waitress—there is a committee of women who belong to an organization called the Sisterhood. It's marvelous. They train unskilled refugees like myself to become waitresses and cooks. You learn to serve at dinner parties and so on. I was quite good, really. You arrange the table and you pass the canapés and the cocktails and then you serve the dinner and after dinner the pitcher of ice water and then the highballs and remember always to empty the ash trays——"

The boy folded his arms on the wheel and put his head down on his arms. She sat composedly, her hands folded in her lap.

"There were many of us in New York. We walked like ghosts

in those brilliant streets full of quick, rushing people. Usually I could detect a refugee the moment I saw one. Not only shabby, but the clothes were different. They hung like graveclothes on them. Their faces were gray and closed like a shuttered house in which someone has died and the rooms are empty of sound and feeling. . . . Now I'm talking like a writer. Perhaps I'm enjoying this—telling you this."

He sat staring straight ahead now. "Have you told it many times before?"

"Never before."

"That's good. These people on the streets. Go on. You weren't like that. You aren't like that at all."

"No. They were the dead ones who walked. I am not like that. They were one kind of refugee. There are many of them. They did not walk quickly, like the people of New York. They paced slowly, without spring in their steps, and the men usually bent forward a little and walked with their hands clasped behind them as hopeless people do in a small space. That's the walk of a concentration-camp prisoner. You walk like that when your spirit is broken. But there are many others of us who are still alive and eager. I wanted to see America. I wanted to be part of America. There were too many of us in New York, huddling together too much, speaking German too much, afraid to strike out into this new stream."

"But how did you happen to come here? That's considered a jump even by Americans. New York to Seattle."

"I had a picture in my mind. A little girl's picture, really, of America. Out of the movies, I suppose, and books. And my mother had read to me when I was very little, and talked of it a lot. I thought it would be enormous spaces and great forests and high, gleaming mountains and water—great lakes that we would call seas. I knew New York was skyscrapers, but that wasn't the way I thought of America. I didn't want to huddle in New York and be a refugee. I wanted it—that thing you said, Michael—free and clear. Free and clear. I came toward the West. Chicago. That wasn't it at all. Kansas City. No. Denver. That was something that had been. I wanted it wild and beautiful and unfinished. Not pretending to be like New York. Then as my train came here, through the Cascade Mountains, and I saw the log houses and the big men in mackinaws and the rushing streams and the wild, great forests I was so happy, Michael. I was so happy I began to sing aloud on the train. I sang 'America' that my mother had taught me when I was a little girl, and I sang about the rocks and rills and woods and templed hills because there they were, it was like a dream come true. The people on the train laughed at me but I didn't care!" She was crying now. "I was happy for the first time since I was twelve years old!"

"Reggie. Darling darling darling!"

14

Saturday, and sunny. Not that alone, sunny in December. And mild, with a pearl pink mist over the bay and not more than one thin layer of gray chiffon over Rainier. There actually were roses glowing in the early-morning opalescence, and in Emmy's rock garden lay brilliant rugs of magenta and yellow, defying the calendar.

Talk about climate, Vaughan thought, surveying his world as usual through the morning half light, those softies from the East always saying Seattle was too wet and too gray and too foggy. Why, there wasn't a climate in the world could touch it. Not for him, anyway. Flowers in December, and snow on Rainier. Look at London, biggest city in the whole world, centuries and centuries of people lived there, and that was a stinking climate for you. But they wouldn't live anywhere else. London way back had been destroyed by fire just like Seattle in Eighty-nine; pestilence had swept through it like in the Bible, and everything that man or nature could think of had tried to kill it, and now those German savages were bombing it to hell. But there it stood, millions of people living in it; they loved it, fog and cold and wet and set apart the way it was. That's what makes a town. The folks in it, building it up and sticking by it, generation after generation. The spirit of the folks in it, though that sounded flowery. Well, that

209

was the way he felt about Seattle. Mountains, water, forests. Fish, fruits, vegetables, game. A finer port than London. Why, hell, London didn't even have a port. Well, the Melendys had stuck by Seattle for ninety years. Maybe that wasn't enough. How did Mike feel about it, wonder? If Lina had her way they'd be living back East, Mike and Dike and her, and that'd be the end of the Melendys in Seattle and the Northwest. The thought sent prickles up and down his skin; it was as though he could feel his hackles rise as he had seen them on the malemutes when danger approached. You couldn't tell how Mike felt. Ask him something and he'd shy off from it like a skittish colt or turn it aside with a joke. He didn't understand Mike. Loved him, but didn't understand him. Whenever he said something of this to Pansy she met it with one of her own odd conclusions.

"That's as should be. Young folks don't want you to understand 'em. You've got no more right to understand them than you have to play their games or wear their clothes. They belong to themselves. I've seen older people try to understand the young ones, and they mix in with them and think they're talking their talk and being just like one of them, comrades and real understanding and sympathetic. And the kids just look at them with an eye that's cold—cold and resentful."

"I don't see any call for their sneering at their elders, or hating them."

"They don't. Not the decent ones, like Mike. They're affectionate all right. They just don't want you to make yourself ridiculous. Kids today are about the best crop we've had since pioneer days."

"Well, now, Pansy, I don't see how you figure that out. What've they done that's so good?"

"Nothing much. But they're so kind of grown up early and prepared. Remember Dike when he was Mike's age? Loose hung in his mind and manners as a jumping jack."

But he had caught at a word. "Prepared. Prepared for what?"

"I don't know. Prepared. For what they've got to do. Waiting."

"Maybe they're waiting for their elders to die. They don't seem to care about making money—that is, really money. All they know is engines. Engines and games and books and walking around half naked or in clothes look like a tramp's."

"Maybe that's all they need to know."

"Need. For what?"

"I don't know."

"Sometimes, Pansy, I suspect you ain't really as smart as I think you are."

"You've been fifty years finding that out, Vaughan," Pansy said, a trifle tartly for her.

Everybody on the Hill seemed on edge lately, Vaughan reflected now. And last night took the cooky. Bunch of womenfolk squabbling and miaeowing among themselves like a lot of cats. It had begun with his mother. Old Exact was cantankerous because Reggie was off for the day; wouldn't go to sleep until the girl got home, and that had been about midnight. Emmy was sore because he had gone over to see his mother when she had telephoned him. Emmy said that girl was paid to stay with Madam, she had no right to go off. Emmy didn't say it was because Pansy was there, but she had meant it. At his age that was just plain ridiculous. Or was it? And Lina had carried on like a loon because Mike was out with little Reggie. A regular three-ring circus. Maybe Lina was right. She said everybody in the family living on top of everybody else no wonder they hated each other's guts.

And now here was Emmy giving one of her family parties tomorrow, a brunch, she called it, at twelve noon because it was Dike's birthday and Sunday and because Mike was home and because Lina was home and because Dave Dreen, Dike's godfather, was in town from Tacoma stopping at the Olympic Hotel and because she had a new set of dishes she had got in one of those china stores in Victoria and wanted to show them off to Lina and Pansy. Emmy was forever giving these family dinners and so on and getting them all together when they were together too much as it was. Nobody on the Hill wanted to come to any damn-fool brunch.

By golly, he'd clear out for today, anyway. Spend the day down at Fisherman's Wharf talking to the boys; fool around down there with the boats and the nets, feel better. Let the bunch of them stew in their own juice up here on the Hill.

Even this morning things had continued to be upset and disquieting. He had slept badly. He had tiptoed downstairs intending to make his own coffee, no percolator stuff but regular logger's coffee, let it just come to a boil and take it off and repeat that three times and your coffee was done, strong and hot and just the way he liked it. But no, there stood Taka in the kitchen in his shirt sleeves and Masako in her white cook's dress neat and appetizing looking as always, and even young William polishing shoes in the pantry. And to cap it all there was Grace, their pretty little daughter.

Vaughan forgot that he had meant to be so mouselike that Emmy would not waken. "Well, what're all you folks doing down here this hour?"

Taka and May sort of tittered and bobbed and said nothing, but William said from the pantry in a tone that was almost surly, "We all slept here last night."

Vaughan was slightly mystified, though genial. "That's nice." He glanced at the girl's round, serious face. "Little Gracie here, too?" Emmy might not like that; Emmy was always afraid that she was being imposed upon. "If you don't watch them, people impose on you," was the way she put it. And, "The more you do for people the more they expect of you." In spite of this watchfulness of hers people always seemed to be doing the very thing she guarded against.

May spoke up, smiling guilelessly. "Work to do—party tomorrow."

"Nuts!" snapped William in a tone startlingly unfilial for a

Japanese. Just like an American boy, Vaughan thought. But William is American, born here and all. Oh, what the hell, let 'em all sleep here if they want to, plenty of room.

"Breakfast ready in a minute," Taka barked.

Resigned, Vaughan said, "All right, all right. No hurry," and trudged heavily out of the room toward the front of the house. From the upper hall came Emmy's voice.

"Vaughan! Vaughan! What's the matter! Is anything wrong? Your mother!" Did he detect a note of hope in her voice?

"No. Nothing's wrong."

"Who's that talking? What's the matter?"

"Nothing, I tell you. I just couldn't sleep."

"Was that Taka and May?"

"Yes. They—uh—they're early. Now don't you get up this hour."

"Oh, really! One little change in their daily routine and they just can't cope. Those Japs are all alike."

"Nobody's all alike."

"What?"

"Nothing."

"I'll be right down."

Damn. From the kitchen came the rasp of the toaster as May pressed down the lever. Everything orderly and exact. Exact. Suddenly he made up his mind he wouldn't eat breakfast at home, he wouldn't call on his mother. He knew he was behaving like a little boy who runs away from home though he will be caught before he can reach the next corner.

He stuck his head in at the pantry door. "Will, bring my car around in front. Right away." A curious look came into the boy's eyes, but Vaughan was too busy with his own affairs to be conscious of it then. Later he took it out of his mind and recalled it and knew it had been a look of fright. "Why?" said William surprisingly.

"Why! Because I want it, that's why!" Sharply, for him. What had got into that kid, questioning him? What had got into every-body?

His leather jacket; might be wet and windy down at the wharf. Out of the house. Among the trees and above the hedge separating his land from Dike's he saw a smooth, dark head moving in Dike's garden. Must be Mike. The kid was like his grandpa, early up. Chip off the old block, like Pansy said. He went down the flagged path at a smart clip; he whipped through the hedge opening; Mike was probably going down to his workshop. Vaughan called, "Hi, young fella!" The head turned; the figure stood in full view now as Vaughan strode past the hedge. It wasn't Mike.

It was an astonishing figure at any hour. At seven or there-abouts on a Seattle hilltop in a sun-and-mist opalescent North-west morning against the background of Dike's big solid mansion it was an unbelievable figure.

A young-old man with a long, sallow face and pointed ears and slanting myopic eyes and a fine upper head on a weak lower jaw; and a too ample waistline. Tied about that waist by a thick cord was an astonishing dressing gown of silk patterned like a leopard's coat. About his throat was an orange scarf. On his feet leopard-skin slippers. He was smoking a pipe. Horn-rimmed glasses ac-cented the whole.

"Good morning!" said this apparition suavely.

"Who're you?"

The leopard padded toward him, light-footed. "You must be the fabulous Vaughan Melendy. My name's Garnett—Cliff Gar-nett." He held out his hand. "How do you do, sir." His handclasp was unexpectedly firm. It didn't fool Vaughan Melendy.

"You—uh—visiting here or——" This sounded foolish. Why, he had seen Lina last night, late. Dike, too. Hadn't said a word. And here was a fella got up like a fat Tarzan or something, run-ning around the yard at daybreak smoking a pipe. "Say, young fella, what you doing here, anyway?"

The leopard dressing gown smiled and Vaughan decided he

wasn't bad-looking. Odd, though. Then the man took his pipe
out of his mouth and laughed aloud. "It's wonderful to find someone exactly as you'd hoped they'd be. Lina always said you
were——"

"Oh. Friend of Lina's, eh?"

"I came in late last night. From Hollywood. I sent a wire but
it hasn't been delivered even yet. Imagine!"

The whole thing had a feeling of unreality. "Haven't you had
any sleep? Out this hour, haven't you been to bed?"

"I never sleep."

Well, my God!

Lina's voice broke in on this rather baffling conversation. Head
and shoulders out of her bedroom window she looked down on
them. Vaughan thought, my, she looks plain!

She said, "What *is* this!"

The leopard waved an arm to take in the garden. "I've looked
the place over, madam, and I would advise you to plant Aquilegia
chrysantha along this wall where you have moist soil well drained
and enriched with well-rotted manure or compost. Now beyond
and behind this, perhaps the Thalictrum glaucum, whose feathery
yellow plumes appear in June and July, blending well with
the——"

"Oh, shut up, Cliff. If you two must get up in the middle of
the night, do you have to hold your convention beneath my window?"

He said, "I urge you to return to your couch, Repulsive. You
definitely are not the Juliet type. Any rate, not at this hour."

Lina then pronounced him a middle-aged faun. Somewhat
mystified by all this, and vaguely uncomfortable, Vaughan sensed
that the atmosphere of seeming insult was perhaps the New York
form of affection. Like certain men who slapped one another on
the back and said, genially, hello, you old sonofabitch. Hurriedly
he now essayed a conventional gesture of farewell. "Well, I'm
going down—uh—— I've got some business to—— You going to
be visiting us for a while, Mr.—uh——"

Lina graciously explained from the window. "Cliff's going to help with plans for the new house."

The leopard waved an arm in the direction of Rainier. "Tell me, sir, isn't there some place in Seattle where one can escape the view?"

Lina paused in her withdrawal to consider this gravely. "We could plant trees to blot out a good deal of it, and just use vistas."

Vaughan stared from one to the other. They appeared to be serious. "Be going," he mumbled. The leopard instantly became stately again and said, "Good-by, sir, I hope I shall see you again, sir."

This form of address made Vaughan feel very ancient. To his own surprise he found himself turning abruptly and vanishing through the hedge gate. As he drove himself down the steep turns and twists of Queen Anne Hill he looked steadfastly straight ahead as he passed Pansy's house. The hell with all of them, he thought. What did she mean, the new house? Dike wouldn't be such a damn fool build time like this with material sky high and labor, too. Sir. Do you think, sir. Well, you're not so goddamn young yourself, sir, if you'll just take a look at yourself in the face some time, sir, especially in that bathrobe at this hour the morning, sir. Having given vent to a few splenetic thoughts and a few mild oaths thus, Vaughan Melendy felt relieved and vaguely elated as always when he was bound for the wharf. Like to get on a tough halibut boat and up to Alaska and not see civilization for a month or more. Civilization! If this was it. Well, no use thinking about Alaska fishing this time of year. A three-masted sailing schooner, that would be the thing, up to Bering Sea for the cod, and gone five months. He guided his car now through the quiet early-morning streets of Seattle down toward the fishing-fleet harbor at Fifteenth and Thurman on Salmon Bay. A sailing schooner —that was the real feeling of freedom and adventure. No greasy engine to nurse and pamper like a spoiled baby. Sails and planks. That was all. Nothing between you and the ocean bottom but your wits and some pieces of canvas and some wooden planks and God.

The Norwegian and Swede fishermen had been complaining the last couple of years. They said you could hear the Diesel engines, the fast, powerful Diesel engines, going throb-throb-throb all over Alaskan waters and Bering Sea; the Japs were pirating the American fishing waters, the three-masted schooners lumbering along were no match for them. They were so fast and sly you couldn't even get a glimpse of them, but you could hear the engines, they sounded like the faint far-off roll of gun explosions. But no one paid any attention to this except the Swedish and Norwegian fishermen, complaining. Oh. well, Vaughan thought, enough for everybody, probably. Still, no sense in making a present of our waters to those Japs, and if they got to sending out a real big fleet of those fast little Diesel-engined fishing boats, why, they could just about take the whole salmon and cod and halibut industry right away from us. He remembered that they had complained of this up at the canneries last year and even the year before. Might be a good idea to look into it. He must remember to take it up with Dave Dreen tomorrow noon at Emmy's shindig.

Across Ballard Bridge and down the roughish road, past the long sheds, the shacks, the shanty lunchroom. And there he was, and there they were, mending the great nets spread on the weather-worn wharf, calking their boats, scraping the oil-soaked decks, painting. Masts and spars and funnels, a forest of them. And over all the seagulls wheeling and swooping. Vaughan Melendy's nostrils were pricked by the tang of water and tar and fish and strong tobacco. This was what he loved. This was good. He loved the hoarse howl of the horns on the big ships when he was snug in bed at night high on Queen Anne Hill, but this was better; this was peace and companionship and silence if you wanted it and talk if you felt inclined, and quiet men with strong blue eyes. And no women. And no fat fauns to call you sir.

"Hiyah, Lindstrom!"

"Hello, Vaughan!"

"How's she making out, Wenn?"

"Well, weather keeps on mild like this I'm going to get her grubbed up take her out."

"Better not. Got a crew?"

"Good men is scarce; looks like I got to get me some native boys. Nick Karluk up to Kodiak he says he can maybe fix me up, but that's too far and too late."

And there were the two oldest codfish schooners with their misleadingly sissy names, *Wauwoma* and *Azalea,* more than fifty years old, marred and battered by the Bering Sea. Scrape and stone as they might, they never could clean those decks, eaten with more than a half century of fish catch and salt. Down in the black hold were their bunks; they slept row on row, piled one atop the other, like the fish they caught. Plenty of air above decks; they wanted none of it; they breathed in the close smell of human bodies, fish, wood soaked with spit, tobacco, kerosene, boots slimed with bilge. Not unless you burned the ship and sank her would those smells leave that hulk.

The *Yakutat* of Ketchikan. The *Norby* of Seattle. The *Nordenskjold*. Big-boned Swedes and Norwegians, the men sat at the dock's edge knotting hooks into the lines. They or their fathers had followed the lumber and the fish to this northwest land of fish and lumber. The sea or the forest, these they knew best. Why hadn't he been down here at Fisherman's Wharf these past few months? And as for the big shipping docks, why, you might as well be living over at Snoqualmie with the ranchers, all you ever saw of real ships these days. Perhaps that was what was wrong with him. He missed the ships.

Now Vaughan sensed a mood of unrest and dissatisfaction. These men were younger than he. Ten years—fifteen years from now their sons would not go out with the cod schooners and the stubby little halibut boats. He had often talked with them about this.

"My boy he's going to the university, he's studying to be an engineer." Or a lawyer. A doctor. He's in the contracting business. Fruit ranch in the Okanagan.

He wasn't having as good a time as he had expected to have. He wasn't having a good time at all. The younger men were silent or surly. They worked at the nets and the lines almost without glancing up as he greeted them. Might as well have his lunch at the shanty and go home. Or to the office. Or drop in at the club. But he didn't want to do any of those things. This was what he wanted, but it had turned sour. The boats were here, the men, the water, the nets, the smell, the sounds, the clean air, even the pale sun through the mist. A vital thing was lacking.

Niels Soderholm sat mending nets on the dock alongside his boat the *Nordisk*. The net looked white and clean as a bride's veil against the weathered gray of the wharf. Niels's gnarled brown fingers were like agile roots. Sixty if he was a day, but he didn't look it, Vaughan reflected. He didn't look any age; he was like a great rock on which sun and wind and water had played with only a surface effect, a painter's brush. Alvar, his son, was on the boat deck, he was busy with hammer and nails and boards, a good-looking fellow with a neat mustache, but he was scowling as he worked; he returned Vaughan's greeting with a monosyllable.

"You're getting in shape early, Niels."

"We're going out early."

"That so? Nielson tells me he's having quite a time getting his crews for my boats. He's fixing to start early, too, if he can make it. Groceries and supplies for the natives, first. Can't let them starve up there. Whole villages up there depending on us."

Niels's hands wove and knotted deftly. Alvar's hammering did not pause. Vaughan felt vaguely uncomfortable. Niels spoke slowly. "Is lots of Japs up there now stealing our fish; some say they are even living on the islands."

"Well, now, Niels, they'd have pretty poor pickings living up there, nothing grows, and the fogs coming down so you can't see your hand in front of your face most of the time. What would they want to go to work and live up there for?"

"Fish—or something. We can't keep up with 'em or get near 'em, even. They got Diesels."

Suddenly Alvar ceased his hammering; he came to the boat's side and leaned over. "I ain't going to piddle round with no goddamn halibut and salmon, anyway. And stinkin' little sardines in August. Not me any more. Sharks, that's what I'm going for, now on."

Vaughan stared. "What d'you mean—sharks!"

"Sharks is what I mean. Liver, shark's liver. They're paying thousands of dollars for a few pounds of it; they make vitamins out of it. Ostergren cleaned up five thousand last season while we was breaking our backs trying to get what the Japs left over for us."

The man's face was grim and determined. Vaughan turned from it to the father's impassive countenance. "What you got to say to that, Niels?"

"I do like the crowd does. We run on shares. If the Japs is undercutting and taking the cream of the catch, why, I do like the crowd does. They say it's shark's liver it's shark's liver. Vitamins out of shark's liver." He shook his head wonderingly.

To his own astonishment Vaughan heard himself shouting in a tone of temper: "What the hell you mending nets for, then? You going to catch sharks in a halibut net?"

"I ain't going to pass by a haul of halibut if we run into 'em."

Alvar at the boatside brandished his hammer for emphasis. "My boy's going on eighteen; he's going to get him a college education, not like me. And for that I got to have money. Same as you."

What had got into these fellows? Still, Vaughan didn't want to quarrel with them; he'd known Niels for thirty years and more, he'd known Alvar from a lad. "Well, that's fair enough, Al. Only

I hope we won't get dragged into this war in Europe before he can make it."

"We ain't going to get mixed up in no German war for the British. Not me. I was too young the last war and Eric he's too young, too, he's seventeen going on eighteen; you don't see me let him into any war against the Germans or anybody."

He went back to his hammering. Above the sound Vaughan yelled, "You'd fight for your country, wouldn't you?"

"Germany"—bang!—"ain't"—bang!—"nowheres"—bang!— "near this country!" Bang!

Vaughan turned and walked away; the men here and there on the boats or the wharf spoke to him or hailed him and he returned their greeting, but the day had no savor. He looked in at the wharfside lunchroom; there was a smell of frying onions to make your mouth water, but the place looked empty, he saw no one he knew; there was a new girl, a waitress instead of Joe, and she looked frowzy, her hair was down on her shoulders like the girls in the movies, that was a fine way for a girl to fix her hair around food and cooking and the lunch counter all day, and her face was painted up like an Indian's.

He clambered into his car; his body felt heavy; he was conscious of a feeling of oppression, of some evil thing surrounding him, unseen. He had been up in the Aleutians in the fogs; he had experienced the blind groping in which there was always danger lurking ahead, but you were powerless against it, it was in the air, you could not see it until it struck and then it was too late. Today, he thought, was like that.

15

MADAM EXACT MELENDY was the first to arrive. Emmy had been
afraid of that. "There she comes! There's your mother. They're
getting into the Mac, your mother and that girl. And it's hardly
half-past eleven. Lunch—I mean brunch—isn't till twelve or
after."

The faded pink-and-white face was tight-lipped as Emmy
stared through the great plate-glass window. She could plainly
see Exact being helped into the Mac by Reggie. It was quite a
process. The girl's bright head bobbed this way and that as she
tucked in the voluminous skirts of her ancient charge, threw a rug
over her knees, adjusted her collar. "My land!" Emmy snapped,
"two minutes down the hill in the Mac, you'd think she was going
to Alaska in a dog sledge."

Vaughan looked up from the Sunday paper. "Ma's age, it's
kind of wonderful she can go anywhere, let alone dressed to the
nines out to a noon lunch and coasting downhill to get there."

Now Reggie stepped into the little carriage; she adjusted the
lever; smoothly they sailed down the grade, the old lady sitting
very straight, her head tied round with a warm wool scarf. On
her face was a look of delighted expectancy. At the bottom of the
incline Reggie gathered up rugs, shawls, scarfs, robes. Vaughan

had thrown down his paper and striding out through the garden was there as the Mac came to a standstill.

Dutifully, like a small boy, he kissed his mother. He patted Reggie's fresh fair cheek. "You're early, Ma. I was going to come up and fetch you a little before twelve."

The matriarchal figure strode with her son, step for step, toward the house; she had refused his helping arm, indeed had pushed it aside vigorously. "Saw Emmy gawping out of the window, I thought everything must be ready and getting cold."

She planted her great feet firmly as she walked; the hooded head was held high. She wore a venerable mink cape, yellow with age, whose edge was trimmed with tiny mink tails, and her hands were thrust into a mink muff similarly festooned. It had the look of an ancient tribal garment.

"Dave Dreen come?"

"Not yet, Ma. He'll be along any minute now."

"Emmy's possessed to give parties all the while. Her ma was the same way before her. Abbie wasn't happy unless she had a dozen people eating her out of house and home."

"Well, Dike's birthday. Just the family. And Dave. Emmy really hasn't had the family since Dike and Lina got home. And Mike being here, too, why——"

He thought to himself, as he had a thousand thousand times in his long life, here I go explaining and apologizing to her for something that's none of her business.

"And Reggie here. That makes nine," trumpeted the old lady triumphantly. "Pansy, I suppose."

"Why, yes. Pansy and Reggie and Dave, Dike—Lina—oh, there's a fellow visiting Lina, that makes ten—my God, what difference does it make—counting!"

"What fella?" They were in the front hall. Reggie was unwinding her charge, who now emerged a butterfly from her cocoon. Beneath the woolen head scarf was her second-best lace cap; the removal of the mink cape revealed slate-gray satin, no less, and amethysts. "Whee!" exclaimed Vaughan. "That ought to fetch Dave Dreen."

Emmy came forward, her face set in a smile of greeting. "Good morning, Mother Melendy." This was a form of address that Exact loathed. She ignored it.

"What fella?" she persisted. She surveyed herself in the hall mirror; she adjusted a lace ruffle; she glanced at Reggie; the girl smiled and nodded. Perfection. "What fella?"

"I don't know. From New York. Hollywood. He's out in Hollywood, pictures. Garnett his name is. Cliff Garnett."

Reggie turned quickly, her face brilliant with interest. "Cliff Garnett! The playwright?"

"That's right. Lina's been in a couple of his——"

"But he's very good! He's wonderful. Not profound, but wonderful."

"I'll say he ain't profound," Vaughan agreed, recalling the leopard dressing gown.

Reggie flushed a little. "Perhaps that's not the word. I meant, not serious, but sharp and amusing and sly, too. And a little bitter. I saw one of his plays in New York—Black Widow. And I've read them all. And at school, of course, we——"

Out of nowhere Vaughan recalled a phrase that young Mike had used when Lina had been playing in a Garnett play. Two years ago. What was it Mike had said? Oh yes. "Mike says he's a road-company Noel Coward."

"Well, what are we all standing around here for?" Emmy said. "Talking about nothing. Here, Mother Melendy. Sit here."

They had moved into the big bright living room with its vast window framing the View, its gleaming mahogany, its glistening ornaments, its rich curtains, fold on fold.

"Sit where I please," retorted Madam Melendy, moving toward a straight-backed chair whose uncompromising lines were exactly the opposite of the great overstuffed armchair which Emmy had indicated.

"Now, Ma!" Vaughan remonstrated mildly.

Emmy tossed her head, the blue eyes snapping behind the glittering pince-nez. "Excuse me," she said with elaborate politeness. "I've got to see to something in the—— I don't know what's got into Taka and May today, you'd think they'd never served company——" Her voice trailed and was lost as she disappeared kitchenward.

"Emmy's a kitchen-fidget. Those Japs don't know how to get a company meal by this time I'd fire 'em."

Reggie's lovely low voice flowed into this rasping scene. "Would you like me to turn on the radio, Madam Melendy? Perhaps there's some news."

"Haven't read the news in the newspaper yet. I don't want to hear the news till I've read what's in the Sunday-morning paper. That's what comes of going to dinners, middle of the day. Upsets your whole morning."

Vaughan gathered up the sheets that lay beside his chair. "I'll read you the first-page news, Ma."

"No. You mumble. Reggie, you read it before the others get here. The front page, anyway."

The girl crossed the room; she smiled at Vaughan as she stooped beside his chair. "You're a dear child, Reggie," he said. "A good child."

"Yes, she is," boomed Madam Melendy, the chary of praise. "You've got to admit she's a good child."

The girl laughed; she looked from one to the other, the old man, the ancient woman. "Do I seem a child to you?"

"Seem!" echoed Exact, her voice sounding through the endless corridors that separated her from this girl by almost three quarters of a century.

Reggie smoothed the crumpled first page, she seated herself in a chair by the window near Madam. "I suppose I am young. I forget." She looked fondly at the bizarre figure of the nonagenarian in her laces and satins and jewels.

The keen eyes narrowed; they seemed to search the girl's face. "You look younger today than ever. Your face. You've got a candle lighted behind your face."

"Well, Ma!" Vaughan shouted. "You're getting real poetic in your old age."

"I'll thank you not to refer to me as old."

Reggie retired suddenly behind the newspaper, but a moment later her voice, clear and distinct as Exact Melendy liked it, began its brief recital of the Sunday-morning news.

"King Leopold of the Belgians marries Mademoiselle Mary Leila Baels, daughter of a former Belgian Cabinet Minister."

"Poor fella," observed Madam. "What a life he's had! That German Kaiser ought to be hung." Then a startled look came into her eyes. "I forget. It isn't the Kaiser this time, is it? This is another war. It's that Hitler."

Vaughan Melendy sat with his eyes shut, only half listening. He had read the paper, he wished Dave Dreen would come, lots of things he wanted to talk to Dave about. Dave had a head on his shoulders all right; funny thing Dave hadn't married after his wife died. Sometimes he acted as if he was kind of sweet on Pansy. Shucks, Dave must be old as I am that's ridiculous but is it I'd marry Pansy tomorrow if heh wait a minute that's no way to talk think about your own . . .

". . . Russians advance thrust to coast beyond Taganrog. . . . The Australian Government has completed preparations in concert with Britain, the United States, and the Netherland Indies. . . . British forestalling measures of great strategic importance are already under way. The official view is that Japan is trying to ascertain how far she can go without provoking war. . . . Navy is superior to any, Knox says . . . has at this time no superior, Secretary Knox stated tonight in rendering the annual . . . I am proud to report that the American people may feel confident . . . Strategic gateway at the Burma Road and the Malay Peninsula. . . ."

"Fiddlesticks!" shouted Madam Melendy. "Nothing in the paper! Burma! Netherland Indies and stuff and nonsense! I don't even know where they are."

Reggie began to gather the loose sheets tidily. Vaughan opened his eyes. "Wonder where the folks are."

"What's on the radio?" the old lady trumpeted. "Besides all this Australia and outlandish places and war war war! Sick of it!"

Reggie picked up the amusement sheet. "Uh—well—there's the New York Philharmonic, Artur Rodzinzki conducting—oh, and Rubinstein playing the Shostakovitch First—no, that isn't until twelve, it's not quite—and anyway you probably wouldn't care for——"

"There's Dave," Vaughan interrupted, and strode to the front hall. You heard the two exchanging overhearty greetings of affectionate insult. Well, you old soandso! You old buzzard! You didn't show up last week you been in jail again I suppose why don't you try living honest! Ha ha! Madam Melendy preened her finery, spread her skirts; she sat waiting like a queen who is prepared for audience.

Now, entering the big bright room, Dave Dreen said, "Well, well!" He walked over to Exact; he took her withered hand in his. "Ouch!" screeched Exact, and slapped his hand. "Well, well, young lady! And how's my girl? Doggone it, you look younger every time I see you! When you going to marry me, Madam? Look at her! Look at those eyes!"

Madam Melendy was nursing her crushed hand and pouting, but incredibly it was plain that some portion of this banter was penetrating the region of belief.

"Can't say the same of you," retorted this beldame. "My land, you've hardly got a hair on your head. Somebody must have snatched you bald-headed; some girl you were making up to."

Dave Dreen roared at this as at an exquisitely witty sally; he slapped his thigh and wagged his head in admiration and said what a girl what a heartbreaker you don't care how you treat your beaux, but his pale blue eyes had wandered to Reggie, young and slim and lovely. "And who is this young lady?"

Vaughan united them with a wave of his hand. "Reggie, meet Dave Dreen. This is Reggie."

"Hohoho, I must say you don't look much like a boy. No sir!" Reggie instantly made up her mind that she didn't like him. "I'm Regina Dresden." Then decided that she had sounded stuffy and ridiculous.

"That's more like it. A pretty name for a pretty——" But Emmy, flushed of face, came rushing through the dining room; a ravishing scent of cookery was wafted with her; the door between dining room and pantry whished and whooshed behind her.

"Dave! Nobody told me you were——"

"Well, well, this is mighty nice of you, Emmy. Having an old beau to dinner like this. Mighty nice!"

The political boss. That was it, Reggie decided. He looked exactly like those cartoons of the political boss, except for the almost-bald head. The head was egg-shaped, the upper head rounded and tapering down to a grim chin. His skin was eggshell, too; his eyes a very pale blue and cold, cold; the hands stubby and hairy; the nails spatulate and very clean and white. A gold nugget hung from his fine watch chain. That meant he, too, was a sourdough. She tried to imagine that bloodless face, those secret eyes in the rough-and-tumble of the Klondike as she had learned of it from Pansy and from Vaughan.

But old Exact was sulking now; she felt neglected; she wanted attention. "Cold. It's real cold in here. Reggie, where's my fur scarf?"

"Oh, we didn't bring it. I asked you if you didn't think we should, remember? And you said——"

"I didn't hear you. Of course I need it. Emmy's house is always like an icebox." Then talk and concern concentrated on her. I can give you a wrap, Mother Melendy. . . . Don't want your wrap.

. . . Start a fire in the fireplace, eh, Emmy? . . . Vaughan, you know I hate all that smoke and dust in my living room. . . . I'll get it, Madam Melendy; I'll just run up the hill; I'll only be a minute.

Reggie was off; you saw her golden head flashing among the firs and madroñas as she ran lightly up the hill toward Exact's house.

Lina, Dike, Garnett entering all in a rush and flurry of greeting now. Birthday congratulations for Dike, trite phrases, many-happy-returns-of-the-day. Dave Dreen said well well Dike you're getting to be quite a big boy now pretty soon you'll be a help to your folks ha ha. Emmy, presenting him with some horrible haberdashery, essayed to sing Happy Birthday to You, but gave it up on the high note. Lina looked young and slim in slacks and jersey and great incongruous blobs of very precious jewelry.

"Who's that?" trumpeted old Madam Melendy suddenly, pointing a long, bony finger. "Who's that young fella in the purple pants?"

Cliff Garnett was presented; he was very continental about it for a native of Kansas; he bowed low, he even gave the effect of clicking his heels in those soft brown doeskin shoes. He murmured something appropriate. "What say?" demanded Exact. Aghast at the awful necessity of repeating an empty phrase, Garnett retreated a step. Dike, the gentle, the charming, came to his rescue.

"Mr. Garnett writes plays, Madam. He's very famous. Lina has been in his plays, you know. He's visiting Lina and me. From New York."

"What's the matter with his neck? Got a sore throat?" Cliff Garnett's throat was swathed in a brilliant rose-and-green silk scarf this morning; here and there was just a fleck of purple in it to blend with the Hollywood slacks. Dike endeavored to explain Hollywood fashions sotto voce but old Exact, whose hearing was miraculously keen, affected not to hear.

Garnett, taking refuge with the impish Lina, who was, he knew, already rehearsing this scene in her mind for Hollywood and New York dinner parties, scarcely took the trouble to lower his voice as he vented his annoyance.

"What the hell kind of relic of the Paleozoic Age is this family of yours? My God, everybody in it is an octogenarian at least— including you. Aren't there any young people in your family? I hate old people."

"Sh! They'll hear you."

"Good!"

"You'll be old yourself someday."

"I know it. That's why I hate 'em." He suddenly stared fixedly at the doorway. "There's another one. Good God, what's she made up for?"

Pansy. Pansy in a magnificent blue fox coat and long earrings and dated Paris frock. There was unusual color in her cheeks glowing through the badly applied rouge. Her eyes were an amazing blue above the soft, rich pelts. "I walked up." She was laughing a little and her breath came rather fast. "I'm late a-purpose because I wanted to show off my new blue fox."

Lina cried, "Pansy, you rat! Where did you get that heavenly coat?"

"Mike Carney sent me the skins from Kodiak. He trapped 'em up on the Islands."

"Oh!" Lina quavered in a dying voice. "I never saw such color. And soft! You could eat them with a spoon. Do you suppose he'd send me some? Dike!"

"My land, child!" Pansy said. "If you feel like that about it, I'll give you this one."

"Oh no, you don't," Vaughan shouted from across the room where he appeared to be deep in conversation with Dave Dreen. "Dike, make your wife behave herself; taking the coat right off a poor girl's back."

Emmy came forward. "Now they've all seen it, Pansy, let me take it hang it up for you. It's real pretty, but a little young for people our age, isn't it?"

Pansy laughed her comfortable laugh. "I'm so old now I can start to dress young again, pinks and blues and so on. It's wonderful." She came up to Dike now; it was as if she had been postponing this moment with her chatter and laughter and preening. She was still smiling, but her eyes as she looked up at him were starry, enormous. Her cheeks took on a deeper flush; the color flooded up to her brow and down to her throat. "Seeing it's your birthday, maybe an old lady could beg a kiss." He bent to kiss her. Her hand came up to his head with an involuntary movement and rested there a moment. "God bless you and keep you, Klondike, this day and every day."

"Heh!" yelled Dave Dreen. "Whyn't you pick on somebody your own age, Pansy?"

"I don't want my heart broken," said Pansy.

"Say, that's funny, you called him Klondike. Haven't heard him called Klondike since——" He stopped, aghast.

"It's his name," she replied quietly. "Seeing you're his godfather you ought to know."

Taka appeared with a tray of sherry glasses and with canapés so chromatic that the eye rejected their probability. "How revolting," said Cliff Garnett. "Could I have some whisky and water?"

Dave Dreen seemed to welcome this. "Well, well, that's an idea, Mr.—uh—— If you don't mind, Emmy, my liver doesn't handle sherry, but a little whisky, a spot of whisky, as the English say——"

Exact had her rye. Lina took nothing. The amber sherry smoldered in neglect. Glasses in hand, the company turned toward Dike.

"Mike. Where's Mike?" Vaughan demanded.

"That's so," Dave Dreen shouted heartily, as though he had thought of it. "Where's that fine young son of yours, Dike? Don't tell me he isn't going to be here to drink his father's health!"

Young voices in the hall, laughter, quick footsteps. "On cue," said Cliff Garnett out of the corner of his mouth, to Lina.

The two young people came into the room. Hatless, easy, slender, graceful. There was about them a vitality deeper than mere energy. The men and women in the room—the men and women of forty, fifty, sixty, seventy, ninety—looked at these two so young, so alive. They could not have put into words the thing they felt. They did not even formulate in their minds the reaction that now came to them as they looked. The difference lay not only in the normal span of years; it was nothing physical—the healthy blue-white of the eyeball, the way the hair sprang in a strong line from the brow, the glow and resilience of the skin, the effortless grace with which they walked or stood. It was not alone that this was another generation. It was a new era, a new breed that had leaped a half century of time and had left the rest of the world behind, breathless and panting.

Mike came to his father. "Sorry to be late, Dad, on your birthday." He was in grease-stained slacks and a sweater.

"Well, really, Mike!" Lina exclaimed.

Emmy was outraged. The flush of the harried hostess deepened to red. "Michael Melendy, if I didn't know that dinner—brunch —was ready this minute I'd send you home to put on decent clothes. Your own father's birthday and late and looking like a tramp."

"Sorry, Grandma." He greeted his father; he kissed his great-grandmother's parchment cheek; he came toward his mother, his eyebrow cocked at sight of the bizarre figure standing beside her.

Lina stood on tiptoe to kiss him. "Remember me, Mike? I'm your mother."

"I knew we must have met somewhere."

"I wasn't sure. I haven't seen you since heaven knows—you weren't home to dinner last night. Look, Cliff, you've met my son Mike, of course, in New York. Mike, you know Cliff Garnett——"

"Of course," Mike said. "Howdy do, sir." Vaughan across the

room looked suddenly pleased. "Is this your first time in Seattle, sir?" Vaughan looked radiant.

"That'll show him," Vaughan muttered to no one in particular. "Sir."

Very erect and important in her straight-backed chair, as though sitting for a portrait, Madam Melendy, having been given the fur shoulder cape, now refused it. She reached into her bag, took out her pipe and tobacco and tamped it neatly. Stone-gray satin, amethyst jewels, lace cap, ivory parchment face, the effect was incredibly rowdy. Cliff Garnett, the worldly, the traveled, was temporarily startled out of his *savoir-faire*. The myopic eyes bulged still more prominently behind the thick lenses.

"Don't look now," he hissed. "But if you see what I see, your revered grandma-in-law is smoking a pipe."

Lina shrugged. "Pay no attention. She just does it to show off."

"Blunch," said Taka, bowing and smiling. And immediately vanished.

They moved toward the dining room. "What's wrong, Mike?" Dike said under cover of the chatter.

"Will Nakaisuki. When I got down to the airfield this morning he'd been down to the hangar. Tried to take my ship out. He darn near got away with it."

"What for?"

"I don't know. He's never done that before. Of course he's been up with me a lot, and I've let him handle her, but he never tried to——"

"——and you here, Birthday Boy, in the place of honor!" Emmy was gurgling nervously. "Lina—no, you can't sit there, that's next to your husband—you sit here next to Mr.—uh—— That's right —and Dave on the other side, and Pansy, you——"

One by one, all of them except Reggie who stood quietly by, ignored by the hostess. Mike came to her; he stood beside her.

"Where's Reggie?" cried old Exact. "Reggie sits next to me." The girl came forward.

"And I sit next to Reggie," said Mike.

"Oh no, Mike, you are to sit next to me and then Madam and——"

"That's right, boy!" shouted Dreen. "Grab yourself a pretty girl. No thrill sitting next to Grammaw—no offense, Emmy."

Garnett took a vicious bite of sweet green Northwest celery. "Damn!" he muttered, crunching. "This fiesta'll go on for hours. I wanted to hear the Philharmonic!"

"You're behaving like a spoiled brat!" Lina said, under her breath. Then, aloud, "What do you all say to some music with lunch? The Symphony's on from New York."

"I'll do it," Dike said, and left the table. The music came to them from the living room as he returned to his chair.

"I like something livelier," Exact objected.

Reggie said soothingly, "Later, when we go home, we'll turn on something gay."

Taka was scurrying around the table with incredible celerity. "What do you think!" Emmy whispered to Pansy, her tone desperate. "Young Will was to help serve and he never showed up. They're all alike. Ten people to serve. And only Taka!"

"It's all right, Emmy. Everything's just lovely."

Across the table Dave Dreen addressed Garnett. "What's your line of business, young man?"

Dike answered before Garnett's resentful glare could take verbal form. "Mr. Garnett's a playwright, Dave. You've seen his plays in New York and in the movies."

"We've got some fine talent right here in Washington, let me tell you. There's the Penthouse Theater and the Showboat Theater right here in Seattle; you don't want to miss those while you're here, Mr.—uh——"

"I loathe the amateur theater," snarled Cliff.

Vaughan stepped in mildly. "Dike and Lina are thinking of building out Highlands way, Dave."

"What say?" Exact shouted. "Build what? What's wrong with your house?"

Lina turned her head toward the old lady, her air one of exaggerated deference. "I don't like it," she said very distinctly.

Emmy raised her voice as always when talking to Exact. "Lina doesn't like the neighborhood either, Mother Melendy."

"You young folks!" Dave Dreen exclaimed. "Restless as cooties."

Dike spoke up quietly. "Thanks for calling us young, Dave."

"What beats me," Vaughan said, "is the way people turn their backs on the pretty places and go to work and live on the railroad tracks or in the slums or wherever it's uncomfortable. Highlands. The trains run right there below you. Same with New York! Park Avenue's all the go, no air or green and the trains running day and night just beneath the street; you can feel the buildings shake and the crockery rattle and hear the engine clanging. Honest to God, I just stand there, laugh. Or else they go live over by the East River. It would've been a real pretty spot only they thought of that, so they put up a prison would make you blue just to look at it, and coalyards and gas tanks and so on every window you look out of."

"Vaughan darling," Lina interrupted, "dear Papa-in-law, I love you most when you go into your Western routine." She turned toward Cliff Garnett with that eager, birdlike manner which was one of her charm tricks. "You know, Cliff, these Westerners are the most terrific snobs. They're so afraid that the tradition they've built up will be broken."

Cliff Garnett regarded her sourly. "I suppose now I say what tradition?"

"Thanks. The big, homey, slow-talkin,' hard-hittin' rough Western stuff. And carefully illiterate. Ain't and quaint and all that. Pop's an educated guy, ain't you, Pop? Went to Washington U and everything, and probably a Phi Beta Kappa, but he wouldn't exchange that gold nugget on the watch chain for any eddicated——"

"Oh, shut up, Lina," said Cliff Garnett surprisingly. "I knew you when you came out of the Michigan woods and your name was Lena Porter spelled with an *e,* and your *r*s sounded like hail on a tin roof."

But Lina Port was not disturbed at the shout that went up. "Dear Cliff," she said. "My perfect gentil knight!"

"It isn't perfect; it's parfit, while you're quoting. And I'll bet you never read a line of Chaucer in your life."

Very low Mike said to Reggie beside him, "I'd like to take a sock at that guy. Though Mother certainly asked for that one."

The girl said, "Everyone at this table seems unhappy."

"Not us."

"Not us."

"I wonder how they'd all look if I just reached over and kissed you hard for about a minute."

"Michael!"

"It's worth trying. I'll bet on Gramp and Pansy and Madam. Of course Grandma and Lina would pass out. I'm not sure about Dad. I wonder who first thought of family dinners. One of the Borgias, I'll bet."

". . . young folks today," Dave Dreen was saying, very loud. "They haven't got the stamina. That's what they lack—stamina. Look at the old settlers. Look at Madam Melendy here. Her parents crossed this great continent in a covered wagon enduring hardship and danger . . ."

Young Mike said, "They take their covered wagons up in the air these days. Some very good covered-wagons boys over in Europe at the moment."

"Planes!" scoffed Dreen. "Let me tell you the Dennys and the Melendys and the Yeslers and the Borens and the Mercers——"

"Mama was a Mercer Girl," Emmy said to Cliff Garnett, aside, hastily.

"A what?" he demanded, bewildered.

Lina nudged him viciously. "Skip it."

"Pooh!" said Pansy, very loud.

Startled, Dave Dreen paused. "How's that?"

"I said pooh! Those folks had a tough time of it, and they had a lot of courage, I'll say that for 'em. But there's just as good young folks today."

Old Madam Melendy tapped with her fork on the table as she had seen many a Madam Chairman tap for order in her public-platform appearances. "Jotham could have bought the corner of Fifth and Pine for twenty silver dollars when I was a bride. He said it was too far up; I said to him, I said, 'Jotham Melendy mark my words the day will come when you'll find you're mistaken smart as you are——' "

"You're a smart girl, Ma," Vaughan said, and nodded and smiled at her. "We all make our mistakes, but I bet you never made a mistake in your life."

They were not listening, Reggie and Mike. The table talk eddied about them.

"I'd like to take you skiing up on Rainier, darling. Would you like that?"

"Ah yes, but you forget——"

"I'll teach you. You'll be good. Look, how'd you like to hop over to Victoria? We'll fly. It takes no time. You'd love it. It's as British as *Punch;* you wouldn't believe that just a little hop from Seattle a place could be so other-world. You ride around in a. horse cab and the driver keeps pointing with his whip and saying, 'It's a bit of Old England,' and by gosh it is! The girls wear black cotton stockings and the men carry rolled umbrellas and everybody drops everything for tea at five. And Hindus in turbans and robes riding around on bicycles. . . . Do you suppose this lunch will ever end——"

Now the oldsters were, surprisingly enough, on the subject of Alaska. The Melendys were not given to talking about Alaska. Vaughan was holding forth. "Much as your life's worth nowadays to be caught with a ten-dollar gold piece in your pocket. Put you in jail for it, by God! Up in the Klondike we handled gold like it was lard."

To her own surprise Pansy, who avoided Alaska as a topic of general conversation, found herself saying, "Seems kind of ridiculous to me now, everybody up there trudging and sliding around in the mud and ice and snow and water, icicles at the end of their noses, miserable with the terrible cold or the terrible heat, going through all manner of hardship for some lumps of metal out of the ground. All that, just for gold."

"And blue fox coats, don't forget," Lina said.

"Yeh, when did this come on, Pansy?" Dave Dreen said. "You being so snooty about Alaska gold."

Pansy looked at Mike; she hesitated a moment as though trying to remember something. "I guess it was Mike. I guess I must've heard young Mike there say something like that, and I got to believing I'd thought of it myself."

Cliff Garnett's eyes gleamed maliciously behind his thick spectacles. "They've put it all cozily back into the ground at Fort Knox, so *that's* all right; you needn't fret."

It was strange that these older people should be quoting one among them so young. For Mike and Reggie the talk went unnoticed, like the music that flowed out to them from the living room.

"Mike says they're going to drive through here on the way to Alaska or fly up by the hundreds of thousands."

Now the boy became conscious of his name repeated, and he turned from the girl to these others as though coming out of a dream. "Uh—what?"

"Yep," Vaughan was saying. "Alaska certainly doesn't seem as far away as it did years ago."

Exact Melendy had been eating her dinner with enormous relish. In a group such as this she was likely to fall silent. Perhaps the rapid give and take of mixed conversation wearied her.

Though seated among them, she seemed withdrawn as though she were already separate from their world.

"I'd like to go to Alaska," she now said suddenly. "I'd like to go up in one of Mike's airplanes to Alaska."

Through the laugh that went up Mike said solemnly, "And I'm the boy who'll take you, Toots."

"That'll be nice, Michael," the old lady said placidly. "When?"

Dike said, "I'm afraid you'll have to wait awhile for that, Grandma."

That quizzical eyebrow went up as Mike refuted this, his tone quite serious. "Oh, I don't know about that. People are going to stop off in Seattle on their way to that week end in Moscow. Before you're a hundred years old, Madam, Mother's going to say, 'We've got a little summer cottage on the Black Sea; we like to spend August up there.'"

Eagerly the old lady said, "Do you think I'll live to be a hundred, Mike?"

"Sure. Surest thing you know, Madam. And Dad'll go up to Alaska for the fishing on Saturday and be back at the office Monday morning. This town will be as lousy with tourists as New York."

"Yeah!" Dave Dreen scoffed. "And I suppose they'll like the Alaska climate, eh?"

Dike said, "Lina and I went up to the Scandinavian countries in—let's see—Thirty-four, wasn't it, Lina? Norway and Sweden and Denmark. Alaska—a big stretch of it, anyway—is about the same climate, isn't it? We just haven't had the sense to . . ."

"You folks just aren't eating anything!" Emmy complained. "Talk a lot and don't eat. Dave, won't you have another . . ."

". . . certain set a wonderful table, Emmy. Home meal like this is a treat for a lonely widower."

"Oh, I guess you're not so lonely, Dave."

"How about you, Pansy? I hear bachelor girls like you live on crackers and tea."

"Not me. I cook myself a good square meal every day of my life; keep my strength up. A lot of women won't cook for themselves; you can tell women living alone their skin is kind of pithy and their eyes haven't got any snap and their mouths look like they hadn't any spit in 'em. Tea and crackers, like you said, and sardines and maybe a can of those rubbery peaches. Not me. Stews and good liver and onions and hot biscuits and green vegetables and pig's knuckles with sauerkraut and brown Betty pudding with homemade grape jell———"

"Heh, stop! Stop! I give in, Pansy. My gosh, when you going to invite me to dinner?"

Emmy's complaints and instructions to Taka ran like a fretful obbligato through the talk. "Look, Mr. Dike's water glass is empty. . . . Pass the vegetables again; what in the world's the matter? . . . Tell May cut the roast further in this is too well done. . . . You forgot to pass the hot rolls . . ."

Now Vaughan was talking of labor and of Northwest politics. ". . . sometimes I get to thinking maybe we ought've gone more into politics, Dike and me and even my father before me. . . ."

"Jotham could have been Territorial Governor if he'd had a mind to, but he wouldn't bother with any such foolishness . . ."

"Maybe it wasn't foolishness, Ma."

"Say, Vaughan, if it's politics you want, I can . . ."

"Nope, I don't mean your kind of politics, Dave—no offense. I mean people like us we've come to this country and taken out of it and got rich on it . . ."

"What d'you mean—come to this country! To hear you talk you'd think we were immigrants."

"Well, if we aren't our fathers were or our grandfathers or great-grandfathers. My father was named Jotham because his father married a New England woman. He landed here from Ireland; he never learned to read or write in his life. A shoveler he was, and a dollar a day would have looked like a fortune to him if he'd ever seen it."

"Why, say, Vaughan, if I'd known you wanted to go into politics, you or Dike, why I'd fixed you up congressman or senator or whatever you were set on. Can yet, if you say the word."

Dike, so quiet during this meal which had been planned in his honor, spoke up quickly now, almost harshly for him. "That's not quite what Father means, Dave."

Almost invisibly the table talk was making a kind of pattern now, like a cobweb. Pansy's voice, low-pitched and resonant, undercut the men's rougher tones. She spoke leisurely, but her way was sprightly and her mobile face was alight with interest. "Long time ago—twenty years—thirty maybe—I saw Weber and Fields in a show; I've forgotten the name."

"Oh, my God!" said Cliff Garnett to Lina.

"It won't be long now," Lina assured him; "there's Taka with a frightful mold of ice cream. There'll be a lighted cake in a minute and then it'll all be over——"

"Anyway," Pansy was saying, "I got to thinking of it, how it kind of fits in today and has fitted, you might say, the last fifty, sixty years in this country." She turned toward Garnett. "I always was crazy about the theater."

"So glad." Viciously. "You're not going to tell the plot, are you? Because I——"

"There wasn't any plot. It was a bank, see. Weber would go up to the teller's window and the teller would say, 'Put in or take out?' and Weber would say, 'Take out.' Then Fields would go to the window and the teller would say, 'Put in or take out?' and Fields would say, 'Take out.' Well, that went on for quite a while, first one and then the other, and finally the teller caught on; he just bopped them over the head and shut the window; he said, 'You can't take out and take out all the while, you've got to put in *some* of the time.'"

She looked around the table. Their faces were blank. Only

Vaughan seemed to have heard. "Yeah," he said heavily. "Yeah. That's right, Pansy." Almost as if they were there alone.

Then Pansy said a strange thing; at least it seemed strange to the company at table, except, perhaps, for the two young ones, and they were not listening. She looked round the table. "Do you know what!" she said. "We went up to Alaska and the Klondike just for gold. Can you imagine that! When I think of it it seems to me like the only thing in my life I'm ashamed of."

"Say, Pansy——" Dave Dreen began. And then stopped. He coughed. "What's come over you, Pansy? You got religion or something?"

"No," laughed Pansy, "no. Looking back on it, why, it just seems kind of snide."

Cliff Garnett's eyes were ranging the table; he was not even pretending to listen. Lina knew that he was automatically shaping these people into characters, arranging their talk as dialogue. The dramatist's eye, the dramatist's mind were sorting, discarding, building up. She could almost hear his brain clicking as, theater-wise, he dropped these people into slots. Vaughan, rough diamond. Dike, charming lost-generation grown-up weakling. Emmy, conventional stock-company fussy American matron. Mike, younger generation, wise, baffling, drifting. Exact, picturesque old nuisance. Dave Dreen, capitalist posing as labor leader. Pansy, old faithful heart-of-gold stuff. Herself, Lina Port, designing female up to no good.

Through their thick glasses the nearsighted eyes were fixed on Reggie. He was having some difficulty in fitting her into a mold. "You!" he now boomed, addressing Reggie directly. "What are you?"

She had dealt with much worse than this in her brief lifetime. Composedly, quite pleasantly, she said, "Nobody, really."

Anyone noticing could have seen that Mike's eyes and Pansy's deepened to the purple danger signal. Pansy spoke quickly. "Reggie is companion to Madam Melendy."

"Oh." Plainly he was not interested.

"Miss Dresden," Mike said, his accents very clipped, "is at the University of Washington."

"What for?" A flicker of reviving interest. He spoke directly to Reggie again.

Equably, pleasantly, she answered. "I'd like to write plays—though that may seem to you ridiculous."

"Oh, my God!" Then, poisonously, "I'm sure you have a lot of lovely plots. A play for Miss Port, for example."

"No, I don't think so. You see, the one I have in mind is a play about refugees." Cliff Garnett shut his eyes flutteringly. "Of course refugees are rather unpopular, aren't they? But these are not dreary refugees. Amusing ones. They all live together in a heap in one of those big abandoned magnificent closed-up Fifth Avenue mansions. Perhaps two of them began as unpaid caretakers, just for a place in which to live. And then, slowly, friends and relatives and fellow artists drift in and stay. They're all sorts from everywhere—from Vienna and Budapest and Paris and Berlin. Musicians and playwrights like yourself, perhaps, and actors—one of the women was a great actress in Vienna—they are desperate and very poor and gay and brilliant, some of them, and they talk a lot and laugh a. lot and perhaps cry a little—and they are working as taxi drivers and waitresses and clerks———"

Cliff Garnett's eyes were open now. They were staring at Reggie. Then, slowly, his head turned to face Lina Port.

"Sa-a-ay!" said Cliff Garnett.

Emmy had paid no heed to this; she was whispering feverishly to Taka, who was looking definitely distraught. You caught the words cake . . . candles . . . shut off that music . . .

"Whole trouble," Dave Dreen was holding forth, "is that every dumb lout in this country's been told by their ma they'll grow up to be President, so they're pulling down ten, twelve dollars a day out at Boeing and the shipyards at Bremerton with this crazy Lend-Lease and so on, and they figger it's just peanuts; they all

feel—what's that newfangled word?—frustrated—that's it—they
feel frustrated, the poor saps. Same way with the young people.
They say they're frustrated. Well, I say no stamina." You could
see that he was fascinated by the word. "Yessir! Stamina. All that
generation after the war yelling it was our fault, we didn't run
the world right. Now folks like myself working our heads off trying to keep that fella in the White House from plunging us into
this war and what happens? Kids like Mike there rarin' to go in,
wanting to go to Canada and enlist; it's balance they need. Intes-
tinal fortitude. Good old—pardon me, ladies—good old guts."

He laughed triumphantly, a one-man claque. They were not
listening. Emmy's flushed face, strained with anxiety, was turned
toward the pantry swinging door. It began to open, slowly, and
one saw a glow, a flame.

"We're going to sing Happy Birthday and I told you to turn off
the radio music. I told you—— Hap-py Bir-thday to——"

But the music had somehow miraculously turned itself off while
they had been talking and now, in the little silence that fell as
Taka stood, stricken, with the candlelighted cake in his two
hands, the sound of a voice—a voice that was barking in a kind of
controlled hysteria—came to them from the great box in the living room.

". . . early hour this morning a surprise attack on Hawaii . . .
Japanese planes . . . Pearl Harbor . . . Hickam Field destroyed . . . The Philippines . . . All Japanese West coast residents . . ."

The stricken faces. The starting, incredulous eyes. Then a
screech from Emmy as the lighted cake fell to the floor from
Taka's hands and the candles spluttered and smoked and stank
in a shapeless heap of sugar and crumbs.

Of them all only young Mike was cool and quite calm. In the
gabble and shouting he alone said nothing. Indeed on his face was
the look of one who has been waiting a long time for something

that at last has come. A look at once of peace and of relief. Then he took Regina Dresden in his arms and kissed her.

"Good-by, kid. I'll be back." He went quickly toward the hall-way.

"Mike!" Lina screamed. "Mike! Where're you going?"

He half turned; he was smiling. "Going to work." He raised a hand high in a little jerky gesture of farewell. "Be seeing you."

16

THE first time Mike came home in his uniform, complete with wings, the women of the family had grown misty-eyed and yearning. Vaughan overheard him snickering with Reggie as he croaked, "And us so young! Too young to die!" Then they both had giggled, though he couldn't imagine why. He spoke of it to Pansy.

"Why'd they laugh," he demanded, "over a thing like that?"

"That's the modern way of crying," Pansy said. "It saves wear and tear."

These men and women of forty and fifty and sixty spoke of the Mikes and the Reggies as Youth. The Youth of our country they said sonorously. Public speakers and radio commentators of the more emotional school especially were always referring to Our Youth. Mike said, "You'd think everyone under thirty belonged to a separate branch of the human race."

That Voice on the radio at noon or thereabouts on Sunday in December had reached into the dining room of Vaughan Melendy's house and changed the life of everyone in the house. Perhaps Lina and Emmy were least affected. But, then, they always had been least concerned with the world outside themselves. Outwardly you saw little difference in the aspect of this great Northwest metropolis. More sailors down on the Skidroad, crowds on the streets Saturdays and Sundays; thousands of boyish figures in uniform. Every sort of American accent—Southern drawls, the Boston broad *a*, the nasal tone of the Hoosier, the New Yorker's dropped *r*. Over Elliott Bay and over the vast Boeing plant and over the Puget Sound navy yards glinting in the sunshine lazily floated great silver-sided cylinders. They were like giant but benign monsters hovering protectingly over this fabulous region. Looking closely, you could see that they were attached to the land by slender threads. Sometimes, too, you saw them squatting on the ground near an airplane factory or a shipyard, like a herd of mammoth prehistoric animals, resting.

That Voice on the radio had magically thrown Vaughan Melendy back almost fifty years into the past and had made him a ship's pilot again guiding the most valuable human cargo in the world and material cargo as well through the waters of Puget Sound toward the Pacific. His comings and goings were secret; he vanished for days at a time; Emmy did not know when he was leaving or where he might go or on what day or week he might be expected to return. Vaughan's shoulders were squared now, never drooping even when he climbed the hill for Exact's inspection; his step was springy and his eyes alight. But on Emmy's face was the look of a bewildered and frightened old lady. Complaining, she moved about her big house, for Taka and Masako and young Will and Grace were gone; they had been whisked away to a secret place, and Emmy said, quite truthfully, didn't I tell you didn't I always say I always felt there was something I never did trust?

"Whyn't you pitch in, Emmy?" Vaughan said. "Red Cross and bond drives and so on. Get out and help with those jobs. Look at Ma!"

"I believe that my place is to keep the home fires burning."

"You got your wars mixed, Emmy. That was the last one. The Japs and the Nazis are going to keep our home fires burning and our homes, too, if we don't get out and work. Anyway, home fires kept for what? Nobody here but you most of the time." But at that she began to weep, taking off her shining pince-nez and dabbing with her handkerchief which wasn't as exquisitely fresh as it once had been because all the laundresses in Seattle were crouched in the bellies of Boeing Fortresses busy with riveting guns or bucking irons instead of washing machines or flatirons.

When Vaughan had said look at Ma he might have been literally interpreted. Madam Exact Melendy was as public a sight and as easy to view as the totem pole down in Pioneer Square. No patriotic meeting, no rally was complete without her. She occupied a place on the platform beside the Guest of Honor or the Speaker of the Evening. In her silks and laces and jewels she was introduced as a living symbol of the spirit of the Northwest. At the proper time she stood up and spoke a sentence or two in her astonishing trumpetlike tones, and the audience would roar with the shock of surprise and then applaud thunderously. Exact loved it. She became a publicity hound and sulked if a day passed without an urgent invitation to attend this gathering or that. School kids began to ask for her autograph, and happily she scrawled her name on bits of soiled paper thrust at her by grimy fists. Miss Birch, returned now to take Reggie's place, was hard put to it to keep pace with her nonagenarian charge. Madam Melendy complained about this. "I'm looking after Birch instead of the other way around. I'm the one ought to be paid as companion. Here she is, walking with a cane and me helping her down the stairs half the time. Where's Reggie?"

"Reggie's working in the airplane plant. You know that, Madam."

"No call to." A sharp look came into her face. "She's going to have a baby, ain't she?"

"How did you know?"

"I guess I've got eyes in my head. See better than you, any day."

They had been married at Madam's house, Mike and Reggie, after Lina had behaved so badly, and Emmy, too. "What'll the newspapers say?" Emmy had wailed.

Pansy had said, "The newspapers have got something bigger to write about than two more kids getting married in a hurry."

"In a hurry!"

"Mike's probably going off any minute now. You know that."

"Nobody tells me anything." The eyes red-rimmed again, the handkerchief in action. "How can Mike marry that girl? He can't, I tell you!"

"And why not?" Vaughan inquired with a badly assumed mildness.

"Why not? Because he's a Melendy and she's nobody and Jewish besides."

"Oh, she won't mind, Reggie won't. She's real democratic in her views. More than a good many American born. Besides, the Melendys need some new pioneer blood in the family. We're getting stale."

"Pioneer!"

"Well, sure. What she's gone through is worse than the Pilgrims, and if she didn't come here to escape religious persecution I'd like to know."

"That's different. You're just talking to aggravate me. What will the newspapers say?"

"My guess is they'll say the usual stuff; this is a historic event in the annals of Seattle's foremost pioneer family and the bride wore the lace veil that was an heirloom in the Melendy family——"

"I won't let her have it."

But Emmy needn't have bothered. Madam Melendy insisted on having the wedding in her own great grim mansion. "This," she trumpeted, "is the home of the bride, isn't it?" The bride's blonde head was as hatless as the bridegroom's, and the two skedaddled off for a three-day honeymoon somewhere up on

Rainier. Exact had made up for the bride's informality by appearing in full panoply including all her diamonds set in thick gold. On these Lina cast a lustful eye. "It just proves," she said, "that if you keep a thing long enough it'll come into style again."

The ancient looked herself over as one would regard the sparkling gems in a showcase—the massive bracelets, the jewel-studded chains, the brooch, the blue-white stones flashing on her withered fingers; she felt of the perfect solitaires screwed into her ears. "I'm giving Reggie some of these as a wedding present." It was as though she were speaking of sharing a mess of beans from the garden.

"Oh no!" cried Reggie. "No!" And looked down at herself in the slim blue dress that was as simple as a sheath. "I wouldn't know what to do with them."

"I would!" cried Lina, anguished.

Exact ignored her. "You'll learn," she said to Reggie. "Michael's a good boy, but there's nothing sets a woman up like knowing she's got a handful of good diamonds to fall back on in case anything goes wrong."

They shouted at this, and Mike touched the withered cheek and said, "Madam, do you know what I love best about you?"

"No. What?" Eagerly.

"I love you because you're not a lovable old character."

She wagged her head delightedly. "I know it. I'm real tough. They don't come like me any more."

Now like pawns in a game each was moved to his place. Dike was very handsome in his uniform as colonel, but the Quartermaster's Department on the bay was not exactly to his liking. And Lina, in New York, was acid on the subject. Dike was in authority on the loading of ships whose cargo was destined for Alaska and for Russia. In his well-tailored uniform and his shining boots he moved among mountains of piled-up cases and boxes containing Vienna sausage and coffee and mixed pickles and baked beans and canned tomatoes. Lina was too occupied in New

York to write regularly. She telephoned across the continent or telegraphed, but occasionally she managed a letter.

. . . your photograph on the table in my dressing room next to Mike's and everyone wants to know which is my beau. I must say you both make wonderful pin-up boys. Those visors are so becoming they make men's eyes look so kind of compelling and cruel and stern and everything. I can't imagine why Montgomery persists in wearing those silly berets. . . . The play goes on being the smash hit of the season; we're sold out until next year; there's a line in the lobby from morning till night. Sometimes I go through just to gloat. Of course Cliff the stinker says it isn't me and it isn't the play; it's just that people will go to see anything that isn't the war; but if you could hear the applause when I take my last-act curtain calls . . . Why can't you get transferred to Washington? Everybody who is anybody is in Washington this year. . . . Dolling, can't you wangle me a pair of those fabulous Alaska-issue gloves that I saw when I visited that day? I should think you could, after all, Commanding Officer and everything. I mean those simply stunning elbow-length black wolf gloves that the boys in Alaska use to brush snow off their faces; you remember I tried on a pair when I went through your department. When I slipped my hands into the cuffs of my coat it was exactly as if I were wearing a huge black wolf muff. And the gloves worn with a shako of black wolf to match would make the most devastating winter costume with my basic black that I got at Hattie's . . .

Before he went overseas Mike had managed—it was his own idea and he might have been court-martialed for it—to say farewell informally with a little hair-raising stunt flying over the cluster of Melendy houses on Queen Anne Hill. He had arranged to convey his plans to the family, so that when he dived and circled three times, skimming the chimneys and swishing the trees, they were prepared though stiff with horror. Then he darted off. The

plane glinted against the blue sky and the mountains and the brilliance of the bay and he was a dot in the direction of the unseen Pacific.

In the beginning Pansy and Reggie practically never saw each other wide awake, though they lived in the same house. Pansy's house. It had come about simply and naturally. Vaughan's house? But that was Emmy's house, too. Dike was alone; he shunned his cumbersome mansion and stayed at his club the greater part of the time when he was in town. Reggie had never even contemplated living there. To live with Madam Exact Melendy was unthinkable now. "Your room's waiting for you, Reggie," Pansy had said. "Come on and keep me company over at my house. I guess old age has got me. I don't like living alone any more."

A curious thing had happened on the wedding day. Just as they were about to leave Mike had come over to Pansy standing a little apart, he had taken her face between his two hands and he had said, very low, so that only they two heard, "Good-by, Grandma." And then he had kissed her and the two were gone.

"Your room's waiting for you, Reggie," said Pansy. And Reggie had come. The two women, the one so young the other old, went to work at the vast Boeing plant. "Planes," Reggie said. "That's what I want to help make. Planes." But as Reggie, in the beginning, had worked on the swing shift which was from four in the afternoon until midnight, while Pansy was on the night shift —called the Graveyard—from midnight until morning, they might as well have been living miles apart. But when they knew about the baby they managed a transfer for Pansy, and now the two in slacks and head scarves, their lunch pails in their hands, went off to the plant together at four.

Pansy remonstrated at first. "You oughtn't to be going to the plant now, doing that kind of work."

"I want to. It's all I can do to help."

"How about the baby? I suppose that doesn't matter."

"The doctor said it was all right. I can't use the riveting gun

any more, or the bucking iron. But the air drill will be all right, and later I'll be stock chaser—that's easy. That Myrtle Whatshername worked until two weeks before her baby was born and everything was wonderful."

It was Pansy who first learned of the newsreel. One of the defense workers in her department said he had just seen it. Mike Melendy was in it plain as life. It was one of those jungle-warfare pictures and boy! Did he look tough and rugged with that beard! It was showing at the Pike Street.

Reggie quit work while the picture remained in town; she followed it from theater to theater after it had left the Pike Street; she stayed for every show, and Pansy stopped arguing against it after a while.

Old Madam Exact insisted on going, and the family said it was no more than right that she should, her own great-grandson on the screen in a picture, big as life. She had said she didn't want Emmy fussing around her. It was Miss Birch who took her, and the two infirm ones sat well down front; they arrived early and sat through the feature and the Mickey and the news and suddenly there he was. There was Mike.

Exact said later, shaken and deeply disturbed, but excitedly voluble—he looked a sight. He was wearing dirty trousers that looked as if they were about to slip off his lean flanks. His shirt was open at the throat so that you saw his sweating chest. There was little that seemed martial about him or the other boys with him in their grimy pants and naked torsos and sweat-stained shirts. They might have been Western cowhands or farm laborers or ditchdiggers, to look at them. Of the group Mike was half turned away. Someone must have called to him, for he turned and looked over his shoulder, and that eyebrow went up in the quizzical quirk and he grinned his engaging grin. He had a beard —not merely a stubble but a beard of quite impressive dimensions looking queerly out of place on that gaunt, boyish face. And it was then that old Exact had said excitedly to Miss Birch, "It's

Jotham! It's Jotham!" Miss Birch had had quite a time shushing her. "It's Jotham walking and talking. Jotham come back to life!"

The last time Reggie saw the picture she had to go to Bremerton. She took the ferry and crossed the bay and sat in the little movie house until it closed. By now she knew every inch of the film; she anticipated every move. Now he stood up, his back to the camera; now he stooped and talked to the boy who was tinkering with some sort of equipment in his hands; now he turned; he looked over his shoulder, the eyebrow quirked; he grinned; and now at something someone had called to him he raised his hand in that little gesture of farewell, that little gesture with a jerk of the open hand at the end, the gesture with which he always had said, "Be seeing you." And now the jungle trees would hide him.

It was then that Reggie had stood up and reached out with her two hands as though to hold him there, and she had cried, high and clear, "Michael! Wait for me!"

The scattered audience had laughed. Embarrassed, she walked up the aisle quickly and rather heavily, for she had grown a bit clumsy by now. The child would be born in another three months. When she came out it was dark. She took the ferry to Seattle and she went back to the plant. Pansy would still be there.

The foreman said, "Well, we figgered maybe you thought the war was over."

Reggie shook her head, smiling a little. " 'Thou know'st, great son, the end of war's uncertain.' " Then at his blank look, "Shakespeare said that."

"He sure said a mouthful," agreed the foreman.